NO WRONG MOVES

BECCA SEYMOUR

RAINBOW TREE PUBLISHING

ALSO BY BECCA SEYMOUR

Zone Defense

No Take Backs | No More Secrets | No Wrong Moves

Fast Break

Rules, Schmules! | Facts, Smacts!

True-Blue

Let Me Show You | I've Got You | Becoming Us | Thinking It Over | Always For You | It's Not You | Our First & Last

Outback Boys

Stumble | Bounce | Wobble

Stand-Alone Contemporary

Not Used To Cute | High Alert | Realigned | Amalgamated

Urban Fantasy Romance

Thicker Than Water

NO WRONG MOVES

ZONE DEFENSE
BOOK 3

BECCA SEYMOUR

RAINBOW TREE PUBLISHING

Cover Design: BookSmith Design

Editors: Hot Tree™ Editing

E-book ISBN: 978-1-922679-33-8

Paperback ISBN: 978-1-922679-34-5

CHAPTER 1

EDDIE

At some point I'd look away and stop stealing second glances at Pearce talking to the dark-haired guy. If Pearce wanted to hook up, it was his prerogative. Hell, it was the reason why whenever I headed into Minneapolis to take in one of his home games, I generally stayed in a hotel.

The last thing I wanted was to stop my friend's ability to get laid. It didn't matter that even the thought made my stomach curdle, a reaction I was used to but doggedly ignored and denied.

A text alert caught my attention. Probably a good thing, as the hot guy cozying up with Pearce had placed a hand on his forearm. While it was simple, seemingly innocent contact, they were just a few beats away from making out.

Shaking my head at my ridiculousness, I checked

my phone, in case it was from my daughter. Not that she should be anywhere near her phone at this time of night, but still. I sighed when I saw Wayne's name. Not the best reaction to receiving a message from the guy I was supposedly dating, but he acted ridiculously assholishly whenever I left town to watch one of Pearce's games.

It didn't matter that nothing ever had happened between me and Pearce. Not only was he my best friend, but he was too young for my old ass.

I rolled my eyes when I read the question asking if I was still out.

"Who's that from?"

I jerked as heat pressed against my side with the appearance of Pearce. Flicking my gaze in the direction of where he'd been flirting with the hot guy, I frowned when the brown-haired man was no longer in sight. "Huh?" I angled to look at him. With Pearce sitting so close, it was hard to get a full read of his expression, but apparently he found my confusion amusing.

"Why are you sitting here texting rather than dancing?"

With a tilt of my chin, I shot my right brow high. Pearce knew full well I didn't dance. "I'm not texting. Was just checking my phone and making sure it wasn't Lottie." At the mention of my girl's name, Pearce's gaze softened.

"She okay?" The lilt of concern tickled my chest, just like it always did when he got all soft and sweet about my daughter.

"It wasn't her, and she better be tucked up fast asleep in bed." She was staying at one of her friends' house tonight. Thank Christ for that collection of moms who always put their hands up for sleepovers. I wouldn't be here without that special breed of parent.

He bobbed his head and shifted on the booth seat to see me more fully. "So who had you frowning? Has Wayne got lice again? Good of him to give you a heads-up."

I worked hard not to laugh, but I couldn't stop the slight twitching of my lips. Wayne and Pearce had a love-hate relationship. In as much as they loved to hate each other. From the day they'd met, Wayne was suspicious about my friendship with Pearce. He couldn't understand why I was best friends with someone so much younger than me, for a start. There was no doubt jealousy there too. Not only was Pearce underwear-model-material smoking hot—his deal with CK gave him that status—but he was at the top of his basketball career. Tonight's incredible game being no exception.

And Pearce. Well, his dislike for Wayne stemmed from his argument that he didn't think Wayne was good enough for me, and by association Lottie. His feelings for me may have something to do with his animosity too, but for my own sanity, it was best not to think about that.

"He's just checking in, making sure I'm having a good time," I lied. It wasn't like I was protecting Wayne; rather, I didn't want to be talking about him on my night away from reality.

Pearce's snort made it clear he wasn't buying it. "Tonight's screw must have been a disappointment if he's up in your business."

I winced, hating that he was probably right.

"Shit," he was quick to say. "You know I'm being an asshat. I'm sorry, yeah?" He reached out and squeezed my knee, gaze raking over my face.

I forced a smile, not wanting to get into this with him. Wayne wasn't cheating. His announcement that he wanted an open relationship a while back prevented that. And at the end of the day, for all my ill-thought-out reactions, I'd agreed. In this scenario, I was the chump who didn't want the drama of ending a relationship that wasn't going anywhere. "It's fine. Or it will be when another beer appears in my hand."

For a moment, it didn't seem like Pearce was

going to let it go, which he usually didn't, but whatever he read on my face had him pulling his lips between his teeth. With a huff of breath, his shoulders relaxed. "I can do that, but get your ass up and join me at the bar."

An easy smile formed on my mouth. "Shift your butt, then."

He scooted out of the booth, and I followed, hot on his heels. It had been a while since we'd had drinks with his teammates after a game—the two of us usually slipped away for a quiet dinner and a few beers. That sounded way more couple-y than it was, but I liked spending time with him, a lot. Did that mean I monopolized his time when I had the chance? Damn straight. I was the first person to call myself out for being a selfish asshole.

When we reached the bar, we stopped next to a few of his teammates. They were laughing and talking about something or other Cassius had said or done.

"—lit up like the fourth of July." Cassius grinned and bounced his brows. "Fucking spectacular."

A couple of the guys snorted while Ollie, the Eagles' captain, rolled his eyes. "One of these times you're going to land your ass in jail and get benched."

"Ollie," Cassius answered with a shake of his

head, "I've talked myself out of so much shit I should have been locked away for. Fireworks in my high school coach's office was nothing."

"Dear God," Ollie groaned, "for the love of all that is holy, do not do that to Coach Jenkins."

"Me?" Cassius even pressed his hand to his chest and widened his eyes for good measure. "I like my balls attached to my body, fuck you very much. Coach would cut them off if I pulled any of that shit."

"I'd pass him the tweezers and the itty-bitty blade to help," Pearce said from my side. The group laughed, and Cassius flipped him off.

"Fuck you, Malcolm. Whatever size blade veterinarians use for an elephant or whatever would be the only blade that could cut it."

Pearce's barb was instant. "Damn, is that why you're still not able to do a slam dunk after all this time? Your oversized balls? Shit, Cass, maybe it's time we intervene and organize a medical consult for you."

"Whatever, man. My balls are perfect specimens. I'm thinking about getting them insured."

"Fucking hell." Ollie wiped a hand over his face, then met my gaze. "Bet you're wishing you'd hermitted our boy away tonight rather than dealing with these dicks." He followed up with an amused smile.

Ignoring how it most definitely hadn't gone unnoticed by Pearce's team that I did tend to steal their teammate away after a game, I returned his smile. "It's a healthy reminder of what I'm missing out on."

"Missing out on?" Ollie raised his brows, smirking. "More like a 'thank fuck this part of your life is over.'"

I snorted. "Well, I don't miss having a coach ride my ass or—"

"Who's riding your ass?" Pearce's bicep pressed against mine. Whether he was aware or not, when we were together, he was tactile... seriously so. Not that it was a hardship. At some point over the past five years, he'd used his voodoo skills and trained me to not only crave his touches, but damn if he hadn't gone and trained me to do the same thing with him, and only him.

"Not you," Cassius spat, laughing loudly, while I snorted good-naturedly, trying not to think about what it would be like for Pearce to ride my ass.

Pearce flipped his friend off.

"Talking of riding asses, what happened to that guy who was rubbing up all over you?" Cassius pushed. I'd been thinking the same thing, despite the curdling in my stomach.

"He wasn't rubbing up all over me. Not sure

what skanks you're getting with, but that's not for me," Pearce fired back, voice light and breezy.

I frowned and risked a glance at him, noticing pink in his cheeks that belied just how carefree he'd attempted to sound.

"Since when?" Cassius challenged. "And dude, no skank shaming."

A laugh rumbled out of Pearce, and he raised his hands. "My bad. There's nothing wrong with skanks." He cleared his throat before saying, "I was just talking to the guy is all. He's a fan."

Innuendo dripped off Cassius's words when he said, "I just bet he is." He then made a show of looking around before settling his attention back on Pearce. "Actually, where's your usual hookup?"

I swallowed hard, knowing exactly who Pearce's "usual hookup" was. He actually seemed like a decent guy. Not that I wanted to hang out with the reporter, especially if he was getting it on with Pearce.

Fuck, I hated being such a double-standard dick, but Pearce and I didn't get together half as much as I liked—living states apart made that hard—which meant when we did, I wanted him all to myself. Seriously, referring to myself as a selfish prick was just the tip of the iceberg.

"How should I know?" Pearce said, arm still

pressed against mine. "I haven't seen him for a while. Well, not *seen him* seen him."

This was news to me. Not that we discussed his hookup or Wayne all that much. We had a mutual unspoken rule about not talking about other men. It didn't mean I wasn't morbidly curious, though.

"Huh" came from Cassius, and I didn't miss the flash of something—a warning maybe—Pearce shot his way.

The bartender appeared before us and took our order. While we waited, I nudged Pearce. "You good?" I couldn't help but feel like I'd missed something in all that.

He angled toward me, resting a forearm on the bar. "A win and a beer with my best bud? Hell yes. Of course I'm okay." With nothing but sincerity in his gaze or his tone, I relaxed. He didn't look put out over not hooking up with that guy. "You okay staying for this, then heading out?"

"We can stay if you want to hang with your team." I could be magnanimous when I wanted to be.

"I'd prefer to catch up with you instead. You not getting in till this afternoon meant we missed out on last night's slumber party."

I snorted. "You're such a dickhead. But yeah, having to meet today with the foundation was important, but I would have appreciated it a whole lot more if it had been another day."

He bobbed his head and took a pull of his drink. "How is everything with the foundation?"

"Going great. Pride Youth is going strong. We've got more sponsorships and have finalized a visit to the summer academy again." I'd been involved in the LGBTQ+ youth foundation going on seven years, having first met one of the foundation's directors when doing a stint at Montview during the elite basketball training camp.

"Excellent. Just let me know if you need anything, yeah?"

Warmth flooded me at his offer. "You already do plenty." It was true. Since his first season at Montview as a guest trainer five years ago, not only had he been offered a regular seasonal spot, but he'd also involved himself in Pride Youth when he'd discovered my connection.

"I do a bit, but you know if I can, I'll always do more."

I leaned against him at the bar, nudging him gently, giving him my silent thanks. What continued to amaze me was that while he could easily write a check for them, he preferred being actively involved.

Pearce sure did tend to go all in when invested.

CHAPTER 2

PEARCE

I pressed the app button again, and Cassius whipped his head in the direction of the door, his earlier confusion making way to frustration. With a huff, he grumbled all the way and tore open his front door.

"The fuck." Slamming the door shut, he turned, grouching about "fucking nonexistent doorbells" and something about "selling the fucking place" and "pain-in-the-ass ghosts."

"Just take your shot and stop procrastinating," Joel said, straight-faced. A moment later he shot me the side-eye. From that look alone, it was clear he knew I had something to do with this fuckery.

I swallowed back my smirk. "Yeah, Cassius, get on with your shot."

He flipped me off and lined up his pool cue.

Bending low, he aimed, tongue sticking out slowly, concentration forming a deep line between his brows.

With his focus completely on the pool game, which he took far too seriously, I read that as my signal. Slipping my hand into my pocket, I angled away from my teammates whose focus was on the pool table. Phone in hand, I tugged it out, thumbed in my PIN, and once again pressed the button on the app that I was having far too much fun with.

The doorbell rang, persistent, annoying, and Cassius's shot went wide, the white ball bouncing off the table in a spectacular fashion. It hit the ground with a thud just as Cassius shouted, "The fuck!"

I couldn't take it anymore. My laughter spilled free, immediately drawing my friends' attention.

"You dickbag." Cassius threw his cue on to the felt table and stalked toward me.

Still laughing, I jolted in the other direction. "What did I do?"

"It was you. I should have fucking known. I don't even have a doorbell." He jerked to his right, and with the pool table between us, I dodged in the other direction.

"Hey." I lifted my hands, palms out, not doing the best job at calming him since I directed a cheek-splitting grin at him. "You said you were... what did he call himself, Joel?"

"The god of sticks, and I quote, 'Give me a stick and I can wrangle that piece like it's a serpent and I'm a snake whisperer.' I'm sure those were the words."

I cracked up laughing. "Didn't he proceed to list off the types of sticks he could... uhm... did he also use the word 'rule'?"

Ollie, our team captain, snorted loudly, grabbing all of our attention. "Don't mind me," he said, gesturing to us with his beer. "You say stupid shit about dicks and cues, Cass, you're on your own."

Cassius crossed his arms, narrowing his gaze at me. "And I was whooping your ass at this game. But the fuck has my god status got to do with you and a doorbell, cockhead?"

Asking for trouble, I bounced my brows. "You also said you had the concentration of a..." I clicked my fingers, pretending I couldn't remember the dumb shit my friend said.

"An alligator," Joel added helpfully.

Amusement punched out of me once more. "Maybe concentrated juice. The weak kind," I offered, darting to my left when Cassius made to move again.

On opposite ends of the table, I raised my brow in challenge. Cassius may be an exceptional shot on the basketball court, but I was a lot lighter on my feet. In response, he flipped me off and shook his head, not doing a great job at concealing the twitch of his lips.

"Right, my pains in the asses, you about done here? We finishing, or calling it now?" From the tone of Ollie's voice, it sounded like he was a fan of the latter, and honestly, as much as I loved pissing Cassius off, I was beat too.

We had a game tomorrow. And while every game mattered, tomorrow's mattered even more. It was why a few of us had got together at Cassius's place to attempt to kick back and chill. Nothing heavy, beyond me finding ways to piss off Cassius. But to be fair, he'd set himself up with the whole stick thing.

The douche in him was strong, but he was still loveable as hell, almost as much as he was ridiculous.

"I suppose we could call it, though other than lover boy over here, it's not like we've anywhere to be." Cassius flicked his gaze to me as he spoke, but it still took me a second to realize I was apparently lover boy.

I rolled my eyes at him, not bothering to put him straight, though from the challenge in his gaze, he was really hoping I would.

"What?" he said with a grin, prodding me for a reaction. "You've got the cute journo whose chain you're yanking and the hot DILF on speed dial. Lover boy totally fits."

"Whatever, man, you know it's not like that." I clamped my mouth shut when a spark of satisfaction registered on Cassius's face. The asshole knew how to push my buttons, and he sometimes wore his douche label with pride. The annoying thing was, he didn't even try to get a rise out of me with venom. This was just a game we played. Him teasing, me playing pranks on him.

"Joel, what do you think? Who's going to eventually win our boy's heart here, get him tied down? The DILF or the journo?"

Shaking his head, Joel started putting away the pool balls. "Well, since Eddie isn't a DILF for me, MILFs all the way, I couldn't possibly comment."

"Bullshit." Cassius smirked. "Your five hundred bucks says differently."

I groaned. "Seriously. This is the latest bet in the team?" I wasn't sure why I was so surprised, since I'd been super active in other bets. Hell, I'd won a tidy sum with the whole Jayden-and-Sutton saga.

"Latest?" Cassius shook his head and snorted. "Hell no. Well, since you hooked up with the local journo, the odds changed a little, but the one with Eddie, yeah, that's been around since the moment you returned from Montview like a lovesick puppy talking about the legendary Eddie Phelps in every other sentence."

I dropped my head and rubbed a hand over my face. I could do the generous thing and tell them me and Eddie would never happen. I'd tried to start something up with the man once, but his resolute no, alongside his determination to stay friends, had been my clear answer. And since he was absolutely my best friend these days, I had no doubt that was the way it would remain.

No way I'd be telling the guys Eddie had rejected me a few years back. Screw that. These friends of mine didn't need more ammunition.

The guys weren't wrong, though, about how I talked about the man. Eddie was important to me, as was his daughter. Our friendship had grown exponentially over time, and I'd pretty much cemented myself into his and his daughter's lives. Would I risk it all if Eddie and I had a chance to be more? Fuck yes. The man was lodged in my soul, and whether he knew it or not, when I'd fallen for him, I'd given him a piece of said soul in return.

"What *is* happening with the journalist these days?" The question came from Ollie, surprising me, as he didn't usually pry into my personal life—or anyone's as far as I was aware. To be clear, he was a kick-ass captain and we spent a lot of time together, but personal sharing was minimal.

"Tony's a good friend."

"Yeah he is." Cassius bounced his brows, and if the pool table wasn't between us, he would have earned himself a shove. "The whole friends-with-benefits thing still working out for you, huh? Nice. I knew you were downplaying at the bar a couple of weeks back."

Somehow I kept my eye roll at bay. "We're more like just friends these days. Life's busy, you know?"

Joel frowned. "What, too busy to get your cock sucked? Dude, something's seriously wrong if that's the case."

"Not wrong. It's just… he's a good guy, and I don't want to lead him on."

"He wanting a relationship or something?" Curiosity colored Ollie's words.

"Jesus, what is this, get-the-dirt-on-my-sex-life question time or some shit?" My chuckle sounded awkward, which pretty much was accurate. We never talked about stuff like this, so I had no idea what sparked this conversation now. "What's with all the questions?"

Cassius shrugged. "The pot's big and things seem, I don't know, a little stagnant."

Incredulous, I laughed. "The hell? So this is your intervention to get the dirt and give me a shove so someone can win the pot?"

"Well, when you put it like that, then yeah."

Cassius's grin was far too self-satisfied and ridiculous to ignore. Genuine amusement bubbled in my chest. These guys, though I expected Cassius mainly, were dicks. But they were my... uhm... dicks.... Of the nonsexual variety.

"How about you just use the fund to take us all out after the season's over?"

"What?"

"Hell no."

"No chance."

They all spoke at once, so I had no idea who said what. "Guys, you're being extra, and I'm not even going to ask how much money's riding on this bullshit with that sort of reaction. And on that note, I'm going home."

"For phone sex?"

I snorted at the hope in Cassius's voice. "To sleep and get a good rest before tomorrow's game, god of alligators." I followed up with a back slap, and after saying goodbye to the guys, I headed out, chuckling loudly at Cassius's, "God of sticks. Jesus. How hard is it to get right?"

It took me all of five minutes to get home, courtesy of living in the same gated estate as Cassius. It came in handy, living so close. Though with their weird investment in my pretty much nonexistent love life these days, maybe I needed to move and find somewhere with huge-ass gates.

Once at my pad, I showered, got my running gear ready for the morning, then headed to bed. Tucked up, I opened my phone and call list. Eddie's name was at the top, like it usually was. I hesitated before clicking on his name, feeling called out by my friends and my fixation on Eddie. They didn't actually know we spoke every day. Sometimes it would only be for a minute, another for a couple of hours. But that's what you did with your friends, right?

I ignored the echo of "bullshit" zipping around my brain. There had never been another friend I spoke to every day. Ever. Not even when I was a kid. The thing was, with my heart and soul heavily invested, and friendship the one thing on the table, I grabbed on to it like a lifeline. Wanting and needing and, hell, loving our connection.

Sure, phone sex, just like the real deal, would be a hell of a sweetener, but this had to be it. And I was okay with that, or as okay as I ever would be.

Did I think it was healthy? The hell if I knew, but I wasn't prepared to change a thing. With that thought in my mind, I hit Eddie's name and smiled, waiting for him to answer.

CHAPTER 3

EDDIE

"CHARLOTTE ELIZABETH PHELPS, I SWEAR ON ALL THAT is good and magical that if you don't turn off your light, I'm going to be shipping you off to military school."

Rather than fearing that threat, Lottie snorted and rolled her eyes. "Okay, Dad. Five more minutes."

That was definitely not a question or a request. But it was way past my kiddo's bedtime, and I'd be dealing with a grumpy ten-year-old come the morning if she didn't do as she was told. I counted to ten, thinking how similar parenting Lottie was to wrangling the college basketball players I coached during the summer.

Hormones, egos, and Michael Jordan complexes had nothing on my Lottie.

It was time to bring out the big guns.

"Two tickets are going to be canceled unless your head hits the pillow and darkness hits your eyeballs, and I'm not talking about my flight or my seat at the game."

Wide eyes shot my way. "But Pearce needs me there."

"He does?" Somehow I kept my face stoic and held back my wince, sure I was going to some sort of parenting hell for the threats, negotiations, and juggling I did with my girl.

"Of course he does."

"If that's the case, why am I standing in your doorway having this conversation, Lottie girl?"

"I'm sorry, Daddy. I promise to go to sleep right away."

"You be sure to do that, kiddo. None of us want to be disappointed tomorrow."

A second later, her TV was off and her notepad and pen placed on her side table, next to her already powered-down phone. Thank goodness for the parent control function for that damn thing.

Once she was snuggled down, I stepped fully into her room, and for the second time this evening, I tucked her in and kissed her goodnight. "Love you to the moon and beyond."

I backed away after turning off her lamp, closing the door as she whispered, "Love you more."

With the soft click of the door, I exhaled and smiled. I couldn't really fault Lottie's passion, not when it was one so close to my own. That pad she'd been scribbling away in was all things League related. The girl was only ten and was more hard-core than I ever was.

As I headed to my room with the plan to grab a quick shower, my phone rang. I hurried my steps to pick it up from the chest of drawers, barely holding back my groan when Wayne's name flashed on the screen.

If that wasn't enough of a reaction to tell me that something had to give… "Hey," I answered, catching my sigh before it escaped.

"You sure you can't come over?"

It was a good job Wayne hadn't video called. My sneer and eye roll would have got a reaction and resulted in a fifteen-minute complaint from the man.

"Lottie's in bed."

"Perfect. She's all tucked up and won't even miss you."

The fuck? I tightened my grip on my phone. "She's ten," I deadpanned.

"So more than old enough, right? You need to

stop mothering that kid. Come here so you can get laid instead."

This time there was no holding back my frustrated sigh. For two years, I'd wasted my time on this man. What the hell had I been thinking? Sure, it had been fun in the beginning, but I'd foolishly thought his selfishness was just a single-guy thing, something he'd lose, especially when he met Lottie.

Not that my girl was a miracle worker or anything. My misplaced thoughts were all down to me and my naïve wishful thinking.

Heck, my foolishness didn't even cut it.

I didn't have the will to get into this with him now, though. Not only did I have an early flight to Minneapolis in the morning to watch Pearce's game, but a couple of my investments had turned to shit with the downward turn of a couple of my stocks.

"I'm going to have to pass."

"Fine." The bite to the one-word response was unforgiving, and I didn't give a shit. "Tomorrow then."

Unbidden, I smirked, knowing exactly how he'd respond when I answered him. Jesus, it really was time I cut ties with the guy. "I have an early flight to Minneapolis in the morning. I won't be back till late the day after."

"Of course you have. When you've finished playing with your boy toy, I expect to hear from you… if you can drag yourself away from the attention whore."

"Hey now," I interrupted, pissed off at his bitchiness. He wasn't usually this bad. Jealous for sure, but not like this.

"Of course you'll jump in and defend Saint Pearce."

Another frustrated breath escaped me. "Listen, we need to talk when I get back."

In response, he grunted out a "Yeah, whatever. I hope your team sucks ass," and the phone call cut off.

"Shit." I stared down at my cell and flopped back on my bed, wondering how I got myself mixed up with the man in the first place. While technically he was my boyfriend, last year, I'd half-heartedly agreed to an open relationship. Not something I'd pursued or was especially keen on. But hanging out with Wayne had times of being fun. In the beginning, at least.

Fuck. I stared up at the ceiling, knowing full well I'd been thinking with my dick. Sex with Wayne had been easy and accessible. Even though he could be a douche, he was safe. There'd been no speaking out to gossip columns, though he was happy to play the part of doting boyfriend on the rare occasion a pap took notice.

But he'd never been enough. Not really. I just felt like a dick for going along with an easy lay for so long.

The loud burst of music from my phone made me jump. I fumbled with it, a frown already forming as I glanced at the screen. Immediately, it flipped into a smile, tension rushing out of me.

Pearce.

"Hey."

"Hey, back. Whatcha doing?"

God, it was good to hear his voice. The man had the ability to chase away my frustration and unhappiness with just the curve of his smile or the cadence of a single syllable. "Just put Lottie to bed, then going to grab a shower."

"Thank Christ. I can smell the stench from here. Lottie begged me earlier to make sure you hosed down. The shame of traveling with you tomorrow would have been too much for her. She was threatening legal action."

I chuckled, breathing easier listening to his goofiness. "That right? What kind of legal action we talking? If there's a good deal on the table...?"

"Oooh, you don't want to mess with that girl's

plans. You'd be living on Spam and butter for the rest of your life."

"Uhm… that's quite a combination."

"Right!" He laughed. "She's an evil genius."

"Uh-huh. But considering my girl wouldn't recognize Spam if it landed on her plate and did a song and dance, I have a feeling you're in on this and working out the terms." I pulled myself up, adjusted my pillows, and leaned back, relaxing into the conversation.

"Conjecture." He snorted. "Shit, is that even the right word to use?"

I grinned. "The hell if I know. What have you been getting into?"

"A couple of games of pool with the guys."

"Please don't tell me they took your money?" Pearce may have been a kick-ass basketball player, but his pool skills needed some work.

"Not at pool, but the assholes are aiming to make bank on a killer pot, apparently."

"Huh? What are you talking about?"

Pearce stayed quiet for a beat before clearing his throat. "Uhm, nothing. Don't worry about it. So, what time's your flight?"

Brows dipping in confusion, I wondered why he was brushing off whatever he'd been talking about. A bet, I figured. It was unusual for Pearce to hold back. He said shit without thinking all the time. The outcome was usually hilarious and just a little endearing.

"Just after ten. We'll need to be up about seven to beat the city traffic."

"Good luck with getting that girl of yours outta bed, and on a Saturday too."

"Don't I know it. Though I expect knowing it's because we're visiting you, she'll manage just fine."

I could hear his grin as he said, "Aw, you see how awesome and loveable I am. It's why I'm Lottie's favorite."

"Sorry," I responded, an amused grin forming, "did you think I said visiting you? I said, watching the game. Cassius Britton is having one hell of a season. Lottie won't stop talking about him."

"Dude, take it back."

"What?" Fizz bubbled in my gut as I spoke, the one-eighty in my emotions from speaking to Wayne to talking to Pearce enough to make my head spin and let happiness take over. "Just saying how it is."

"You best be messing with me, man. Lottie's my favorite girl. She's my number one fan."

Nothing but sweet feelings settled into my bones when he talked about my daughter. From the moment they'd met, not long after the end of the college summer training camp we both attended, they'd become thick as thieves.

It was good for teasing him mercilessly, letting him know they got on so well due to his maturity levels, or lack of. The truth was, Pearce was simply an all-round good guy. Arguably the best guy I knew.

Not for the first time, I wondered what would have happened if I'd been in a different head space three years back and had said yes to him when he suggested we hook up when we'd headed out to Australia for Ryan and Nate's wedding. The no had been hard to say and stick to. But at twenty-six and with a couple of years of friendship already under our belt, Pearce had been too young, too in the thick of fame and the industry for me to be getting involved. Romantically, at least.

Plus, I hadn't wanted to ruin what we had with a one-night stand.

Now, hell, I kinda wanted to kick myself for standing by my decision and playing the responsible card. Not that I regretted or didn't dote on our friendship.

Pearce Malcolm was the most important man in my life.

"I suppose she may still hold that number one title," I offered, taking pity on him and the sulky voice that had dragged his words low. "Speaking of, you all set for tomorrow?"

"Yeah. Maybe. Yeah. The… uhm… guys are ready. What time did you say your plane was landing?"

Rather than challenge his doubt, I responded to his question. "Too late for you to meet us. The last thing you need to be worrying about is me and Lottie getting in. We'll be in the crowd, cheering you on."

"And we'll catch up later, right? You won't be dashing off?"

A soft smile lifted my lips, liking a lot that he wanted to spend time with us. "We'll be there, ready to celebrate." At least I hoped that was the case. If they won tomorrow's game, they'd be heading for the playoffs. Pearce may have been acting like the game wasn't a big deal, but he'd trained hard for this moment, and being a seasoned pro and in a team that had finally been making movements in the League, he wanted this badly.

Which meant I wanted it for him just as much.

"Yeah, okay," he said, chasing his words with a yawn.

"And on that note," I said with a chuckle, "get your ass to bed. I'll see you tomorrow."

"Sounds good. See you tomorrow, Ed."

"Will do. Rest easy."

We ended the call, and I stared at the phone. Unable to resist, I opened my messages.

Me: Lottie and I are going to have to share the #1 title. Tomorrow's game, you'll show me exactly why you're worth it.

I hit Send, not sure if the text was too sweet, or dumb, or whatever, but I already knew Pearce was worth everything.

CHAPTER 4
PEARCE

THE LEATHER CONNECTED WITH MY HANDS. WITH A tight grip, I flexed my fingers, darted to my left, slipped past Giles, dribbled, and took a shot.

I swore someone hit slow motion on the remote. I didn't dare look at the timer, sure doing so would make the shot miss.

The buzzer sounded, right alongside the final call for the end of the game. Immediately, I grinned, relief mixing thick and fast with joy. Winning this game meant finally, for the first time since playing in the League, we'd be going to the playoffs.

I didn't have time to search the crowds before the bedlam began. Lucas and Smith were on my back, Jax had scooped me up in a hug, and then there were the press and Coach, and cheers and chants.

I went with it, knowing it was no use digging in

my heels. Sure, I wanted to see if Eddie was still in the crowd, but with the three mics in my face and the manager's arm around my shoulders, giving me a tight squeeze before he left me to it, I forced myself to be present.

"Great game, Malcolm, and congratulations on earning your playoff spot."

I grinned at Tony, the local sports reporter I'd hooked up with for a while. He was one of the few good journos I'd met. "Thanks, Tony. We played a hard, fast game."

"Last time we spoke, sixty was your magic number. This game, you blew your points scored out of the water. Seventy-nine points. That's the third highest in the League, ever. How do you feel about those numbers?"

My heart galloped in my chest. Seventy-nine was incredible. Knowing that made holding back from searching for Eddie even more of a challenge. He'd get such a kick out of it.

"Well, Tony, you know there was so much riding on tonight's game. The Eagles have fought long and hard to get here. I had a great performance, right alongside my team. I wouldn't have been able to make those points without my boys. None of it would have been possible." Tony's smile grew wider. He was a legit fan of the Eagles, and since I'd agreed to give him, a small-time local reporter, the only interview about me coming out five years earlier, his fan status had become more hard-core. Perhaps me liking him was more to do with how we'd hooked up a few times over the last couple of years, though we'd always managed to happily stay friends, neither seeking anything more.

Regardless of the bet my teammates had made.

"And the crowd tonight was intense. Every seat was filled, and a few interesting chants were going around containing your name." There was a twinkle in his eyes as he spoke, and I dreaded to think what he was getting at.

"Was there anyone special in the crowd tonight, someone you played extra hard for?"

The asshole. Somehow I maintained my easy-going smile, though I hoped he could mind read, as I was going to nut punch him when it was safe to do so.

"All of our hard-core fans make it easy to give it our all for."

"I saw a few former greats in the crowd tonight," he continued mercilessly. The nut punch would only be the start of the level of pain I was going to throw at him. He was the only person who knew for a fact about my absolute infatuation with Eddie Phelps.

And apparently, Tony took great pleasure in torturing me.

"I expect some of those former greats have offered you so much inspiration over the years. Are there any in particular you want to give a shout-out to?"

And then Eddie was by my side, grinning and throwing his arm around my shoulders. I soaked in his touch and his happiness, allowing the pride evident on his face to wrap around me.

"Eddie Phelps, what are your thoughts on Malcolm's game?"

"Malcolm didn't hold back tonight, nor did the Eagles. They played like every team should. Seamlessly." He squeezed my shoulder, and somehow I didn't spring wood.

Movement next to Eddie dragged my attention to the left of him and down. A new smile formed, this one just for the little girl at his side. Complete with my numbered jersey and brown ringlets, Lottie was close to being my favorite person. It didn't matter that she was only ten.

I looked over at Tony and gave him a silent plea to wrap this up.

"I best leave you to it."

Relieved, I grinned as he finished off his spiel before instructing his cameraman to switch off and head over to Lennon, then he gave me a quick handshake. "I'll call you soon. Celebrate hard, and don't do anything I wouldn't do." He followed up with a cheesy wink, and I rolled my eyes at him before turning my attention to Lottie.

I scooted down onto one knee and opened my arms for her. She almost flattened me as she charged into my embrace.

"You were brilliant. Did you hear you're now rated third for most points?" Wide-eyed, she pulled away. "Ever."

Pride bloomed in my chest. Hell, having Lottie so proud of me was right on up there with finally heading to the playoffs. "I did. It's pretty awesome."

She nodded, her eyes bright, her expression serious. "I was thinking this would open up new sponsorship deals. I'll start doing some research. Maybe you should tell Dad that I can have my phone out over dinner so I can do that."

Eddie's snort drew my attention to him. "How about wait till after dinner when we're back in the suite?"

I dotted a quick kiss on Lottie's cheek and stood, loving it when Eddie got into dad mode like this. He had the whole loveable stern vibe going on. When I'd first witnessed it, I was introduced to a whole new side of him.

I liked it a lot. Loved he was so caring and open with his daughter.

"But Dad, if I'm going to be Pearce's agent one day, we need to talk through these things in real time." I bit my lip when she rolled her eyes at her dad.

"Ten going on twenty-five," Eddie grumbled, his gaze connecting with mine. "I blame you."

I laughed. "Me? What did I do?"

In response, he quirked a dark brow. I followed the movement, working hard to remind myself that panting after the man was all levels of wrong. While I didn't care he was over ten years older than me, he'd mentioned once that he didn't understand how relationships lasted with age gaps. Wasn't that a fun conversation to be a part of! Talk about crushed.

But more significantly, he was in a relationship. That was the biggest punch to the gut.

When he'd told me a couple of years ago that he'd met someone, I'd been devastated. When he'd told me he was dating a man, I could have cried.

I wanted to be the man he dated, fell for, become a family for Lottie with. Instead, he'd settled on Wankface Wayne, a realtor who was a sleaze, but apparently, Eddie didn't see that side to him.

"Okay," I finally admitted, happily squeezing

Lottie's hand when she placed her palm in mine. "I may have encouraged her a little."

"That's right. Pearce did, Daddy, 'cause that's what you do when you love someone. You encourage them and want them to be happy and follow their dreams."

My heart filled. I loved this girl—and her manipulative ways—just like I loved her father. A quick glance at Eddie, and I froze. How he looked at me and Lottie was enough to take my breath away.

"And that includes using my phone during dinner and then Pearce coming back to the hotel with us so we can talk about it more." She paused a beat. "And I think we'll need cocktails."

I snorted, and Eddie rubbed a hand over his face.

"Dinner. No phone till dessert," he said. "And Pearce might want to go and celebrate with his friends tonight after dinner."

"We're his friends. He can celebrate with us," Lottie said, an edge of defiance in her voice.

"You are definitely my friends," I said, stopping Eddie from saying more. "Dinner, then hanging with my two favorite people seems like the perfect way to celebrate making the playoffs to me."

Lottie's grin was victorious. Making eye contact with Eddie, I shrugged.

"You spoil her." There wasn't an ounce of accusation in his tone.

"Because she's awesome and is going to make a kick-ass agent one day."

He studied me for a beat. "You sure you don't have plans after?" His smile lost some of its shine before he said, "Tony's here. If you have plans…"

Surprise sparked to life in my chest. We rarely discussed my personal life—aka my sex life—me deliberately keeping my cards close to my chest. It had slipped out about a year back that I'd hooked up with Tony, though.

"No, not at all. We don't see each other very often," I clarified.

Eddie nodded and then slowly smirked. "You sure?"

"Gee, Dad. He said he loves us and wants to hang out."

Loud laughter burst free. While I had absolutely not said those words, she definitely wasn't wrong. Ignoring the heat in my cheeks, I focused on Eddie. "You heard the girl. Give me thirty."

I turned on my heel and dodged the crowd, studiously ignoring the reporters, and headed for the locker room.

Once there, I took in the boisterous team,

accepting and giving a few back slaps. At my locker, I nodded at Jax. "Good game, man."

"Playoffs, baby." He smacked my ass for good measure, and I grinned at his antics.

"You know it." I shrugged off my clothes, confident in this space of guys, something I refused to ever take for granted. From the moment I'd come out while at Montview Academy for the college summer workshop I assisted in, my team had been phenomenal.

It wasn't the case for other guys in pro sports. Minnesota Eagles were fucking epic, though. And this moment right here, ass slaps, even more than the qualifying game, were the reason I'd stayed with them, not pursuing the tempting offers my agent waved in front of me, and hoping like hell I wasn't traded.

Once undressed, I headed to the shower.

I stepped into the cubicle, waited till I could hear Jax's shower running, and then went in for my stealth attack. I extended my arm, shampoo in my grip, and squeezed gently. Just enough to not give away the extra liquid I was adding to his head.

I was a pro at this shit and could literally do it without looking. My accuracy was always pretty much spot on. I waited until I heard the shift in the water spray, the change indicating Jax was rinsing.

Smirking, I extended once again and squeezed the life out of the bottle. Satisfied, I quickly rinsed off, wanting to be done before—

"You fucker."

Laughter burst from me.

"Pearce, I swear to God…"

"What's wrong, Jax?" I hollered. "You run out of shampoo? Need to borrow some?"

I heard extra chuckles around me.

"You're an asshole, Pearce."

"I *like* assholes, Jax. There's a difference."

He snorted loudly, and I figured it was enough to distract him so it was safe for me to make a run for it.

Clean, or as fresh as I could get in my haste to get away from Jax and as quickly as possible to Eddie, I dressed, receiving a few smirks from my teammates.

"You do know Jax is going to sulk the rest of the night, right?" Ollie shot me a smirk and a raised brow.

I grinned in response. "He's lucky I went easy with low-key shampoo after what he did to me last week." The guy had filled my socks with glitter. That shit went everywhere. Like *everywhere*! It was a good job I hadn't hooked up. Trying to explain why I had glitter in the crack of my ass would have been awkward.

Ollie chuckled. "Considering you cellophaned his car the week before, were you surprised?"

The memory, of doing just that and how much of the damn stuff it had taken to layer it on nice and thick, amused me to no end. Pranks were fucking fun and hilarious. I lived for this shit. Since Jayden had left the Eagles, it had taken a while for someone to bite and play pranks as hard as I did. Jax was proving to be a fun competitor. Though Cassius was my usual go-to guy.

I had been taking it super easy on Jax, though. I hadn't wanted to scare him off. But with today's win and us having a place in the tournament, it was time to bring my A game.

"You heading out with Phelps and his kid?"

I nodded. "Yeah. They flew in for the game this afternoon and will head back tomorrow."

"That girl of his still determined to rule the world?"

I chuckled. "Yup. Starting with ruling me, I think." My teammates had thought my and Eddie's friendship was a little out there a few years back. Not only were there more than ten years between us, but he was a single dad, an ex-professional basketball player, plus he lived in Chicago.

But we'd just clicked. He made me laugh and was easy to be around. And when I'd come out not long after meeting him, he was a sounding board I appreciated, since he'd come out as bi a year after his retirement, not long after splitting with his wife.

Sure, our lives seemed a world apart, and ignoring the fact he was hot as sin and I was straight-up in love with the man, I'd made my peace once he'd started dating Wankface Wayne.

Well, sort of, or as much as I could since the realtor wasn't good enough for Eddie.

I had no regrets that I'd held on tightly to our friendship, though, despite how much my heart ached at times. I wanted the man in my life however I could get him.

After grabbing my gear, I stopped off for a quick word with Coach, then headed out to find my friend and his daughter. I found them outside the locker room.

Once again, Lottie raced toward me. This time I scooped her up, not giving a damn that she was ten and far too big to be carried.

"You guys ready to go?" I asked.

"I'm starving. Dad wouldn't let me have a hot dog during the game." Lottie made a good attempt at pouting.

"Then you wouldn't be able to eat with Pearce. No dessert, no talking shop, remember. It means you need all the room for your plans for world domination." Eddie quirked his brow at his daughter, sending me a follow-up wink. "Your car in the usual spot?" he asked.

I bobbed my head. Eddie, and sometimes Lottie when my games didn't clash with school, made regular trips to see me play. Every single time, I was overwhelmed he made the effort, all but pinching myself knowing he valued my friendship as much as I did his.

"I booked us in at the hotel restaurant. I hope that's okay." His gaze flicked to his daughter, and I glanced at her still in my arms. Her head was against my shoulder. While her eyes were open, I figured she'd be exhausted. Not that she'd ever admit as much to either of us.

"Sounds good. The perfect place to spend time with this crazy kid."

Eddie's smile was soft, and when my gaze traveled to his face, I realized it was directed at me rather than Lottie.

I held his stare for a beat before glancing away, too terrified he'd see longing in my eyes. The last thing I wanted was him to feel awkward. And the thought of not spending time with either of them wasn't worth the risk.

"You want me to drive?" Eddie asked as we stepped into the secure parking lot. My relieved smile was instant, as was the flutter in my stomach. He knew I always had a mini adrenaline crash post game, where I was overcome with tiredness until I got a decent meal.

"That'd be great, thanks." I passed him the key to my SUV, which I may have upgraded to last year with Lottie in mind.

We got settled in the car, and Eddie started the engine. "With this traffic, it'll take us at least forty-five minutes. Why don't you rest? You know I've got you."

Our gazes caught, a whisper of a smile tilting his lips. I closed my eyes, aware he spoke the truth. The only trouble was, I wish he had me in every way possible.

CHAPTER 5

EDDIE

AFTER A MILLION AND ONE QUESTIONS FROM LOTTIE, I'D finally managed to get her to bed, giving Pearce a break. While food had perked him up, once we'd made it to my suite, he'd played along with Lottie, despite how he obviously flagged.

"She settle okay?"

I picked up my beer and smiled at Pearce, appreciating how much he cared about my passionate daughter. "Yeah. She was pretty buzzed after your game and shop talk." I collapsed on the oversized couch and eyed the man lounging across from me. "You really were incredible."

And there was his blush, as if on cue. Perhaps I was an asshole for enjoying it so much, but with how upside down my life had started to feel, I appreciated the familiarity and comfort of being in Pearce's space.

He was so easy to read and get a rise from. And hell if I didn't bask in every moment I spent with the man.

"The team pulled together," he said. "We held our own."

I quirked my brow at him. "I know that's the party line, but come on," I challenged.

His grin was immediate, his slight flush from my earlier praise morphing to a darker shade of red. "It was fucking awesome. Did you see that three-pointer in the first ten?" He shook his head as if visualizing the play. "Lennox didn't know what hit him," he all but gushed. "Hell, it was amazing." The excitement I loved to hear filled his words and his features.

"The playoffs," he continued. "I can hardly believe it."

"I can. You and the team deserve to be there. You especially." Before we'd first met, I'd paid enough attention when watching ESPN to sit up and take note of the new Eagles forward. Since becoming friends during the summer program where we helped coach players set for the League draft, my opinion of the man had grown expo-nentially.

Not only was Pearce an incredible player, but he was also fun to be around. Our conversations had been as easy and natural as if we'd known each other for years, and definitely not like there was a decade between us.

"You think you'll be able to make it to many games? Obviously depending how far in we get."

I bobbed my head. "I'll make as many happen as possible. Lottie's away at camp for one week when the finals are scheduled. It'll make it easier. I'm not helping with the summer program scheduling at Montview this year." This meant I'd freed myself up for the rest of the month from that additional task I usually had. I paused and took a drink before asking, "Is Montview still on the cards for you this season?" Despite my casual question, his answer mattered. Spending so much time with Pearce over the summer had become one of my favorite things to do.

A frown appeared between his brows. "Yeah, of course. Why'd you ask?"

I exhaled a soft breath, admitting, "With Jayden and Sutton gone, it makes you the only active League player, and with you making the playoffs, I know how that can go. Things get busy. Priorities can change."

He quirked his brow. "You think I'm a flake?"

There wasn't a hint of anything but his usual sweetness and humor in his tone.

"Maybe," I sassed, earning me a throw cushion to my face. I chuckled.

"Is that right?"

Our gazes connected and my laugh smoothed out into a you're-so-full-of-it-but-what-you-gonna-do-about-it smile. "No. No flakiness in sight." The more I'd learned about the man, the more I appreciated that was the absolute truth. He wasn't even thirty, yet he was more together than a lot of guys my age.

It had only been in the last year or so I'd fully realized or accepted that.

"But to answer your question, yes, I'll be there. I may not do the full six weeks every year, but for the moment, it's doable." He shifted on the couch opposite me and threw his long legs up, getting himself comfortable. "How about you?"

"How about me what?" In response he quirked his brow. I huffed, knowing exactly what he was getting at. "Yes, I'll be there. Moira can only take Lottie for two weeks, though. The rest of the time she'll be in Hong Kong."

"So does that mean Wayne's taking care of her?"

I didn't miss the tic in his jaw when he said Wayne's name, nor the distaste at the possibility of him looking after my girl.

"Or is Moira taking her to Hong Kong?"

I couldn't help but laugh at the look of horror when he said those words.

"She's not that bad. She's Lottie's mom and loves her."

"I'm not saying she doesn't. I'm just worried she'll leave her in a meeting or add her to a deal in a merger or something."

Humor touched his words, but I understood the undercurrent of seriousness in his tone. While I had joint custody of Lottie, for the last year, Lottie had lived with me full-time since her mom's work had taken her overseas.

Moira's business made for a busy life, one that didn't gel with being a shared-custody mom.

Whenever she was local and had the time, my ex would swoop in, clouded in Chanel perfume, and spend time with our girl, spoiling and doting on her. She loved Lottie unconditionally but preferred to love from afar through five-minute video calls.

Lottie and I had a great life and bond, though. Sure, she missed Moira, but my love for her was enough. At least I hoped it was. "I'm actually thinking of sending her to my parents."

When Pearce went bug-eyed, I choked on my sip of beer. "Fuck," I spluttered.

"You deserve to choke if you send her to Alabama."

I gasped for breath while snorting out a harsh laugh.

"She hates it there. Last year your mom tried to get her in that beauty pageant. How'd that turn out?" Nothing but pure, unadulterated glee reflected in Pearce's face, and he knew he had me.

"She cut up Dad's church suit and wore that while chanting 'beauty pageants suck' on stage."

A soft smile formed on his mouth. "Proudest day of my life."

My heart clenched, thinking the exact same thing. Pearce would be an amazing dad someday, something I knew he wanted. I ignored the taunting voice telling me if I'd accepted his offer to hook up, maybe he'd be an amazing dad now.

That ship had sailed.

"Just bring her to Montview."

"Are you crazy?"

"She'll love it. Hell, just think of the profiles she'll make on the college kids. She'll get them signing contracts with her, promising she can be their agents after college."

I raised both brows at him. "Make that after high school, if she has her way."

"Just speak to Emily. She'll make it happen. Plus, you know I miss Lottie like crazy over the summer." He shrugged, a look appearing on his face that I knew all too well. "That or you can ask Wank—" I quirked my brow, clamping down on my bottom lip to keep from laughing. I shouldn't encourage his dislike of Wayne, but he got such pleasure from it. "—*Wonderful* Wayne to look after her. I'm sure he'd jump at the chance."

I flipped him off. "Fuck off."

I didn't need to elaborate; it would only encourage him further. And after yesterday's conversation, something I wouldn't be sharing with Pearce, I didn't expect Wayne to be in the picture for much longer.

It was time. Not only because of the shit he pulled last night, but Lottie wasn't a huge fan of him.

I'd let all that slide because I knew we wouldn't be lasting the distance. We didn't chat about the future, and then there was the whole open-relationship thing. Something Pearce had scoffed at.

I thought Pearce would have loved the concept, a young, hot guy like him. I'd been wrong. "Fuck sharing" had been his exact words. "If a guy is lucky enough to call you his, the last thing he should need is anyone else. Your love would always be enough." His words had been so earnest, I'd struggled to catch my breath. When he'd finished up with "Hell, your love would be everything," I'd fought hard to remind myself how hooking up with a guy in his twenties and trying to make it work was a fool's task.

Pearce was incredible, but he was too young to be

trapped. That on top of being with a guy my age with a kid whose age gap to him was almost the same as the gap between us... nope. All I saw in that future was heartache. For me and for Lottie.

I sighed, shoving away the what-ifs and thinking about Wayne. "Okay, I'll chat to Emily and see if it's possible."

His smirk turned self-satisfied, and he snuggled deeper into the soft cushions. "I'll make sure I tell Lottie it's my idea."

Warmth battled it out with amusement in my chest when I realized his breathing slowed. Rather than waking him, I went to the master bedroom and collected a blanket. The overlarge couch wouldn't be too cramped, and unsurprisingly, Pearce falling asleep when he was in my space wasn't that uncommon.

Back at his side, I picked up his cell resting on the couch, turned it to silent, and placed it on the lamp table. I carefully wrapped the blanket around him, taking a sneaky glance at just how peaceful he looked.

He'd played his ass off tonight. A pang of guilt jolted my chest, knowing he should have gone out and celebrated with his teammates. I was a greedy bastard, holding on to our friendship the way I did. Hell, I coveted it.

No matter how many times I tried to convince myself that after I'd turned him down, his promise of us being just friends was honest, I knew it wasn't.

I shook my head, disappointed in myself that I couldn't let him go. While I'd never offered him anything beyond friendship, I didn't discourage how much time we spent together. Nor did I push him to go out and take advantage of his youth as hard as I knew I should.

Just what an asshole I was sat heavily in my gut. Looking at him now, all relaxed and comfortable, I couldn't find it in me to challenge myself too hard.

The truth was, my half-assed relationship with Wayne had been the only thing holding me back recently. But the more time passed, the more difficult it was to remember why holding back was such a good idea.

PEARCE WAS STILL OUT FOR THE COUNT WHEN I WOKE. A soft snore drifted from the couch as I organized coffee. I understood that level of exhaustion after a game.

It wasn't until Lottie headed into the kitchen, asking, "Do we really have to head home today?" that his snoring stopped, and he shifted.

At the movement, I struggled to pull my gaze away. When he sat up, shirtless and hair mussed, I was so glad I was unsuccessful. Was I gawking at the guy? Absolutely. Was I grateful that at some point in the night he must have undressed a little? Heck yes. I figured I had to get my Pearce fix whenever possible.

"Dad."

My attention snapped to my daughter, the arched eyebrow and her intent stare making it clear she noticed my focus was not where it should be. I swore Lottie seriously was ten going on twenty. She was so much sassier than I remembered being at her age.

"Yes." I smiled, even knowing my answer wouldn't make her happy. "We're not changing our flights."

"But I want to hang out with Pearce."

Me too, kiddo.

Instead of saying what was on my mind, I shrugged. "That's not going to happen."

"And my tummy hurts."

I frowned and angled my head, raking my gaze over my girl. She did look a little tired, but she'd had a late night. "Since when?"

She shrugged. "A little while ago."

Not sure if she was trying to con me since she didn't want to leave or if she was telling the truth, I asked, "How much does it hurt?"

"A bit."

"So it's best we get home sooner, then. Maybe an earlier flight?"

"No," she answered immediately, shooting me the stink eye.

"Morning."

My attention switched to a sleepy-looking Pearce.

"Morning," I responded, focusing hard on making eye contact. "Coffee?"

"As if you need to ask."

I grinned, more than aware Pearce didn't function well without his morning caffeine fix. I set about organizing his coffee, half listening to Lottie trying to convince Pearce to talk me into us staying.

"… and he said no." A dramatic huff followed. "It's not like he doesn't talk about you all the time and visit you," she continued.

I cleared my throat, ignoring the heat rising up my neck. "Lottie, enough." I narrowed my gaze at her before smoothing my features and handing Pearce his coffee.

"What did I do?" I had a feeling she was rolling her eyes, especially based on Pearce's low chuckle. "Okay, he doesn't talk about you *all* the time," she drew out. "Not when Wayne's around."

She made her feelings for Wayne completely clear from her tone alone. I struggled to hold back my wince, knowing when I got home, I'd have to follow up with the "talk" I'd promised Wayne.

Convenience wasn't worth it.

"Oh yeah, what's wrong with talking about me in front of Wayne?"

I caught Pearce's gaze and stared at him pointedly when he attempted a wide-eyed innocent expression. I wasn't buying his nonchalance.

"Let's wrap up this conversation," I interrupted with a clap of my hands. "Lottie, you stink. Go shower."

Lottie twisted her lips before lifting her arm high and taking a whiff of her armpit. "I do not." She shot me a pointed look that reminded me of her mom. "But I will shower, simply because hygiene is important."

"You do that, and I'll order breakfast. Pancakes?"

She grinned, her eyes widening in delight. "Yes, please. With strawberries and a ton of maple syrup."

I chuckled at her enthusiasm. Pancakes were my girl's weakness. Well, that and basketball. "I'll see what I can do."

"You're the best, Dad." She spun on her heels, but paused, whipping her attention to Pearce. "No messing with my pancakes."

I clamped down on my lips to stop laughing as

Pearce held up his hands, palms out. "Hey, what did I do?"

"The last time I had pancakes you exchanged the whipped cream with cottage cheese." Lottie gagged for good measure.

"What, a man can't make an honest mistake?"

Pearce was so full of shit. The guy was renowned for being a pain-in-the-ass prankster. Sure, they could be super funny, but I'd never tell him that. It was more fun to grumble and act put out.

"Hmm." Lottie apparently wasn't buying it as she did the whole "I've got my eyes on you" finger point at her eyes, then his. A beat later, she headed to her bedroom, leaving me and Pearce alone.

"I'm up for pancakes too."

I quirked my brow at him. "You are, huh? Without cottage cheese?"

He smirked, looking ridiculously handsome when that butter-wouldn't-melt look appeared on his face.

With a roll of my eyes, I challenged, "Haven't you got, you know, another important game coming up? You sure pancakes are wise?"

A cocky grin appeared on his mouth, and he lifted both brows high. "You think I need to worry about the calories?" He indicated his bare chest, his lips twitching.

Unable to stop my traitorous gaze, I gave a far too slow perusal of his chest. Jesus, I was a glutton for punishment.

The reminder of just how young he was and how much of a brilliant future he had slammed into me. Sure, I appreciated every hard ridge and the expanse of skin on display, but comparing it to my own and the handful of grays starting to sprout, it was a rude fucking reminder.

"Yeah, yeah, hotshot," I settled on. "Pancakes it is."

CHAPTER 6
PEARCE

I AGREED TO HANG OUT WITH EDDIE AND LOTTIE UNTIL their flight. We spent our time the way we usually did when in my town—went to my place and shot hoops with the two of them.

Perhaps it wasn't what some would call the most exciting way to spend my time the day after a big win, not just for the team but for me, but honestly, I didn't want to do anything else.

"I'm going to sit this one out. You guys are getting all sweaty and gross." Lottie scrunched her nose, letting us know just what she thought about that.

Eddie shot me a smirk, and we played some one-on-one.

"What are your plans when you get home?" I swooped around him with ease and scored a point.

"Not much." Readjusting his cap, Eddie got back in position. "I have a couple of meetings. Lottie has her school camp soon, so I need to get whatever gear she needs for that at some point."

I laughed. "I bet she's looking forward to that," I said, knowing she wasn't a fan of school trips at all.

"You know it." He shadowed, just a few inches between us. "It was only the promise of last night's game that stopped her sulking and agreeing to go with no fuss. I swear she plays me something fierce."

I dodged right, but he was on me immediately. "It's her job to keep you on your toes." I twisted, found my opening, and landed another point. "She's a kid who knows her own mind. That's a good thing, right?"

A warm smile tilted his lips. "Yeah, it is." Eddie passed me the ball. "She knows when to push it and not to. She can also handle me saying no without too much fuss."

Bouncing the ball, I nodded. "She's an awesome kid, and you're an amazing dad."

At my words, he beamed at me, a touch of pink touching his cheeks. Rather than call him out, I changed the subject. "So, home alone when she's at camp? What are your plans?"

"Other than watching you in the finals, you mean?"

I smiled, excitement springing to life, right alongside hope that we got that far. "Obviously," I said.

"You know me, tucked in by ten most nights."

I chuckled. "There's nothing wrong with that."

"Says the twenty-nine-year-old whose idea of an early night is before midnight."

It was true. I was usually a bit of a night owl, but I could sleep pretty much on cue.

"That doesn't mean I don't appreciate a chilled night at home." I didn't add that if it was a chilled, or even better, an early night snuggled in bed with him, I'd be more than up for it.

Such comments pushed the friendship boundary a shit ton too far, so I wisely kept them to myself.

Dribbling the ball, I paused at the sound of Lottie calling for her dad. The voice sounded off and had both of us whipping our heads in the direction of the house. Zeroing in on Lottie's small frame in the open garage doorway, I started to move, Eddie a couple of steps in front of me.

"What's wrong, baby?" He went down to his knees as I reached his side.

Pink-cheeked, Lottie's bottom lip wobbled as she clutched her stomach. "My belly really, really hurts." A pained groan escaped her, tears tracking down her cheeks.

"Hurts as in a tummy ache and too much ice

cream?" Calm bled through Eddie's words while my gut clenched. With sweat beading Lottie's brow, this looked so beyond a sugared-up belly ache.

"No," she sobbed, the sound tearing through me and shoving me into action. "I've been trying to ignore it."

I needed my keys. Something wasn't right. I had no idea how I knew that, but for one, Lottie was not a complainer. Sure, I knew she didn't want to go home, but this was so much more than that.

"Let me get my keys and get the car started."

Eddie peered up at me, wide-eyed and letting me see his worry.

"She's burning up," he said, and I noticed his palm on her forehead. "Something's not right."

I got moving, calling over my shoulder, "I'll meet you in the car." Taking action, I raced into the house, collecting my wallet, keys, and phone. I tore my sweaty tee off when I stepped into the laundry room, tugging on a fresh T-shirt and swiping Eddie one too. By the time I reached my SUV, Eddie sat in the back, strapped in, Lottie snuggled into his side.

Our eyes met, and I pushed every ounce of emotion I could into trying to reassure him before I settled behind the wheel and headed toward the local emergency room.

We rode in silence, the speed of the last ten minutes running on repeat in my head. Add in Lottie seeming A-okay first thing this morning. A glance in the rearview mirror reminded me that I wasn't over-reacting. Hunched over, Lottie sniffled quietly, the occasional whimper and groan escaping her.

Eddie whispered against the top of her head, stroking her sweaty brow.

My gut clenched, hating this. The speed, the adrenaline, the unknown. And fuck, I could only imagine how Eddie was feeling.

Traffic, thank God, wasn't horrific. There were two hairy moments, but I tried my hardest to keep my cool. In under fifteen minutes, I pulled up outside the ER and jumped out, opening the rear-side door.

Ashen-faced, Eddie all but stumbled out, reaching in and tugging his girl into his arms. Our gazes connected, and hell if my heart didn't lurch. The man screamed lost. Panicked. Rather than scooping them both up in my arms like I wanted, I ushered them toward the entrance, more than aware that it was likely my car would be towed.

The fuck if I cared. Not when Lottie and Eddie needed me.

The next fifteen minutes were a whirlwind. And right or wrong, I was relieved when the receptionist recognized who I was and raced us behind an examination curtain practically in moments.

Another thirty minutes was all it took for a scan to reveal the problem. Appendicitis. Eddie sagged at my side. "She complained this morning and I ignored her."

Somewhere in the last half hour he'd held my hand, clinging tightly, his other hand holding Lottie's. I squeezed his palm. "Hey, you couldn't have known. She said an ache, not full-on pain."

"But I should have—"

"Nope. Let's focus on what's happening now. Everything else is insignificant."

The look on his face almost brought me to my knees. "Okay, you're right." He returned his attention back to the doctor, saying, "You can sort that, right? Appendicitis?"

"We can. We'll get her to surgery," the middle-aged doctor explained. "We just have more paperwork to complete, but we'll make sure Charlotte is well taken care of."

A rush of breath escaped Eddie, and he hung his head low. Certain there were more questions to add and confident Eddie needed a moment, I asked the ER doctor, "How long will the surgery take?"

The doctor gave a reassuring smile, gaze dipping

momentarily to our joined hands. "She'll be out within a couple of hours at the most. As soon as she's in recovery, we'll reach out and let you see your daughter right away."

I nodded, not feeling the need to correct her, especially if it meant I wasn't going to be cleared out of the ER anytime soon. "And healing? She'll be okay? Not in too much pain?" A rope tightened around my heart at the thought of Lottie in prolonged pain. Hell, in any form of suffering. I wished like hell I had the power to take it away from her. I'd take it on myself twofold if I could.

"She'll be sore for a while and need to take it easy. But we'll go in laparoscopically, so it should mean healing time is faster. Normal activities should be fine in maybe two or three weeks."

Already my brain was going over her recovery, working out what would be best for her. There was no way they'd be able to head home, go on a fight. Was it bad I liked the thought of the two of them in my space way too much? That I liked the idea of keeping as close an eye as possible on Lottie while she was healing?

Paperwork signed, explanations given, I white-knuckled Eddie's hand, not quite sure I was doing a great job at being supportive, not with the way my heart slammed in my chest and sure if he let go, I'd sink to the ground.

And all this for my best friend's kid.

With a farewell of false smiles, we walked with Lottie as far as we were allowed.

"You know she's going to be okay, right?" I managed, knowing I really needed to step up. This was ridiculous, right? This type of operation was as common as scoring a three-pointer. If only my common sense would let my worried heart know. But at least I tried.

"I know."

"Give it three hours and she's going to be asking for her cell and looking at rankings and ratings and making predictions for the playoffs."

When Eddie snorted, warmth bloomed in my chest. I grinned over at him. "And you know, two or three weeks at my place means she's going to be absolutely in her element and lapping up every moment of her recovery."

"What? But we c—"

The shake of my head cut him off. "Just think how happy she'll be recovering at my house. No school." The leap of my heart as I waited for his response was as ridiculous as it was dangerous.

A few weeks in a shared space was my idea of bliss. Obviously, the reason wasn't ideal, but if it made me an asshole that I was happy about it, I'd wear a pin with pride.

"You sure?"

My nod was immediate. "Of course. You know you guys are always welcome."

"What about your schedule?"

I mentally went over my next few weeks. "I've got five days before our first playoff game. It's at home. All the rest after the first round depends on if we win—"

"You'll win."

My heart flipped at the steel in his voice. Fuck, I hoped we did, but we were playing the second seeded team, so who the hell really knew what would happen?

"Well, when we do play away, it won't be for long before I'll be home again for two or three days. You being at the house for me to come home to? Hell yes! There's not a lot of hardship in that. It'll make up for you guys not being able to watch in person."

And I meant every word. Eddie's gaze roamed my face, his attention drifting between my eyes. Whatever he saw seemed to make him relax.

"Okay, yeah. Thanks."

"It's more than okay."

I led him away to the private waiting room, still gripping his hand. From the way he squeezed and didn't let go for pretty much the whole two hours of waiting, I was more than happy to pretend this was normal, and that both Eddie and Lottie were mine to take care of.

The problem was, after two or three weeks, how would I let them go?

CHAPTER 7

EDDIE

"I don't know when. It'll all depend on her recovery."

"It all seems so convenient that it happened while you were in Minnesota so you can cozy on up to Pearce."

My skin flashed hot, anger thick and fast as it clawed up my throat. "You think my daughter being in agony and needing fucking emergency surgery is convenient?"

"No, of course not." Wayne's tone turned placating. "But it's only appendicitis, right?"

I couldn't take anymore. Not from this asshole. It would be a shitty thing to do to break things off on the phone, right? But I was oh so tempted. "I have to go. Lottie's napping and will be waking up soon."

"I have to go too. I'm due at Lionel's party in a couple of hours."

Of course he fucking was. "Uh-huh." It was all I could manage before ending the call. Pulling my phone away from my ear, I shot daggers at the thing, wishing Wayne and I had been face-to-face so I could do what I should have done a long time ago.

"That sounded like it went well."

I jumped at Pearce's voice. Leaning against the doorframe of Lottie's hospital room, he looked every bit as pissed off as I did. I'd ventured out into the corridor once Lottie had settled into a nap after another dose of painkillers, to give Wayne a call and let him know what was happening. We'd been due to go the Lionel's party together tonight, which clearly wasn't happening for me. Not that I wasn't relieved. Lionel, one of Wayne's friends who I knew he hooked up with, was a certifiable asshole.

"You young guys," I started, "you're all okay with calling things off via phone, right?"

There was a widening of Pearce's eyes at my question, and he swallowed hard. "Well, I think a lot of people don't even bother with a call. Text messages do the trick." His gaze lowered to the cell in my hand. "You need help working out the right text message etiquette to tell Wayne to fuck off? If so, I'm your man."

My lips twitched, liking too much that Pearce didn't hold back his pleasure. "I can't, right? Do that, I mean? Tell him it's over by text?" I rubbed a hand over my face, exhaustion creeping in.

"Hey."

I opened my eyes and dropped my hand, startling at Pearce's proximity. For a big guy, he moved far too quietly, getting into my space.

"Maybe don't even worry about this now. It's been a long twenty-four hours. I know there wasn't a chance you slept for more than a couple of hours in that tiny bed in Lottie's room last night. Why don't you head to my place and get some sleep?"

I shook my head. "But Lottie—"

"Lottie has me. She'll be fine. She's healing brilliantly and the nurse said it's likely the doc will be releasing her tomorrow. They just need to get her temperature under control. We'll hang out here and talk basketball when she wakes. You come back for dinner. Pick us both something up."

My heart stumbled in my chest, my shoulders sagging in relief that Pearce was here. Moira was obviously in Hong Kong. Yesterday when I spoke to her, she'd said she'd be able to jump on a late evening flight, but by that time, and I knew she was going to be fine, so what was the point? When I'd told my ex to not worry about it and that I'd send regular updates, her gratitude had been immediate.

It wasn't something I understood myself—her not being desperate to see her daughter—but I was used to single parenting. That didn't mean it couldn't be tiring or lonely. It made Pearce's offer mean so much more, especially as it was genuine. Not only that, but I believed he cared for Lottie.

"You sure?"

He nodded. "Absolutely. It's only just after one, so you can get a decent nap. I'll keep my phone on, and if anything changes, I'll call you immediately. I promise."

"I know you will." Unable to resist, I stepped closer and wrapped my arms around him. Pearce hugged me back, his arms strong and warm, and when he squeezed, I sagged a little into his embrace. Such simple contact fed my soul, providing me with comfort I didn't dare dream I'd receive. Not pulling away, I gave myself the moment, drinking in Pearce's support.

From the moment it was clear something had been wrong with Lottie, he had stepped up and taken control. And thank Christ he had. I'd been running on autopilot, everything frozen beyond the rapid beating of my heart and stone-cold panic. Without

Pearce… I relaxed into his touch, not wanting to finish that thought.

"He's an asshole. Okay." Pearce squeezed me lightly. "Whatever you decide will be the right thing for you."

I nodded, my thoughts flicking to my conversation with Wayne.

He hadn't even asked about Lottie. Not once. Hadn't asked how I was or if I needed him. It wasn't even as though the last six months we'd been fucking very often. Was I relieved he'd been getting it elsewhere? That my answer was a resounding yes meant it was finally time to let go.

"You okay?" Pearce whispered the question close to my ear, the warmth caressing my skin and giving me goose bumps.

I nodded against him, sure that was my cue to step out of his arms. But it was comfortable here. It was rare that we hugged—well, not like this. We always greeted each other with a handshake and a half hug, but like this—up close, bodies connected, his body heat pressing against my skin—it was enough to remind me why we didn't.

Pearce was temptation personified, and if we'd done this regularly, I wasn't sure I could hold back from making a move and possibly screwing up our friendship. That was the last thing I wanted. And after him stepping up like he did with me and Lottie, there was a whole lot of hero worshipping happening right now. And holy hell if it didn't make my heart beat that little bit harder for him.

Reluctantly, I eased out of his hold. Our gazes connected. "Thank you," I said quietly. "For this, for everything."

He squeezed my forearms before releasing. "You know I'm always here for you and Lottie. Now get your ass out of here." A chin uplift followed his words, along with a curve of his lips. "You know how I like my burgers, right?"

I snorted and shook my head. "So, grilled chicken and salad. Got it."

Pearce groaned and passed me his car keys. "It's like you're mirroring Jake, our nutritionist."

A smile lifted my lips. "Twelve years' experience in the League will do that. You've got training first thing. Then your first big game in four days."

"Shit, these days go fast."

I winced in sympathy, remembering all too well that five days between games initially sounded awesome, but between training and life, they passed by in a blink. "Just think, a few more weeks and it's the off-season. That's your time to kick back."

The narrowing of his brows took me by surprise.

"That's if we get that far. It could just be a couple of weeks."

"Hey," I said, surprised. Easygoing was Pearce's middle name, and I was sure his teammates would have added several more choice descriptors alongside that. Prankster being just one of them. He wasn't known for taking life too seriously. Between this unusual negativity and him being completely in control with Lottie, I was seeing unexpected sides of the man. "That defeatist attitude stops now. Screw that. You're in the playoffs. The aim is to make it all the way."

A slow smile formed on his mouth. "It's like having my own personal cheerleader. The guys are gonna be so jealous when I tell them Eddie Phelps waves his pom-poms for me."

An amused snort tore out of me. And there he was. The Pearce who'd managed to claim a section of my heart just for himself. "You go ahead and see how well that works out for you."

Pearce arched a brow at me, looking far too delectable when he did so. "That right? What possible threats could you bring to the table?"

My stomach somersaulted thinking about all the possibilities and the direction of this conversation. More than that, the tone of the damn thing. There

was no doubt this teasing ventured into flirting terri-
tory, and hell if it didn't feel good.

"You do remember I'm staying at your house for
the foreseeable future, right?" I quirked my brow and
didn't know how far to push this. Between my worry
for Lottie, my frustration at Wayne—and certainty in
ending it—and how good spending time with Pearce
made me feel, I needed something positive, something potentially amazing to cling to. Ignoring all
previous concerns I had, I leaned forward a fraction,
rightness settling in my chest when I settled on, "By
the time I get back to your place, I'm going to be
single." Despite the widening of Pearce's eyes, I
pushed on. "So if you don't want to see how exactly
that works out, by all means, have at it."

I swept on by him, skin flushed, ears ringing. I
quickly checked on Lottie before hightailing it out of
the hospital. That I'd left Pearce looking stunned and
red-faced didn't escape my notice. That I'd flirted so
outrageously, despite my hesitancy in trying to
pursue anything with the man, filled me with…
Fuck, there was no dread, simply excitement. Pure,
stomach-fizzing excitement. Something I hadn't felt
since I was nineteen.

I didn't even know if he was interested anymore.
Well, not for sure. Was I being a presumptuous
asshole?

I stepped out into the early afternoon sun and exhaled heavily.

What if Pearce wasn't keen for anything beyond friendship? If he wasn't, I'd truly screwed up the best friendship I'd ever had. I angled my neck from side to side until a satisfying pop filled my ears. It would be fine. I had to believe that. I hadn't outright propositioned the man, and if things were awkward, I'd apologize and work my ass off at making it right.

Since that's what had happened when Pearce indicated he'd like to be more than friends and we'd survived that, I figured we'd be able to again if need be.

I sighed and tugged out my phone, knowing I had a call to make. Since my parents had never met Wayne, they'd never need to know I was breaking the gentleman's code they'd drilled into me. And fuck it. Wayne didn't deserve my energy or a face-to-face, not when he was such a cockhead.

Wayne answered on the fifth ring. "Yeah?"

I rolled my eyes, pissed that I'd wasted time and energy on this man. "I know you're getting ready to head out to your friend's, so I'll keep this brief."

"If you could, I'm kinda busy at the moment." The sound of a deep chuckle filtered down the line. It wasn't Wayne's.

"Right. When I get back, we won't be seeing each

other again. It's time for a clean break." The words flew from me with ease—smooth and controlled.

"So I was right about Pearce." He scoffed. "It'll never work."

Clenching my jaw, I ground my back molars, trying my hardest to keep this civilized and not call him out on all his shit. "That's nothing you need to worry about."

"If there's nothing else…?"

I hated the curl of disgust settling in my chest. Hated I'd put up with his shit simply to distract me from my growing feelings for my best friend—and wasn't that a nugget of realization that slammed into me. Fuck, it was enough to take my breath away.

But Pearce had it so right calling him Wankface Wayne. The thought made me chuckle. There was no way I could keep it in. "Nope," I managed to say, my amusement loud and clear. "That's i—" He cut me off. The action dragged even more laughter out of me.

Fuck, it felt good to be free. Free from Wayne making me think he was doing me a favor. Free from denying my feelings for Pearce.

Grinning, I opened Pearce's car door, relieved he'd had the sense to move it yesterday so he wasn't towed. Once settled, I opened the built-in SatNav, pressing Home. A tug in my chest surprised me when I did so. Creating a home with Pearce, for the three of us, was a future that was exhilarating and terrifying. And… I was getting way ahead of myself.

Just because I'd finally admitted that my affection for Pearce went way beyond that of friendship, it didn't mean that something would happen. I was a dad with a shit ton of responsibilities. Pearce still had an amazing future laid out before him.

Fuck. Adulting was hard. It meant I had to be stupidly sensible and talk this shit out at some point… if he was interested.

But it wasn't like I could just say, "Hey, you wanna go steady? Well, yeah, we haven't even kissed, but how do you really feel about being a step-dad?" There was pressure, then there was *pressure*.

As I pulled out of the parking lot, I focused on breathing and calming my thoughts. There was little point in being fifteen steps ahead of myself. I needed to take each day as it came. Plus, Lottie was the most important person I had to focus on. It was difficult when my dick spent so much time responding to Pearce. There was only so much my body and brain could handle.

But still, focus was necessary.

I had a feeling that was going to be difficult until Pearce and I talked this thing out.

CHAPTER 8
PEARCE

HOVERING IN THE DOORWAY WITH A HARD-ON WAS ALL levels of wrong. It was all Eddie's fault. The asshole knew it too. It was the reason why he'd raced out of here after throwing all those words my way. Every word he'd said, the tone he'd used, had hit their mark. Caressing my skin before seeping through and finding a home in my chest.

Hope. The motherfucker had made hope surge to life. Well, that, and my dick.

Getting a chub while in the corridor outside his daughter's room was not okay. But taking steadying breaths, thinking of gross things, hell, even digging my short nails into my palms weren't helping.

"Daddy."

But that voice right there worked wonders.

"Hey, Lottie girl." I eased away from the doorframe and stepped properly into her room, making a beeline for the chair next to her bed. Groggy-eyed, she peered over at me, a frown dipping her brows before she yawned.

"Pearce, where's my dad?"

I relaxed into the chair, placing my feet super carefully on the end of her bed. "I managed to kick him out so he could sleep and we could have us time. You know how rare it is to have you all to myself without the grown-up around."

A drowsy giggle escaped her. "Does that mean you'll let me have my phone to see what's reporting on ESPN?"

This kid right here was incredible. Her dad had done the best job raising her. While he grumbled at times and begged her to focus on her friends and encouraged her to seek other interests too, it didn't mean he didn't support her dream. Considering she was ten years old, Lottie was more clued in than some adults I knew.

"Even better, we can get ESPN on this fancy TV you've got here." I tugged the TV hanging from the ceiling closer so we could both see it, then swiped the remote and found the station.

"Sweet," she said, following up with another huge yawn. Reflexively, she stretched, which was quickly stopped with a yelp.

"You hurting, Lottie?" I was on my feet immediately, hovering over the poor kid, wishing once again I could magic away her pain.

She bobbed her head. "Yeah. It's really sore." Her hands stopped short of touching her stomach where I knew her wound was.

"Let's see if the nurse says you can have any different painkillers for that, okay?" I pressed the buzzer and sat back down, refocusing on the TV and adjusting the volume. "So, the first game's at the end of the week," I said, trying to distract her while waiting for the nurse to arrive. "What are you thinking?"

"Roosters are up against the Cardinals. The Cardinals have it in the bag." She glanced over at me, and I nodded in complete agreement. The Cardinals got to the finals last year, and they'd kicked ass most of the season too.

"What about the Wolves versus the Mavericks?"

She scrunched her face together as if hard in thought, covered her mouth with her hand, and tapped her index finger above her lip. My heart warmed at the sight. It was something her dad did whenever he was figuring something out.

"It'll be close. Wolves may just tip it though and take the win."

"Huh, you don't think—"

"How are we doing in here?" A nurse I'd not seen before entered the room, gaze flicking briefly to me before settling on Lottie. "Charlotte, my name's Jamaal. I'm one of your nurses this afternoon. You doing okay?" He kept his attention on her as he paused by her bed.

"My tummy's hurting." She glanced over at me, looking decidedly sorry for herself.

"Is she able to have more painkillers yet?"

Jamaal picked up her chart and nodded, offering me a smile before turning back to Lottie. "I think we can absolutely get you some more painkillers. Can you take a look at this chart for me and tell me which face you're on right now?" He held out the pain scale chart and waited patiently for Lottie. She examined the diagram carefully and pointed at the amber unhappy face. Jamaal offered a sympathetic smile and jotted down a note. "Okay, let me go and get a doctor to sign off on those, and I'll get them right on over. While you're waiting, how about ordering yourself a snack?" He turned to me. "If she could eat something, it'll help with the next lot of painkillers."

"Absolutely."

His attention then flicked to the screen, and I followed his gaze, heat hitting my cheeks when I realized footage of my last game was playing.

"Right, well, I'll be back as quickly as possible," he said, once again talking to Lottie.

Once he'd left the room, Lottie said, "Let's get this snack ordered and get to work."

I chuckled, loving that she was focusing on anything rather than her discomfort. "Deal, as long as I get something too. Have you seen how awesome this menu is?" I flicked through the TV until I got to the food ordering service. "I vote chocolate cake, Jell-O, and ice cream. What do you reckon, kiddo?"

"For me sure, but you can have a protein shake. Don't think you can use me as an excuse for slacking off."

Lightness flooded me, my smile extra wide. "You know, it's a shame I'm going to retire before you can be my manager. Truly," I deadpanned.

She narrowed her eyes at me. "Well, that's definitely going to happen if you keep trying to eat chocolate cake. Your plan should be to be the oldest player in the League." She sighed, all dramatic like. "I totally blame Mom and Dad for not having me five years earlier. It's all their fault I'm not old enough to be almost finished with school."

Amusement bubbled in my chest. "You're totally right. Your parents suck."

FROM THE MOMENT EDDIE RETURNED, I WAS ON ALERT. What that meant was I turned into a stumbling, bumbling idiot.

Case in point.

Eddie: "I brought you a coffee. Be careful, it's hot."

My mind lingered on "hot," which led me to thinking how hot Eddie was, which led to the words "so fucking hot" spilling from my mouth and my face setting on fire. This led me to spilling said coffee on my pants and Eddie helping me clean up.

Of course this encouraged my dick to misbehave, pop a boner, at which point I sat down so hard on the chair to cross my legs to conceal said boner that I misjudged, missed, and landed on my ass.

Fun times were had by all.

Except me, who wanted the ground to open up.

But hearing Lottie's sweet laughter did the job of calming me—in every imaginable way—and making me so damn happy that she managed to laugh despite her shitty couple of days.

I didn't miss the barely concealed amusement on Eddie's face. Heck, who was I kidding? Barely concealed… what a crock. The guy busted a gut laughing before helping me up. With the way his hands lingered in mine, though, it was totally worth it.

After that, we stuffed our faces. Them with juicy burgers, me with a chicken salad. Was it bad that I loved and hated Eddie for being so damn thoughtful? But seriously… a chicken fucking salad.

"It's getting late, and you have an early start tomorrow."

We'd just finished another game of bullshit, where I'd destroyed my opposition. Lottie had since plugged her earbuds in and was watching something or other on YouTube, her eyes drooping and her skin looking a little paler than earlier.

A quick glance at the time told me it was past her bedtime and definitely closer to mine, since I'd committed to an early run with Cassius and Ollie in the morning. "Are you going to be okay?" My gaze roamed over Eddie's features. He looked a lot fresher than earlier. He'd showered and shaved and wasn't looking as bleary-eyed as this morning.

The smile directed at me was soft and sweet and all mine. "Yeah. The sleep this afternoon helped. Thanks for looking after her." His gaze darted to his daughter, who remained completely focused on her phone, before returning to me. "You sure you're okay with us sticking around?"

"Of course. Why wouldn't I be?"

His shrug was too stiff to be carefree. "You've got a lot on. I don't want us being a distraction."

Leaning forward in my seat, I captured his gaze. "It'd be more distracting not having you there, wondering how Lottie's healing, not being able to make sure you're both okay."

When he swallowed hard, my focus shifted to his throat before snapping to his mouth as he darted out his tongue and swiped at his bottom lip.

We were quiet for a moment, and when he didn't speak, I realized he was thinking about something hard. Five years of spending every spare moment I could in this man's company had taught me a thing or two about reading his tells. "What's up? Has something happened?"

An awkward laugh escaped as he ran his hand over his head, gaze once more darting to Lottie, then back to me. The clearing of his throat caught my attention even more. He was nervous? About what?

"I spoke to Wayne again."

I stiffened at the mention of the man's name. Fuck, what if they'd worked out whatever was going on between them? A couple of years was a long time together to be calling it quits. I hoped Eddie wasn't asking if Wayne could stay too. How would I be able to say no to his request without coming across as a prize prick?

"Yeah?"

"I called it off with him. It was long past due. His

reaction to Lottie...." He scoffed, and my brows sprang high at the derision in the sound. "Or lack of... Yeah, it was something I should have done a long time ago."

As he spoke, my mind buzzed and my skin prickled. Would it be bad if I fist-pumped? Probably. Instead, I didn't hold back my wide-ass grin. "Oh no," I deadpanned. "How devastating. He's such a good guy and so worthy of your company and time. How will you possibly cope without such a great guy in your life?"

The sarcasm dripped off my tongue, earning me a loud laugh and a "Fuck off. Tell me how you really feel."

I could barely form additional words with just how big my grin spread across my face. "I can if you need me to."

Eddie rolled his eyes, and I tried hard to rein in some of my glee, offering a more genuine "But you are okay, right? Not cut up about it?" I hoped to shit I'd read this situation right, even though hearing this was something he'd been considering for a while took me by surprise.

"Yeah. I really am. The last six months or so, and probably since having Lottie full-time—" After a glance to ensure Lottie was still focused on her screen later, he carried on. "Well, we haven't really seen each other all that often. We were just going through the motions, you know?"

Air whooshed out of me. I wasn't even subtle about it. Since we rarely talked about our romantic lives, sex lives… whatever… I'd had no idea the state of his. Knowing that their relationship had been degenerating for a while shouldn't have made me so happy, but I'd be a liar if I said it didn't.

"I'm happy you're not cut up over it. And let's get this straight. Wankface was never good enough for you. You know that, right?"

With twitching lips, Eddie nodded. "I know, but it happened, and it's done."

My grin was back. "When you're home tomorrow and Lottie's tucked up in bed, we'll celebrate."

"We will?" His brows lifted high. "And how exactly will we celebrate, since the countdown to your first playoff game is on?" There was a hint of teasing in his voice that I liked entirely too much.

While he was right and I couldn't get wasted, nor could he really since there was Lottie to consider, I'd think of something. "You let me worry about that. Just know that you not having Wankface in your life anymore deserves to be marked by something epic."

I couldn't very well let him know my first thought was me on his dick; that would be all levels of hot—I meant wrong… right? So with that potentially, maybe, probably off the table, I'd work something else out.

"Why do I have a feeling I should be nervous about whatever you're proposing?"

Flames lit my cheeks. "Shit, did I say me on your dick aloud?" At his widening eyes, flushed cheeks, and with the way his mouth gaped, I figured not. *Fuck.* "Shit, fuck... uhm—"

"Daddy, I need the bathroom."

My salvation came in the form of a ten-year-old. I jumped out of my seat, startling both Eddie and Lottie. Both pairs of eyes were locked on me. "Uhm... okay. I'll leave you guys to it. See you both tomorrow." Pointedly ignoring Eddie, I focused on Lottie, dotted a kiss on the top of her head, and ran like my ass was on fire.

Holy mother of cock. I swore I was going to duct tape my mouth. How the hell did I come back from that epic brain spew? On autopilot, I left the hospital ward, heading toward the exit.

I supposed the only thing to do was distract Eddie with a celebration so he'd forget what an idiot I was, because surely to God, the idiot in me was strong. It wasn't the ideal way to reassure the man I'd make excellent boyfriend and stepdad material.

CHAPTER 9
EDDIE

PEARCE DROPPED HIS SUV AT THE HOSPITAL THIS morning so I could get Lottie back to his place safely. While I didn't ask him to do so, I was grateful for how considerate he was. This caring, thoughtful side of him didn't help diminish my growing feelings for him.

It was only now, with the changes over the years and our developing friendship, I was able to look beyond what was once the young, carefree twenty-four-year-old I'd first met to finally see him as a man who I could depend on.

It wasn't just his age that reflected that. It was his love for my daughter, his desire to care for us both. He'd changed in so many ways, while remaining in that relaxed, almost happy-go-lucky state of mind.

As I settled Lottie in the bedroom she'd claimed as her own about three years ago, my heart swelled beyond comprehension when I found a bag of new clothes and toiletries for her. In "my" room—one of the guest bedrooms I slept in when staying over—I'd discovered a note letting me know I could help myself to his closet alongside a bag of new underwear.

It made sense since we were almost identical in size. While I'd gained a few pounds and was nowhere near as firm as I had been in my pro days, I made an effort to stay in shape.

The note led me to standing in the kitchen preparing a salmon salad wearing a pair of his gray sweatpants and one of his Eagles training tees. Had I liked putting his clothes on? That'd be a firm yes. I wasn't even that embarrassed that I'd sprung a boner when I'd luxuriated in tugging on the sweatpants, remembering him wearing the exact same pair and thinking how fucking delectable his ass looked in them.

At the sound of the garage door opening into the laundry room, my heart ratcheted up. The words he'd blurted yesterday remained burned in my memory, and unintended or not, there was no erasing them.

Not that I would, even if that was an option.

"Hey," he greeted, entering the kitchen.

Looking over my shoulder, I raked my gaze over him. He looked freshly showered and tired. Not surprising since he'd been training for hours.

"Hey, everything go okay today?"

He nodded, dropping his bag next to the door and untying his laces before kicking off his Nikes. "Yeah. It was full-on. Watched a fair amount of tape, practiced until I thought I was going to keel over." While he chuckled, his exhaustion was easy to read.

"You hungry?"

"I sure am." He tugged open the fridge and pulled out a protein water. As he chugged it back, draining the whole bottle, I forced myself to look away. This was getting ridiculous. "This" being my attraction, my horniness, my regressing into an awkward teenager.

"Where's Lottie?"

"Where do you think?" My words earned me a light chuckle.

"Bed and glued to ESPN?"

"You know it."

Venturing over to me, he asked, "Is she doing okay?"

Meeting his gaze, I nodded, welcoming the

warmth and concern in his voice and eyes. "Tender, demanding, which means she's going to be just fine." I picked up the lettuce to return to the fridge, turning fully toward Pearce for the first time. His brows shot high, eyes widening, and I realized he was looking at what I was wearing.

I fought hard to push away the heat traveling through me at his attention, but it was useless. This was the reason I never should have shaved my beard.

Pink touched the apples of his cheeks before he cleared his throat, a shit-eating smirk appearing. "Holy shit. Let me grab my phone. Eddie Phelps in an Eagles jersey…"

"Fuck off." I grinned and pushed past him toward the fridge. "As you're more than aware," I said pointedly, "I have so many Eagles jerseys and paraphernalia that I have nightmares."

He chuckled. "Most with my number on. I know."

I glanced back, and he bounced his brows up and down. "Uh-huh. For your birthday you received what from me and Lottie, and what did I get in return?"

"VIP Tickets to see Tay Tay, which, I'll say giving me three tickets was awfully generous of you." He leaned against the countertop, grinning. I smiled back, remembering what a great night the three of us had.

"And?" I prodded.

"You were the lucky receiver of forty items of Pearce Malcolm merch. Eight of which are one-of-a-kind, I'll remind you."

Perhaps this wasn't the best thing to be joking about right now as it was doing nothing to distract me from what an incredible man he was. Forty gifts for my fortieth birthday. Nor was he exaggerating about the one-of-a-kind merch either. Throw cushions, beach towels, a pack of condoms, even a bottle of lube, to name just a few of the special items with Pearce's face or Eagles number printed on them.

I kept every single item. Admittedly some—the PG stuff—had been swiped by Lottie, but did I like relaxing in clothes with his number printed on them when at home? Maybe a little too much. It was no wonder that Wayne was convinced there was something going on between us.

We stood for a couple of beats, smirking at each other.

"So, dinner?" he asked, breaking the spell, and I noticed a new spread of red on his cheeks. "What do you need me to do?"

I shook my head. "Nothing. I've cooked up some

fries for Lottie, so keep your hands off them," I said, heading to the oven to pull out the tray.

"Why does Lottie get fries and I don't?" He pouted, his bottom lip sticking out so far, I was tempted to nip at it.

"You really need me to answer that?"

A dramatic huff pushed past his lips. "Nope. I can be a responsible adult when I need to be."

"Uh-huh. And an athlete who has the first of many incredible playoff games of his career coming up."

"Yeah, that as well." He eyed the plates I finished preparing. "I, um… promised you a celebration."

I fought hard not to get flustered, remembering exactly how he'd wanted to celebrate.

"That's a little tricky, what with Lottie and her wound. So I thought, Lottie won't be able to come sit with us, right?"

"Not today. Maybe in a couple of days, but she's not up for it at the moment."

"So, I thought maybe a picnic in her room. I know it's cheesy and not exactly a proper celebration, but…"

A fizz of happiness bubbled in my stomach. "She'd love that."

"And you?"

It took me a moment to answer, too surprised by

his tentative tone. Clearing my throat, I answered, "I'd love that too."

"Awesome." A grin appeared on his mouth. "I'll go get it set up." He raced out of the room, his heavy steps pounding up the staircase. Alone in the empty kitchen, I stood there, listening to Lottie's sweet laughter and the deep rumble of Pearce's voice.

Only a few hours here, and this was a version of domestic bliss that was both terrifying and something I didn't dare dream of. There was something brewing between the two of us. The last forty-eight hours or so had made that crystal clear.

I needed to be brave enough to go for what I wanted, find a way to push aside my joke of a relationship with Wayne, and swallow back my concerns of destroying my friendship with Pearce while not breaking my and Lottie's hearts in the process.

Pearce Malcolm was worth the risk.

I just needed the dust to settle from the emotional and absolutely terrifying two days I'd had. That way nothing would be clouding my judgement. When I made my move, I needed Pearce to know I meant every word and gesture.

DINNER WAS FUN, LOTTIE IN HER ELEMENT BEING DOTED on by the two of us. Pearce and I sat on a picnic blanket. Where he'd found it, I had no idea, but it had made us all smile and provided the perfect setting to finally be able to unwind, knowing that Lottie was safe and healing.

"How's the team feeling about your first game?" I asked after pushing my plate to the side.

"Good. Everyone's still buzzed and trying hard not to get ahead of themselves. It's really something to finally be making the playoffs. To go the whole way…." He trailed off with a sigh that spoke of dreams.

"Your team is strong. You've been playing like champions all season. There's no reason why you can't get to the finals and win this thing."

"You think?" Uncertainty dipped his voice, and from his tone, he wasn't seeking an ego boost.

"I know it."

"Dad's right," Lottie added. She'd given up on her half-eaten dinner and had been resting quietly, flicking through her phone. "Your stats have been amazing this year, and anyone who knows a thing about the game only has to see you on the court to know you're one of the top ten players in the League."

As I grinned at my daughter, a surge of love filled

my chest. I loved that she was so invested, but more than that, that she wanted to offer Pearce the reassurance he needed.

When I focused on Pearce, it was impossible to miss the tenderness etched in his features. He reached out and fist-bumped Lottie, saying, "You're the best, Lottie girl."

Her smile was sleepy, cluing me in to her really needing to get a good night's rest.

"Right, kiddo," I said as I stood. "Let's get you washed up and back to bed."

"I'll get her pain meds," Pearce said before I could even ask.

I shot him a grateful look. "Thanks."

"Anything for my girl."

Every time he said that, offered such effortless affection, emotion slammed into me. I'd never been an overly emotional guy... well, not until I became a dad. From the moment I set my gaze on Lottie, a dam wall or something that had held back a side of me I'd never known existed all but burst free. And with it was this ball of emotion, ready to roll on a dime.

"I'll get this cleared up too."

"You don't have to. You've got an early start tomorrow."

He shook his head. "I can handle getting this

done. It's not my bedtime just yet." He quirked a brow at me as he gathered the plates.

It didn't take long to get Lottie ready for bed. She was washed up as best as we could manage since we needed to keep her small wounds dry. But we'd all survive her not being squeaky clean for a few more days. The pain meds and a bottle of water sat on her bedside table, and her room was straightened out from our picnic dinner.

It had been a long time since I hadn't needed to manage by myself. Moira and I had split when Lottie was just three. It made sense for me to retire when that happened, knowing that while we had shared custody, Moira's business was taking off and her international travels had started to become more regular.

It meant no nanny, no after school care, just the occasional time out when Moira was around, and the twice-yearly visit to my folks. Being a single dad could get lonely. It didn't take a genius to under-stand why I'd attempted to give it a shot with Wayne, but looking around the tidy room, seeing the tendrils of care from Pearce, brought things into sharp perspective. Wayne had never done anything like this.

Rather than dwell on the whole Wayne saga and wishing I'd ended things before they'd even begun, I focused on tucking in Lottie, hoping I'd get a few minutes alone with Pearce before he crashed.

"Night, kiddo. You call out to me if you need anything, okay? If it hurts to call out for any reason, just use your cell. I'll keep mine switched on."

"Okay, Daddy."

My heart melted. She rarely called me that anymore—generally only when she was super tired or feeling unwell.

"Love you." I dotted a kiss on her forehead.

"Love you more."

I smiled as I backed away, turning off the over-head light. Once the door was closed, I took in a breath before slowly exhaling.

Exhaustion beat at me. Despite my drooping eyes, considering the craziness of the past few days, I was glad I was here. Sure, today I'd had to deflect a few calls and rearrange meetings, but doing so from Pearce's house, a place I was comfortable, was kinda nice.

As I headed downstairs, I tuned in to Pearce's voice. Since I hadn't heard the door, nor did I hear another voice, I figured he was on the phone.

"… another time." Laughter followed and a pause. "Just keep it in your pants." Pearce snorted, and I hesitated from entering the room. "No. A couple of weeks probably. I can come to you." He quieted. "We'll see how it goes. Listen, I need to go." And now I felt weird standing here like this, listening in. Shrugging off the weird discomfort that settled over me, I stepped into the sitting room, finding Pearce lounging on the huge sectional, bottle of water in hand and his phone to his ear. He offered me an up-nod when I entered. "Just stay out of trouble, and I'll see you for the first game. See you, Tony."

I tensed at the mention of Tony, resenting the fact that I did so since I had no right to react. After Pearce ended the call, his focus turned to me.

"Lottie okay?"

"Yeah," I answered with a bob of my head, eyeing the couch and feeling weirdly out of sorts after listening to the tail end of his conversation with a man I knew he hooked up with. "I expect she's already fast asleep." My smile was more like a wince, and from the concern dipping his brows low, Pearce spotted it.

"And how about you? You doing okay over there?"

I remained hovering a few feet from the doorway. "Sure, yeah, just tired."

"You want to watch some TV, have a drink, or anything?"

"If you have plans while we're here, please don't change them on my account." The words rushed out of me, strangely formal. I internally rolled my eyes at myself, disgruntled that I was such a dickhead, but a touch of green settled in my stomach like a murky, heavy weight.

"Huh? What plans?"

"Uhm… with Tony or whatever. I just… Me and Lottie being here, I don't want it to distract you or for you to change your routine, or hell, cramp your style or something." Babbling was never a good look, but I couldn't stop my messy, insecure words.

"I can catch up with Tony whenever. It's no big deal."

The truth of the statement did nothing to ease that tinge of green. Jesus H. Christ, I was too old to be jealous. Right? If not, I was surely too old to be chasing after a guy who could have any man he wanted. My time with Wayne had taught me several things. One of the major ones was that I wasn't cut out for open relationships. Not anymore.

I needed, *wanted* stability. Craved a man or woman to come home to. Did I like the idea of Pearce being that person? Maybe a little too much and too eagerly. But I wasn't sure he was in the right place to be there with me.

While we had chemistry and mutual attraction, I wanted the whole package. Asking Pearce to think about his future and know where Lottie and I fit in to it seemed crazy unfair of me. Hello, pressure much!

"It's fine. You don't need to explain yourself." My words seemed to cause even more confusion from his deepening frown, but I rallied. "Honestly, your focus is the playoffs and carrying on your business as though we were never here."

"But I—"

"I'm going to crash. Two nights in the hospital cot was not good for my back. If you need me to do anything around the house or pick anything up tomorrow while you're at training, just drop me a text." I nodded for good measure and forced a smile. "Night, Pearce. Thanks again for letting us stay."

Without another word or giving him time to respond, I headed to my room, got washed up, and dipped beneath the covers.

Tonight had not gone as I'd hoped, but hearing Pearce rearrange things with Tony was the unfortunate reminder I needed that our lives, our situations were worlds apart. Maybe in a few years things would be different. For now, though, it would be sensible to bury my desire for wanting something more and instead focus on my healing daughter and being a good friend to the man I shouldn't be getting a hard-on for, right?

Even as the question bounced around in my tired

brain, I wasn't quite sure I believed the answer should be yes. What I did know was I spoke the truth to Pearce. The last thing I wanted was for him to be distracted. Me getting on my knees and offering to suck his cock would be that for sure, so maybe instead, I just had to keep my dick and my heart in check for a little longer, before I distracted the man so damn good, he wouldn't know whether he was coming or—

I snorted at the thought. Pearce would definitely know that.

CHAPTER 10
PEARCE

With no idea what caused Eddie to act so weird and brush me off the other night, it took Coach threatening to bench me to pull my head out of my ass and get it on straight.

With everything between us—me and Eddie, that was. I sure as shit didn't mean Coach, who seemed close to losing his cool—that first night with him at my house distracted me.

But fuck if I'd be benched. It was a wake-up call I begrudgingly needed. With the game taking place in a few hours, I couldn't afford distractions. Not a chance would I let my team down. We'd worked so hard to get to this point. Playing in the championships wasn't just my dream. Every single player was thirsty for the win.

"Malcolm."

I barely caught my grimace hearing Coach call my name. We'd been practicing for an hour, keeping it light, but since my name had been a cuss for Coach for the past seventy-two hours or so, I expected I'd screwed up again.

Neutral expression in place, I turned. "Yeah, Coach?"

"Go speak to that local reporter I always see you with. You've got ten minutes before I want you cooling down and icing your knees."

"Sure thing, Coach." With a rush of relief, I hooked the ball under my arm and headed over to Tony, who I spotted a few feet away from the major reporters and networks who were spending some time at our training session.

"Hey." I greeted Tony with a smile before swooping him up for a friendly hug. "I didn't see you arrive."

He patted my back and pulled away, a grin plastered on his face. "You were busy goofing off with Cassius."

I snorted. "I don't know what you mean. I'm too busy busting my balls preparing for tonight's game."

Bright eyes were directed my way, and Tony grinned even wider. "I'm seriously happy for you, Pearce. I know how bad you want this."

"Thanks." I bobbed my head, trying to fight back

the nerves attempting to claw to the surface. "So you're here in official capacity, right?" I bounced my brows for good measure, earning me an eye roll.

"I could do with a quick sound bite if that's okay."

"Sure thing, and we seriously do need to catch up soon."

"Tonight? After the game."

I hesitated, my thoughts drifting to Eddie. Whenever Eddie came to a game, Tony and I never got together. He knew the score and understood when my friend was in town, my time was his.

When I didn't answer immediately, his brows drew together. "I didn't think Eddie would be coming, since his daughter's recovering."

"He's not."

His eyes widened, and a half-smile formed. "Huh, but he's at your place and you need to rush home and do the domestic stuff."

"Not need; more like want."

"I get it. You said a couple of weeks, right, him staying?"

"It should be, yeah." My stomach clenched knowing half of that time I wouldn't be at home, so I'd be missing out on hanging out with them. I also knew what Tony was getting at. "Listen." The back of my neck prickled. "Maybe we should officially cool it and stick to being friends for a while." Which in all honesty we'd been veering toward for the past few months.

Mouth twitching, he quirked his brow. "A while, huh? Or do you really mean for good?" He waggled his brows for good measure, and thank fuck he was such a good guy and wasn't making this awkward.

"Probably for good. Just sticking to friends. Things with Eddie… well, I'd like there to be all the things with Eddie."

"Friends I can do." He snorted. "Well, not *do* do, but we can absolutely be just friends. I hope you figure things out with Eddie. I really do."

The stumbling of my heart coincided with my head snapping to movement over Tony's shoulder and my gaze connecting with Eddie's.

He was here. Now. And close enough to hear exactly what I'd just said. I was sure of it.

Tony's "Oh" after my movement led to him saying, "Well, uhm… I'll give you a couple of minutes before that sound bite," before he scurried away.

As soon as he was gone, Eddie stepped toward me. Red colored his cheeks.

"Hey, you're here." Surprise and happiness filtered through my voice. Perhaps a little embarrassment too that he'd overheard me, assuming he had.

But after his slight distancing, if that's what it was, perhaps this was what was needed. Unintentional or not, he'd finally heard what I wanted.

In his silence, worry snapped to attention in my gut. "Lottie." I glanced to his side. "Where is she? Is she okay?"

"She's fine," he answered, a softness forming in his eyes, the norm whenever we talked about Lottie. "Ollie stole her away." Angling to his right, I followed the line of direction. Seeing Lottie in an Eagles courtesy wheelchair, a grin on her face and three of my teammates fawning over her, I relaxed, exhaling heavily.

"Thank Christ." I rubbed at my heart, the pang of worry slowly dissipating. "Lottie's out and about."

"She is. She doesn't need the wheelchair, obviously, but it was the compromise to come and see you, knowing she wouldn't be jostled by accident."

"Good idea." While it wasn't busy like it would be in a few hours, there were still plenty of people around. "And you guys came to say hello?"

"Lottie wasn't sure if you'd be coming home after practice and before tonight's game. She wanted to wish you luck."

"Lottie's pretty great at her pep talks."

Eddie snorted. "She has her moments."

"You guys can still come tonight, if you think she's up for it. I can make sure she's safe and—"

"Maybe the next home game." The seven days between now and then would give her more recovery time. "I'll be so focused on worrying she's okay, I won't be following the game properly. I don't want to miss a thing."

Disappointment warred with relief. I didn't want Lottie here for the same reason—the whole being fragile thing, not just because I wanted all her dad's attention. "I'll be home straight after the game." The words rushed out with no real purpose other than to remind him I wanted to spend time with him too.

"You don't have to rush back. It's important you spend time with your team."

I snorted. "These guys get enough of me when we're away. Give them the chance, they'd be begging you to take me off their hands."

His brows shot high, eyes flaring. "That right?"

"Ha. Don't you know it." Cassius appeared out of nowhere and draped his arm over me. "We'd pay for it to happen. Give us a break from his dickish ways."

"You know, there's plenty of time away from my 'dickish' ways without selling me off, right?"

"Meh." Cassius shrugged, hand squeezing my shoulder. "Selling you off implies we'd get paid. Did you miss how desperate we were to pay someone to take you?"

My elbow in his side made him grunt. "Whatever, asshole. Eddie would pay a tidy sum for my fine ass." My nod was firm. "Isn't that right?"

Between the pulled-in lips and the frown, Eddie didn't seem in agreement.

"Don't you give this dick any fodder. You're my friend and would happily pay for my time."

"Pimping you out. Sweet," Cassius added. "Though I don't think Eddie needs to pay for something you'd give so willingly."

I jerked my head to look at Cassius, mouth gaping, heat spreading up my neck. "Dude…"

Cackling, Cassius wisely backed away.

"The fuck? Not cool, man," I added, my ego demanding I at least attempt to not appear as needy and desperate as apparently my teammates knew I was.

Blowing me a kiss, Cassius continued backing away. "Just calling it like I see it. And Coach said 'hurry the hell up.'"

I closed my eyes, wondering how just a few moments ago I liked the idea of Eddie hearing my conversation. Being called out, though, made me wish for the ground to open up and swallow me whole. It was something I was used to feeling recently. You'd think it would get easier. But nope.

Instead, I forced myself to look back at Eddie. His gaze was already locked on me.

"Can I borrow you for a minute? Somewhere private. I know you're busy, but just… a minute." The serious expression on his face did nothing to ease my desire to disappear, but still I nodded.

A glance at Lottie reassured me she was okay, but I needed to be certain. "Ollie."

He peered over.

"You good for two?" I indicated toward Lottie and received a nod and a thumbs-up. After giving him an up-nod, I turned to Eddie and signaled for him to follow me. There was a collection of storage rooms just off the locker rooms. While I didn't know what he wanted to talk about, his "private" plus the intensity in his eyes told me enough that I didn't want an audience.

Two rooms were locked. A huff of relief escaped at the third door being open. After looking around the room to check it was unoccupied, I headed inside. Eddie followed, hot on my heels, the soft snick of the door the only sound beyond my anxious breaths.

I turned, saying, "Everything o—" The words caught in my throat, cutting them off.

Everything was not okay.

Not when Eddie stood barely an inch away from me.

Not when Eddie's pupils were blown so damn wide I'd likely get lost in them.

Not when Eddie closed the remaining distance between us, his mouth descending toward mine.

No. Things were far from okay. Things were motherfucking incredible.

Our lips connected, smooth and warm, before he cupped the back of my head, urging me to move, to press against him, to accept his tongue.

I did so willingly, drinking in his kisses, memorizing his groan as I dipped my tongue into his mouth, brushing it against his own. Winding my arms around him, I held on for dear life. This kiss... this moment... was everything. *Everything* I'd wanted from the moment I'd met him.

Our mouths moved in rhythm, in perfect synchronicity, as though we'd been enjoying this touch for longer than the mere seconds, or minutes, or hell, it could have been hours we were connected like this. I fell into his kiss, never wanting this to end. Never wanting more than this moment right here.

Which was total bullshit, as my hand on his ass, squeezing tight, fuck if that wasn't what I wanted too. I squeezed, earning me a grunt and a hiss when his denim-clad cock rubbed against mine, barely constrained by the thin material of my training shorts.

I swallowed his hiss, absolutely wanting more and everything Eddie would give me.

We kissed, hands roaming, breaths ragged against each other. My dick ached to be free, desperate to explore, to be discovered, to—

A bang in the corridor jerked us to a stop, though hell if I was letting go. Wide-eyed, I stared at the man in my arms, and when he smiled, his lips glossy from our kiss, I went in for a repeat. Our lips found each other again, this time sweeter, softer, but whatever the noise from the corridor was, it wasn't stopping.

With a sigh, I eased away, soaking in the blissed-out look in Eddie's eyes. I swore he'd never looked hotter with glistening lips, ruffled hair, and heat in his gaze that was a hundred percent directed at me.

"So," I started, "if this is what you wanted to borrow me for, you can make this request of me any time you want."

His lips twitched, which was totally unfair as all I wanted to do was kiss him again.

"I'm good with that, as long as you know I want all the things too."

With happiness flooding my chest, I didn't have it in me to be embarrassed that Eddie had absolutely overheard my conversation with Tony.

"All the things, huh? Whoever thought of such a thing is a genius."

"That's one word for him."

"And another would be?" I fished.

"Trouble, and he's going to find himself in a heap of it if he doesn't get his ass back on court."

Rolling my eyes, I sighed. "I do kinda have an important game tonight."

The amusement on Eddie's face dropped. "And here I am distracting you."

"Hell no." I tightened my grip. "You're here giving me an incentive to kick ass so we can celebrate tonight. If you want?"

"I want."

Those two words slammed into my chest, threatening to buckle my knees. The only way to stay upright was to give in to the need rushing through me.

I kissed him again, absorbing his heat, welcoming the way my head started to spin. Lightness filled my chest while simultaneously feeling fit to burst. His grip was firm, controlled, enough to keep me from floating away.

Eddie broke the kiss with a heavy breath and even heavier eyelids. "We should go."

The reluctance in his voice bled into the gravelly need.

"We should." I pulled myself together, easing away, knowing Coach would definitely kick my ass if I didn't get a move on. Plus, Lottie was out there.

I smoothed out my hair and dipped out my tongue, wetting my bottom lip and savoring the taste of Eddie. When he groaned, my gaze snapped to his.

"Come on." He shook his head, as though waking himself up or perhaps trying to make sense return to his brain.

As I bobbed my head and followed him out, my mind reeled. Not only had he kissed me, he'd chased me down and said he wanted more. Exhilarated that this was finally happening, I couldn't even begin to tame my grin. By the time we returned to the court, it was still there and not budging. Not even when Coach yelled my name so damn loud the roof shook.

"Don't run off," I called out to him as I backed away. "I still need my pep talk from Lottie."

With his gaze fixed on me, he nodded, an intensity etched into his features that I'd never seen before, but fuck if it wasn't the hottest look I'd ever seen on him. I'd just started to wonder what his come face would look like when Ollie grabbed me by the shoulder.

"Where's Lottie?" I immediately asked.

He pointed over toward the sideline, where she was with a couple of the guys and now with her dad.

A breath of relief escaped when I realized she hadn't been abandoned.

"Seriously, Coach is close to having a fucking aneurysm. What the hell, Pearce?"

Dragging my focus away from Eddie and Lottie, I looked at my captain. He stopped short from wherever he was maneuvering me to, eyes narrowing before widening. "You… Holy shit, man, now, seriously *now* you get yourself some?" He shook his head, though from the twitch of his mouth, he wasn't as pissed as he pretended to be.

"Where'd you just drift off to?" Cassius joined us, ball in hand.

Before I could answer, Ollie butted in. "Having a pre-celebration, apparently."

Still grinning, I rolled my eyes, not bothering to confirm or deny.

Cassius snorted, then froze for a beat, doing this weird wide-eyed, shaking-his-head thing. "Holy shit!"

"What?" Ollie glanced between the two of us.

"Pearce disappeared with Eddie."

"Noooo," Ollie dragged out. "For real?"

"And I'm out of here." I made to turn, but Cassius clamped down on my shoulder.

"No fucking chance. You really hooked up with the DILF *now*?"

"Guys, get your head focused on tonight's game." Somehow I kept a straight face and stopped my giddy excitement from showing. "Now is not the t—"

"Fuck that," Cassius cut in, loud enough to get more than one head whipping in our direction. Unfortunately one of them was Coach's.

"If the three of you don't quit whatever the hell you've got going on, I will not be held responsible for the level of pai—"

"Got it, Coach," Ollie hollered back, taking the ball from Cassius and indicating for us to follow him quick smart.

We did immediately, but not before Cassius mouthed, "I've so won the cash."

CHAPTER 11

EDDIE

With the taste of Pearce on my lips, I relied on autopilot to get me to Lottie. After keeping away from the man for the past few days in an attempt to not distract him, I'd done a piss-poor job of that by mauling the guy. And a few hours before his game, no less.

If it wasn't for the fact he'd melted in my arms and kissed me back, I would have felt guilty. Perhaps I should have anyway, but how could I when his kiss was the best I'd ever had?

By the time I reached Lottie's side, the players she'd been with were on the court and Tony was next to her. Guilt barreled into me. Not only had I abandoned her, but with the way Tony was looking at me, he had a fair idea of why I'd dragged Pearce away from him.

"I'm so sorry," I rushed to say, my gaze first on Lottie and then on Tony. "I didn't mean to be so long and—"

"Dad, Tony was just telling me about an interview he did with Josie Spellman."

It took me a moment to catch up and redirect my focus to my daughter. Excitement filled her features, making me realize that she hadn't even noticed I'd been gone.

"He said he'd reach out to her and see if she'd be interested in talking to me. That would be so awesome." She peered up at Tony with stars in her eyes, and he chuckled.

"I think Josie would be more than happy to chat with someone so dedicated to the game and looking at following in her shoes." Flicking his attention to me, he smiled. "I hope that's okay?"

My brain finally cleared from its kiss-drunk fog, and I smiled back, this time remembering my manners and reaching out my hand. Tony took it and shook as I said, "Tony, that would be incredible. Thanks." When I dropped his hand, I cleared my throat, trying to will heat from spreading in my cheeks. "And thanks for looking after her."

Still with the same friendly smile on his face, Tony shrugged. "It's more than okay. It gave us an opportunity to talk about tonight's game. Lottie said you guys aren't watching?"

"Well, we are, but at home… uhm… I mean at Pearce's place."

Tony glanced at my girl, concern dipping his brows. "How are you healing? Pearce said you were recovering brilliantly."

"I am," Lottie said with the confidence of a girl who knew exactly who she was. "Dad said we can definitely attend Pearce's next game, which will be another win."

"You're that confident about tonight's win, huh?" he asked.

"Absolutely. Pearce is going to kick ass."

I winced, wondering how it was my ten-year-old was making excellent progress at sounding like a sailor. "Lottie, no cussing."

Her pursed lips told me she was fighting to not roll her eyes at me. "Sorry, Dad. Butt, I meant butt." She grinned.

"I actually have to get back to work," Tony said. He focused on me, saying, "I don't have your details. Should I get in touch via Pearce?"

The embarrassment I'd been trying hard to hold on to spread quickly to my cheeks. "Yeah, sure, thanks."

"No problem at all."

After our goodbyes, he headed away, and I peered down at my girl. "How are you feeling? You ready to get out of here?" She looked a little peaky.

"I still haven't spoken to Pearce."

Just the sound of his name had my pulse picking up speed. "Okay, let's quickly find him again, then we'll grab something for dinner tonight to eat before the game." I turned and searched for Pearce. It took barely a beat for me to spot him. He was in the middle of doing some basic ball work with Cassius and Ollie.

While we waited for him to finish, Lottie talked nonstop about Josie, a super successful agent. Sure, my kiddo was only ten, but she knew her own mind and had ambition. And from everything I knew about Josie, she'd be a pretty impressive role model.

A good ten minutes of Lottie's gushing later, I snagged Pearce's gaze. It wasn't necessary to indicate I needed to go or that Lottie wanted to wish him luck, as he immediately said something to Cassius, which he followed up with a smack to his teammate's gut when he laughed. Then he was jogging over to us. Each footfall of him getting closer, heat licked over my skin. Who knew unwavering eye contact could be so damn intense?

By the time he reached us, my body vibrated with the need to scoop him close and lay one on him. It took everything in me to keep my hands to myself, but one kiss did not make a relationship.

"Hey," he greeted. "You guys heading home?"

There went my crazy pulse again. "Yeah." I bobbed my head, aware that I hadn't blinked yet. I cleared my throat and forced myself to look away and take a much-needed blink. Fuck, I needed to get myself under control, but Pearce running toward me had been the start of what dreams were made from. It was kinda sad he was strapped down so I couldn't see his swinging dick.

"Uhm… yeah, so Lottie just wanted to wish you luck," I said, the thought of his dick taking up residence in my overactive imagination.

At the slight widening of his eyes and then the quirk of his brow, it was clear he knew my thoughts weren't perhaps suitable for public sharing. When he flicked his attention to Lottie and lowered to a knee, I took a steadying breath.

Pearce Malcolm was tying me in knots or simply turning me on, and while I was on board with that as he was fucking hot and one of my favorite people in the world, I didn't know how to behave. Not when we had so much to say and explore. My hands twitched at my sides as they carried on chatting, tempted to haul him into me. Somehow, I resisted.

"—got this."

"Thanks, Lottie girl. I'll see you in the morning."

"I can stay up so we can celebrate."

Pearce grinned, his gaze briefly flicking to mine. In the short connection, warmth brushed across my skin at the promise obvious in that one look. He was absolutely wanting a follow-up to what I started earlier. I dragged my bottom lip in my mouth, releasing it slowly and being as subtle as a wrecking ball. Pink hit his cheeks, and I grinned.

"I think it's best if you go straight to bed after the game. You'll need to be as healthy as possible if you want to be here for the next game, right?"

I smirked at his save and would make sure she was sound asleep by the time Pearce got home. Thoughts of how to celebrate bubbled to life. "Pearce is right, Lottie, so no arguing, okay?"

Despite her loud sigh, she bobbed her head. "Okay."

With a wink, Pearce leaned forward and gently hugged Lottie. "Love you, kiddo. Cheer hard for me, okay?"

"Always," she answered seriously, and my heart squeezed when she followed up with "Love you."

Emotion colored Pearce's face as he squeezed her and stood. He didn't give me time to hesitate or over-think. In the space of a breath, he was in my space and wrapping his arms around me in a tight hug, his nose buried against my neck.

Hugging him back, I barely held back the ripple of longing racing through me, but when his lips pressed against my neck, I gulped. "You'll do brilliantly," I finally whispered. "Focus," I managed to say, a reminder to the both of us that in this moment, the game was everything. "Keep your eye on Lemington."

Before he angled back, he placed another kiss to my neck. Goose bumps broke free, and I eased away.

"I've got this."

"You do." I squeezed his arms, reluctant to fully let go but knew I must.

"I wish you could stay." Guilt attempted to spark to life. But before it could take shape, Pearce continued, "But you both at my place is an awesome close second. I'll be home as soon as I can."

"You don't have to rush b—"

The incredulous look on his face had me cutting myself off.

"Or you can get home as quickly as you can, and I'll be up waiting for you."

My words earned me a heart-flipping grin. He leaned forward once again, his mouth moving close to my ear. "Feel free to look in the second drawer in my bedside table. You know," he said, pulling away to make eye contact, "if you get bored."

With those final words, he winked, ruffled Lottie's hair, and jogged back to the court.

DISHES DONE AND LOTTIE IN BED, I COULDN'T WAIT ANY longer. Curiosity had a reputation for sure, but it had been Pearce's tone that did it for me. I didn't expect anything but heat and orgasms.

Still buzzing from the Eagles' win, I opened the door to the room I'd never spent any time in, for all the obvious reasons. The scent of Pearce's bodywash greeted me, familiar and doing nothing to reduce the electricity zipping through me. From the doorway, I easily spotted the bedside table. I gulped as a flush of anticipation raced to my chest.

Fuck, this was really happening. Pearce and me. I was about to rifle through his drawers, and even though it was with his permission, it was another step in the direction of something so much more than I'd anticipated with him.

With each step closer, my dick throbbed, swelling in my pants. Tempted to squeeze myself, I zeroed in on the drawer instead, welcoming the rush of anticipation. If the evening went as I hoped, the only hand touching my dick would be Pearce's.

I opened the drawer, my eyes widening before a soft chuckle escaped. There were enough toys and lube in the oversized drawer to rival a sex shop, and what was even better was several were still in their packages. Sitting on Pearce's unmade bed, I pulled out the four different bottles of lube. One I was familiar with, my favorite brand. The other three had me snorting. Who knew lube could add an extra tingle to my prostate?

I placed them back in the drawer, all except for my favorite brand, and smirked at the varying dildos. It seemed like Pearce liked to have fun and enjoyed variety. As soon as that thought settled in my mind, I blanched. Variety was awesome, but it didn't mean he wasn't after something more or not interested in monogamy, right? Rubbing a hand over my face and pissed off that I was getting way ahead of myself, I cracked my neck and peered once again inside the drawer.

I snagged a plastic-wrapped package, mouth lifting immediately and my ass clenching in anticipation. Now this I could totally get onboard with, and I half expected it was what Pearce may have had in mind too.

I stood and made my way to close his bedroom

door, creating an additional barrier should Lottie come hunting for me. As I closed it, a text alert made me jump. I chuckled as I tugged my phone out of my pocket, then read Pearce's response to my congratulatory text.

My already hard cock turned to steel, my breath picking up as his words sank in.

Pearce: That last point all I thought about was sucking you off. On my way.

Fuck, Pearce teasing like this was a whole new side that I was eager to see more of. My grip tightened on the sealed package, and my pulse fluttered.

Back at the bed, I threw my phone on the mattress and tore the package open after a couple of attempts. The glue or whatever the hell it was that they sealed the damn thing shut with was stupidly secure. Finally freed, the plug felt smooth in my hand. Only once had I tried a plug before, and after I'd gotten over my initial embarrassment, it had been sexy as hell and had done the prep work nicely. Me doing this now with Pearce not only on my mind but on his way home? Heck yes, I was absolutely up for it.

Snagging my phone, I reopened the messages and flicked on the camera symbol. I aimed at the plug, the empty packaging in the background. With the photo taken, I typed: *That last point all I thought about was you in me. I best put this to good use.*

I hit Send before I could second-guess, barely hearing the whoosh of the message being sent over the pounding in my ears. Taking a deep breath, I placed my cell back down and focused on the smooth black plug. "Right," I said into the empty room. "I've got this."

CHAPTER 12

PEARCE

NOT ONLY HAD WE WON OUR FIRST GAME, BUT EDDIE and I had sped through all the bits between our first kiss and what I hoped like hell was a fuck when I got home. Talk about Road Runner speed. I was more than up for it. Even my usual post-game crash was nowhere in sight.

For a moment after I hit Send, letting him know in no uncertain terms I wanted to suck him off, I'd hesitated, wondering if I'd dreamed the whole thing. Since the moment I'd met the man, I'd crushed hard, then fallen fast over the edge of knowing I was in love. That point of no return had happened when we kissed just before my game, and it was the tingle of my lips that reminded me it had most definitely happened.

That connection buoyed me and made me fly

high during the whole forty-eight minutes of play time, and all the minutes in between. The fact that I'd sweated my ass off and had also showered, yet the taste of him was still there... yeah, it was enough for me to race out of the stadium like I had the man I craved waiting for me. Happiness bubbled in my gut, hardly believing that I could finally tug that "like" out of my thoughts.

Eddie Phelps was waiting for me, and as I slipped into the back seat of the car I'd organized, since I'd let Eddie use my SUV while he was here, I fought hard to control my dick that wondered if he'd explored my bedside drawer. It had been a risk, directing him there, but at least this way he'd known completely where my head was at.

Once settled, I tugged out my phone, seeing a text notification that I hadn't heard come in. My heart raced when I opened it. Head spinning as the words blurred from all my blood rushing to my cock, I swallowed hard.

Holy fucking butt plug.

Did I dare consider he'd be greeting me stretched and ready?

My dick strained against my suit pants, hard enough to tear through the fabric if my mind kept up with the visuals. I'd take Eddie any way I could get him. I was vers as fuck and loved nothing more than the idea of him pounding into me, but hot damn if going to town on his ass didn't make my head spin with want.

Forcing myself to steady my breathing and take control so I didn't come in my pants, I stared out the window. Ten more minutes and I should be home.

Each minute dragged on as the driver eased through game traffic, and I'd never been more grateful that I wasn't driving, or that I'd bought a place close by. Driving myself while my dick ran the show would have been dangerous.

Finally pulling into my estate, we passed through the gated security, and I hit the fob to my gates. Once we'd stopped, I said my thanks and all but threw a fifty-dollar bill at the guy as a tip. Each step to the front door was one closer to me losing my mind. My mouth dried at the thought of Eddie greeting me at the door. Naked would be awesome, but I expected Lottie just being a closed door away from a nightmare show of me dropping to my knees and sucking her dad off wouldn't be the best thing ever. The poor kid would be scarred for life.

I let myself into a quiet house. Most of the lights were off, except for the kitchen and the stairway. A quick glance in the kitchen, my heart beating heavily, showed it was empty. I smiled, hoping on all that was lubed and hard that it meant Eddie was in my room.

I took the stairs two at a time, trying not to make a noise. Mission accomplished, I barreled into my bedroom and stopped short.

Skin. So much fucking delicious skin on display.

With flushed skin, an unwavering gaze, and honest-to-God quivering limbs, Eddie was every fantasy I'd had right here in the flesh.

"Holy fucking Christ." The words spilled out of me as I shut the door, flipped the lock, and tugged off my tie.

"Twenty minutes is a long time." He moved his right thigh, angling it out. His soft gasp had my gaze shooting to his face, desperate to see his expression.

Want. Unfiltered, raw desire stared back at me. Never did I truly imagine seeing him this way, especially not so fucking wanton and needy. Eddie was the epitome of control. Sure, we had a shitload of fun, but him laying himself out for me like this, like he was some exquisite banquet to be savored, had my heart beating triple time.

"You just going to stand there?"

Hearing his teasing tone, I smiled, shoving off my jacket and unbuttoning my shirt. "Have you had that in you this whole time?"

He clamped down on his bottom lip and bobbed

his head. I couldn't handle not looking anymore. My gaze drifted down his toned body, taking in the splatter of fur on his chest, his abs, and the trimmed hair around his junk. I licked my lips like a needy fucker, desperate to fulfil the promise I'd made in my text.

The shifting of his thighs, slight jerk of his hips, and his deep groan almost stopped me from hitting jackpot. But no way could I pull my attention away.

Black and smooth and looking so perfect in his ass was the plug I hadn't dared hope he'd really have fun with. And fuck, was I glad I teased him about it earlier.

"Pants off."

I snapped my attention to his face, meeting his blazing stare and quirked brow. Of course Eddie was topping from the bottom, and hell if it didn't crank me up even higher.

Making quick work of the rest of my clothes, I was on the bed, kneeling by his feet. Perhaps I should be greeting him with a kiss first, but with the plug right there, I couldn't resist. "This," I said, reaching out and touching the edges of it, "is the hottest thing I've ever seen." Leaning down, I pressed kisses along his inner thigh and nudged at the plug with my nose. His whimper was absolutely worth it.

"That kiss," I continued, this time mouthing his cock, "I never expected."

When he groaned, I flicked my attention to his face. "Unplanned too." His half-mast gaze was fixed on me.

There was much to say, unspoken words between us, so much to figure out. But the last thing I wanted to do was think. With my dick leaking like a faucet, I bobbed my head. "You want me to replace the plug?"

A flash of heat appeared in his eyes before he nodded. "Yeah, right after you kiss me."

My grin was immediate. Dotting one last open-mouthed kiss on his cock, I shifted, lips touching his. Like the first time our mouths met, familiarity and rightness swept through me as our tongues touched and we worked a perfect rhythm. We kissed until I struggled to breathe. Kissed until the only thing keeping me alive was our mouths connecting and the certainty that if I stopped now, my brain would short-circuit completely.

He thrust against me, rubbing against my cock, giving me no choice but to ease back and gasp for air. "I want you so fucking bad." The words escaped me, sounding like a plea.

"You have me," he whispered, cupping my cheek. The touch centered me, pulled me away from the desire racing through my veins to focus on the man before me.

Perhaps I shouldn't have questioned it and simply taken what he was offering, but Eddie was everything to me. Sure, I'd always thought I'd grab whatever he offered with two desperate hands, but the truth was, whatever this was that was happening, I didn't know how I'd bounce back from having just a piece and having it only once.

While my eager cock cussed me out, begging me to shut up and bury it deep inside the man beneath me, my heart urged me to speak. "I have you for how long?"

His searching gaze bounced between my eyes. "You're too important to me," he finally said, his words kickstarting my heart, "to fool around and it mean nothing."

It was all I needed to hear before my mouth crashed on his, my fingers seeking the black plug. When I skimmed the smooth surface, I swallowed his grunt. "This," I said, easing away, my breathing choppy, "seriously is so fucking sexy."

A fresh flush covered his cheeks.

"Do I need a condom?" I asked. I was pretty sure he was on PrEP, but still…

At my question, his eye twitched.

"Hey, no judgment and worries either way," I said quickly, wanting us to be both safe and comfortable.

"We should before I get tested again," he said, a hollowness in his voice I hated to hear.

Before he could get inside his head, I kissed him again, rubbing around the plug once more for good measure. With a satisfied grin at his moan, I eased back. "I can definitely wrap up if it means I get to be buried deep inside you." I gyrated against him, trapping our dicks between us, luxuriating in the feel.

But I needed more. Moving quickly, I made to stand to grab the condoms I kept in the bathroom.

"I have them here." Eddie's words stopped me. Reaching out, he angled toward my drawer, tugged it open, and pulled out a packet.

I took it off him with a smirk, ignoring my trembling hands. It wasn't nerves that had me struggling to tear open the foil. Instead, a rush of need pulsated through me, making it hard to get my shit together, but I needed to do this and get inside the man before I passed out from lack of oxygen to my brain.

Convinced only an orgasm from coming hard deep inside Eddie was the solution, I doubled down on fumbling with the packet, giving a triumphant "Thank fuck" when I finally got it open. Eddie chuckled, the same look in his eyes he'd had since the moment I entered the room.

"You doing all right there?"

"I am now." I bounced my brows and slipped on the latex before focusing on the plug. "I'll be even better when I remove this." With my fingers on the end, I flicked my gaze at him. "This okay?"

"Yeah." As I pulled, the air punched out of him, but honest to God, I only had eyes for his open hole.

"Fuck me." My dick throbbed, and I gulped.

"I actually thought you'd be the one doing the fucking tonight," he sassed.

My lips twitched and I stole a glance, taking in his quirked brow. "Now that I can do." Swiping the lube, I lathered myself up, then gripped his cock for good measure. His deep, needy sigh was worth it as I applied the slick and gave a few slow strokes.

"Anytime now," he said with a deep groan.

"Needy, huh?" So not what I expected from him, but I was definitely a fan.

"Pearce, I swear— Nngh…"

Two fingers slipping inside him cut him off beautifully. "What were you saying?"

He attempted narrowing his eyes, but adding a third finger stopped that with a moan fierce enough to have my dick bobbing. He was loose and so ready for me. I pulled out, positioned myself, and pushed in with one slow stroke. There was no resistance, just his sweet, soft gasp, and a delicious heat engulfing my cock that I swore I would combust.

"Daddy."

We froze, held our breaths, and I swore my heart stopped beating. The sound of a door opening shot a bolt of adrenaline to my heart, and I moved, tearing out of Eddie so damn fast that I teetered on my knees and fell backward. Mildly aware of Eddie's grunt and the horror in his gaze, there was nothing I could do, not when my arms windmilled and I disappeared off the edge of the bed, my ass hitting the floor with a thump.

Crumpled on the floor, I gasped for breath before a groaned laugh escaped me. I slammed my hand over my mouth just as a naked Eddie appeared at my side, his eyes wide. His lips twitched and he opened his mouth—

"Daddy, I had a nightmare."

"Shit," he mouthed, and my amusement died down when his face blanched. "She can't see me coming from your room."

I swallowed back my hurt and nodded, reluctantly understanding that this thing between us had escalated so quickly that my head was still spinning. It made complete sense that he didn't want Lottie to know. But a fool she wasn't. "Go to the bathroom. I'll get her to bed, then you head to your room, okay?"

Some of the color returned to his cheeks as he spoke. "Yeah, okay. Thanks." Realizing I was still on the floor, he reached out for my hand and helped me up. "You okay?"

"Not the first bruised ass I've ever had," I whispered, then called out, "Hold on, Lottie. I'm coming," when I heard her again.

Eddie squeezed my hand and backed away, shooting me a grateful smile. I offered him a chin lift, then reached for my sweatpants that were draped on my oversized chair. Once I tugged them on and wiped my hands quickly on the towel I'd dumped on the floor, I unlocked the door. Lottie stood in her open doorway, her eyes wide and immediately connecting with mine.

"Hey, kiddo." I stepped toward her, cuddling her close. "Bad dream, huh?"

"Yeah." Her quiet voice held a tremor I'd never heard from her before. "I called Dad."

Tightness lassoed around my gut. Guilt that he hadn't been able to rush out to her immediately was a shit of a thing. "Let's get you to bed. He must be in a deep sleep. I'll wake him before I go and get you a glass of water, okay?"

She nodded against my stomach, and I gently squeezed her arms before guiding her back into the bedroom she'd claimed as her own. The soft light of her bedside table lit her disordered bedsheets. The poor kid must have really been active in her sleep.

"Are you sore?" I thought to ask. So much movement post-operation couldn't be good for her, right?

"A bit." As she climbed onto the bed, I saw her wince. I imagined "a bit" meant that she was in pain. Lottie was so much like her dad, it was scary. He didn't like people fussing over him, just like he never admitted to feeling unwell or being hurt.

"You going to be okay here a sec while I get your dad and sort some painkillers?"

Indecision warred on her face. I hated seeing it there. This girl was a warrior, and seeing her vulnerable hurt my damn heart.

"It's okay, I'm here." Eddie stepped into the room wearing shorts and a tee.

"Daddy." Lottie's voice cracked, and I winced, shifting out of the way so Eddie could get to his daughter. "Where were you? I called."

Fuck.

"I'm so sorry, baby girl. I was fast asleep."

I looked away, not able to bear seeing Eddie's wince or the guilt I was sure would be evident in his features. "Uhm… I'll go get pain meds and some water." I headed for the door, hearing Eddie's soft "Thanks" just as I stepped into the hallway.

Once by myself, I shook my head and closed my

eyes, barely comprehending how one second I'd been buried so deep into the man I secretly loved and then next I was wracked with guilt. Oh, and supporting a legit bruised ass. That fall had been hard.

With a deep breath, I set about my task, not liking one bit the guilt I felt over the delay in getting to Lottie, or the fact we'd both lied to her. Feeling shitty wasn't the best thing ever.

Drink and painkillers in hand, I headed to Lottie's room, peering around the doorway, weirdly nervous. I was never nervous around Eddie or Lottie. Ever. Not even when Eddie had shot me down three years back and we'd met up the next day for a beer. This was new. And not so dissimilar to the guilt churning in my gut. I didn't like it one bit.

Both Eddie and Lottie were stretched out on the double bed, Eddie stroking her hair and talking too softly for me to hear his words. He flicked his gaze at me, and I held my breath, not sure if I was welcome or not. When a gentle smile lifted his lips, a whoosh of air escaped me.

"How's it going in here?" I asked, my shoulders relaxing a little. Reaching the side of the bed, I held out the tablets.

"Thanks." Eddie took them off me and helped Lottie sit and take her pills before they settled back down.

"Thank you, Pearce."

Affection flooded my chest when I looked down at Lottie's tired eyes, her skin pale in the soft light. "Anytime, pumpkin. You going to try to get back to sleep now?"

"Yeah." Her shoulders shuddered a little, and I frowned, concerned that whatever her nightmare had been about had really knocked her around.

"Okay, well if you need anything, just—"

"Will you stay too?"

My eyes widened in surprise at her request. Hesitating and not sure what the right thing to do here was, I sought her dad's gaze. His smile was tender, and he gave me a small nod, indicating it was okay. And I knew he meant if I felt comfortable doing so.

"Of course I will, Lottie girl. Let me just go throw on a sleep shirt, and I'll be right back." I left the room feeling lighter, relieved Eddie was welcoming me in the task of comforting his daughter and touched that Lottie trusted me enough to care for her. Without a doubt I loved this girl fiercely, wanting nothing more than for her to be happy, healthy, and safe.

I threw on one of my old team shirts I used for lounging in and headed back to the bedroom. Lottie's eyes sprang open when I entered, the sweetest of smiles sent my way a heartbeat later. Since I'd been gone, she'd scooted to the middle of the bed.

Getting into bed without jostling her, I turned on my side and stroked her brow. "You have sweet dreams now, kiddo."

"I'll try." Her words were a soft mumble, her eyes already firmly closed.

The gentle caress of fingers on my head startled me, then I relaxed into the touch, my gaze connecting with Eddie's. My heart squeezed as I took him in. He was also on his side, his one arm holding his daughter while the other continued to stroke my hair. It was his eyes, though, that threatened to unravel me, and the affection boldly on display in their depths.

I reached out and wrapped my arm over Lottie, hand settling on Eddie's arm. While this was far from the celebration I'd hoped for, being close to the man I loved and the girl I doted on, it didn't even feel like a close second. Screw that. This here was the perfect way to end the night.

CHAPTER 13

EDDIE

I woke with an elbow in my face and to the sound of light snoring. Typically these weren't the most pleasant things to wake up to, but that didn't stop my content smile from forming or the uptick of my pulse.

Yesterday I'd been out of my mind with lust for Pearce, putting myself out there, emotionally and physically, in a way I never had before. For an all too brief few minutes, it had been perfect. How we'd connected. How I knew he'd be wringing out an orgasm from me to eclipse all previous orgasms.

Sure, that had all ended pretty dismally with Lottie's nightmare, but I couldn't regret cuddling up with my two favorite people in the world. Peace was a funny thing, something I'd been certain I'd previously felt. Last night, though, after tasting Pearce's kisses for the first time, then falling asleep the way we had, peace took on a whole new meaning. And holy shit, I was totally on board with the buzz of contentment running through my veins.

It was early, too early to be awake after a late night. With dawn breaking and soft light filtering through the curtains, any chance for falling back asleep was gone. Usually I'd get up, enjoy the quiet dawn afforded, but the soft snore coming from Pearce and Lottie's breathing provided the best type of calm.

That was until Lottie shifted and kneed me in the nuts.

I grunted at the contact, my mind whiting out for a moment as my eyes watered. Clamping down on my lips and dragging them between my teeth to stop from crying out and waking everyone up, I cupped myself, turned, and focused on breathing.

Jesus, my kid was trying to kill me. Either that or she was determined to remain an only child.

Once my mind calmed and my vision cleared, I realized the snores had stopped. The mattress moved and dipped. I angled around to see Pearce sitting up, bleary-eyed and frowning.

I huffed out a pained breath and pressed my face into the pillow, not quite ready to do anything beyond cradle my crotch and consider what I'd done to deserve a wake-up call like this.

Pearce's hand touching my shoulder jolted me into awareness. Having not heard him move, I wondered if for a moment I'd blacked out there.

"You okay?" With his mouth close to my ear, I figured he'd got out of bed and was beside me.

I managed a nod and pried my eyes open, turning to face him. Once our gazes met, he smiled that brilliant damn smile of his that was far too cheery and perfect. There wasn't a chance my bruised balls could handle him looking so irresistible.

When I indicated I wanted to get up, he backed away, giving me room. The moment he figured out my predicament was obvious. The asshole's shoulders shook, lips twitching, but at least he reached out to help me up. We maneuvered out of the room, and without discussion, headed to Pearce's bedroom. The second the door shut, I grunted. "Holy shit."

"She got you good, huh?"

At my nod, he winced. "You need me to check them over? Maybe kiss them better?"

I huffed out a laugh and cringed. "Stop, you fucker. I can't handle a stiffy or laughter while I'm cross-eyed and still debating throwing up."

He snorted and ushered me to his bed. "You need ice or something?"

"Nuh-uh." I shook my head. "Just need to curl up and feel sorry for myself for five minutes."

Needing the comfort of his soft mattress, and maybe the scent of his sheets that had wisps of our combined lovemaking from last night, I scooted up to rest my head on the pillow.

"Room for me there?"

My gaze snapped to his, kinda surprised he asked and didn't just join me. While he smiled, an unfamiliar hesitation was evident in the slight frown between his brows. But what I didn't see a lick of was regret. It was enough to have me reaching out for him.

Taking my hand, he curled around me before I could take a new breath. When my back connected with his front, I relaxed in his hold.

From the moment we'd landed in Minneapolis, my life had spiraled. Everything had flipped upside down, barely giving me the chance to take stock and breathe. Hell, less than a week ago I'd been in a failing relationship, or at least a version of one. Then there was Lottie, and now this.

"You seem to be thinking really hard." Pearce gave a light squeeze. "I would offer to blow you so you'll stop, but I'm not sure your dick could handle it right now."

I huffed out a laugh and hoisted my elbow back a

little to nudge him. "Shut up." Rather than voicing the thoughts flying about my brain, I focused on Pearce's steady breaths, on the heat radiating from his body as he spooned me. Just the thought of being a little spoon to Pearce pulled a giggle out of me, which I was sure startled us both.

"The fuck was that?"

"Fuck off," I said with a laugh. "I have no idea what you're talking about. Now shh. I need my five minutes."

I closed my eyes, trying to calm my weird reaction. A legit giggle. When the hell had I turned into a pubescent kid? The desire to roll my eyes at myself was strong, but I could also be remarkably stubborn, so my eyes remained shut.

Five minutes to stop my nuts from throbbing and to let my brain settle. It was all I needed.

"You're thinking, aren't you?"

I lowered my head, chin to chest, and sighed in defeat. "Yeah," I admitted. "When did you get to know me so well?"

A soft kiss pressed against my neck, and I thought I felt his smile as he did so. Pearce shifted, easing up, and peered down at me. "You want the honest answer to that?"

The way my heart bounced around in my chest, you'd think I'd never been looked at the way Pearce was doing now. But I supposed that was the thing. Pearce's intent, his emotion had never been as open as it was right this second. Vulnerability I rarely saw from him pierced his gaze.

"Always." And I meant it. Pearce was the most important man in my life. The only way we'd be sure to navigate our way through what was happening was to communicate. Fuck, I hated this adulting shit at times, but since being a dad, it was my life.

"Since the day we met, I like to think I could read you pretty damn well." He raked his gaze over my face as he continued, "Most of the time I get it right, understand where your head or heart's at. Just the once I got it wrong."

Not willing to have this conversation without seeing him fully, I turned over. When I did, Pearce settled his head back on the pillow so we lay face-to-face.

"When you asked me out."

"On a date. Yeah."

I brushed my fingertips over his forehead. "I didn't want to say no."

"You're fucking with me?" Indignation, quite possibly surprise, and a little self-satisfied amusement flooded his features. Then he frowned. "Why'd you say no? Turn me down?"

Jesus, even thinking about how to respond made

me feel like a prize prick. Pretty sure my hesitation and reluctance were clear to read on my face, too, so I wasn't surprised when he arched his brow at me. "Honesty, right?"

I wrinkled my nose. "Yeah, I know. I'm going to sound like a dickhead." At least my words had him grinning. "You were twenty-six, just a few years in the League. Plus, I already valued your friendship." I tried to hold back my grimace, but I still winced. "My old ass came with a kid and a stable home. We didn't even live in the same state."

"We still don't." His brow quirked high, and I huffed out a breath.

"Yeah. I don't need reminding."

"Plus there's still, what, ten, eleven years between us. That hasn't changed." The fucker's smile grew. "And then there's Lottie, who you now have full-time. That's the only thing that's changed."

Refusing to look away at him calling bullshit without saying the words, I nodded. "All true. But you're now twenty-nine, and are..." I searched for the word. "...seasoned."

Loud laughter burst out of him, his eyes crinkling with amusement.

"Yeah, yeah." I nudged at him and rolled my eyes. "Laugh it up."

After a few false starts of him half-assed controlling his amusement, he said, "Really, you're saying I was an immature asshole."

"Well, not an asshole necessarily."

He snorted. "I think we know that's bullshit, as almost everyone on my team has called me out for my assholish ways a time or fifty." Pearce reached out and stroked my arm, leaving goose bumps in its wake. "You know my maturity levels are still questionable, right?" Even though amusement lit his words, a glimmer of uncertainty rippled underneath.

Pearce wasn't the only one good at reading people, and I could read him pretty damn accurately.

"I'm not going to fight you on that statement," I said with a small smile. When he raised his brows, I continued, "But you're so much more than your age. You're one of the most caring and considerate people I know." Pink touched his cheeks as I spoke. "Your ability to play the fool, play pranks," I said with a pointed look, "is part of what makes you ridiculously, brilliantly you."

When I stopped speaking, we stared at each other in silence. Behind his brown eyes, I could see my words hit their mark. He all but sank deeper into the mattress and edged closer into my space.

"And why now... apart from the obvious?" The whispered question puffed warm air against my cheek.

Moving my hand to his waist, I looked him directly in the eye. I wouldn't mention Wayne, as we both knew my ex was the "obvious." "When Lottie fell ill, there was a moment there that I couldn't breathe. Couldn't think." Just the thought of it tugged at something lodged in my heart. "But I didn't need to. You were doing it for the both of us. You were there. You always are." I swallowed hard before huffing out a light laugh, one that didn't scratch the surface of how surreal my realization had been. "You wrenched my eyes wide damn open, Pearce. And now that they're open and I see what we could be…" I shook my head and brushed my lips against his before saying, "I want it. I want you. I want everything. I have no idea ho—"

He swallowed my words with his mouth, cutting me off, and I'd never been more grateful for him shutting me up.

He skimmed his tongue over my bottom lip, and I opened for him immediately. We kissed until I couldn't imagine another's mouth on mine ever again. We kissed until I didn't need to worry about air, since he was breathing for me. We kissed until I didn't even pretend to resist as he pushed against me and his heavy, perfect weight settled on me.

Wrapping my legs around him was as smooth as the way our lips worked in synch, and as I bucked my hips, searching for friction, he pressed and moved against me, giving me exactly what I wordlessly asked for.

We bucked and groaned and rubbed, the whole time our mouths never disconnecting. I held on tight, my palms on his ass, dragging him against me, harder and faster. We rocked and moaned, and fuck if the tingling in my spine and the tightening of my balls didn't make my head spin.

"Nngh…." The nonsensical word tore out of me, breaking our connection as my lips parted. Our gazes connected. So close, the tiny flecks of hazel seemed brighter, but I didn't have time to memorize the variation in color, not when I was captured by the heat and intensity in his gaze. "Fuck." I bucked again, squeezing his ass, not sure if I was holding on for dear life or was urging him on.

Pearce's gaze dipped to my mouth as he ground harder, his dick rubbing against mine. "Fuck, Eddie." He punctuated my name with a fierce kiss. It was hard and messy and my complete undoing.

Light exploded behind my closed lids, my balls drawing up so high, I had no idea if I'd ever see them again, and I was coming. Coming so hard my mind blanked as pleasure crashed into me. Pearce stiffening above me had my eyes springing open.

Mesmerized, I watched as he spiraled. And fuck, Pearce orgasming... best thing ever.

Collapsing in my arms, Pearce was a welcome dead weight. I kissed his neck, his cheek, his temple. With a soft sigh, he turned his face my way so I could reach his lips. Just a gentle, exhausted press of mouths, and it was perfect.

We were sticky and tired, and I expected my dick was raw from friction, but still... "I haven't come from dry-humping since I was a teenager."

Burying his face against my neck, Pearce snorted. "I'm not sure my dick survived."

A content grin settled on my lips. "Totally worth it."

Warm breath danced across my skin when he chuckled. "Definitely." He eased up onto his fore-arms, taking some of his weight. His gaze searched mine, and I kept my smile in place, reaching up and stroking his back.

"You good?"

"Yeah." He flicked his gaze to the side where I knew his phone sat. "You think we have enough time to shower before Lottie wakes?"

Unable to give a straight-up yes, I hesitated, earning me a frown. Without him saying a word, I knew what he was thinking. The flash of disappointment in his gaze was too obvious to ignore. I hated seeing it there.

"It's not that I don't want to tell her," I said slowly, calmly, for me as much as for him, "but we have to do the adult shit and work out what this is first, right?"

When he shifted, I froze, thinking he was going to pull away. Sure, being sticky wasn't comfortable, but I didn't want him leaving. Instead, surprise flitted through me when he leaned into me and pressed his mouth against mine for the sweetest of kisses. When he angled back, he said, "I get it. I can totally do this adulting shit."

"Yeah?" A relieved grin spread across my mouth.

"Jesus, don't sound too surprised." There was no bite to his tone as he quirked his brow at me.

Rather than bullshit him and deny it, I simply smirked. "How about for now you focus on your next big game and getting to the semifinals? After that, we'll get everything figured out."

Eyes narrowing, he frowned. "But if we make it to the finals, that's another four weeks away, and you'll have flown home by then."

Aware he was right, I realized we couldn't just pocket this for a month. "Okay, since I really need to shower—"

"—with me."

"With you if you get your ass off me and hurry, we'll at least attempt to figure this out, okay?"

His face brightened. The sight had my heart squeezing and bubbles fizzing to life.

"Okay. Ass up, pronto." With that, he moved so fast a laugh burst free from deep in my gut. Then he manhandled me into his shower, soaking me and soaping me, and somehow making my cock come to life once again until we were both groaning far too loudly and coming in each other's palms.

While we hadn't left room to talk, blowing my load twice in under an hour was nothing short of a miracle for my old ass. If this continued, Pearce may just kill me. But as I rinsed him off and took extra care of making sure he was unwound and relaxed before his practice in a few hours, I couldn't help but dream that we figured out a way to make this work and that this became our life.

CHAPTER 14

PEARCE

I COULD BARELY FEEL MY LEGS LET ALONE MY DICK BY the time we finished in the shower and dried off. There was little time to rejoice in the fact that we'd picked up almost where we'd left off last night before Lottie joined us downstairs while I was on my first coffee.

Bleary-eyed and holding her side more than she had done the past few days, she looked pretty rotten.

Eddie saw her at the same time. A frown dipped his brow low, worry etched on his face. "You feeling okay?" He led her to the large couch set just off the kitchen, a place of comfort where my grandfolks would usually rest up on their twice-yearly visit while I cooked.

"I'm okay." As she sat, a wince wrinkled her forehead.

"Uh-huh. Let's just check your wound."

Her exasperated sigh made me smile. While this kid could play her dad well and had us both wrapped around her little finger, she wasn't one for fuss. But dutifully, she lifted her sleep shirt a little and lowered the waist of her pj's.

"Pancakes?" I asked, drawing her attention my way.

It won me a smile. "Yes, please."

"You got it, kiddo." I got to work while Eddie checked her over, giving them a semblance of privacy and trying to downplay the crackle of nerves I could feel radiating off Eddie. Sure, we'd been distracted this morning in the best possible way while Lottie was sleeping, but in the bright morning sun, reality came knocking.

"It looks a bit red this morning."

Concerned, I peered over as I whisked the eggs. Eddie glanced over at me, and I paused.

"I think I need to get this checked out." As he spoke, clear-as-day worry settled in his gaze.

"Does that mean I have to go back to the hospital?" Despite her frustrated tone, her voice trembled a little, reminding me Lottie was only ten. It was so easy to treat this kid as older with her wise-ass sass and confidence. Next to her dad, peering up at him with glassy eyes, just how young she was hit me in the solar plexus.

"Hey, it's just to get you checked over. Nothing to worry about." The reassurance rushed out of Eddie. "We'll make a call first, so you don't need to do anything beyond eating your pancakes, okay?"

"Okay." She bobbed her head.

"Do you want to get her settled in front of the big screen, and I'll get the number for you?" I reached for my phone as I spoke, trying to figure out if I just called my own doctor or if I needed someone else since Lottie was a kid. Shit, maybe she just needed to go to urgent care. I had no clue the best person to call.

"That'd be great, thanks." Eddie offered me a smile, apparently completely unaware that I was freaking the fuck out not knowing who to actually call.

I shot him the most reassuring smile possible and angled away, focusing on my phone. When I heard him leave the room, I hit my mom's number and headed to my walk-in pantry so Eddie wouldn't figure out how out of my depth I was.

"Hey, beautiful boy. You were so amazing last night."

The sound of my mom's voice relaxed my shoulders and had me releasing a steadying breath. "Hey, Mom."

"What's wrong?"

I huffed out a laugh and shook my head, not for the first time wondering how she did that. "I think Lottie has an infection maybe, and I don't know who I'm meant to call. Like, do I just take her to the hospital, call Doc Mathius, find a pediatrician, what?" As I spoke, my words became gradually faster, anxiety pitching them higher than usual.

Fuck, just this morning Eddie said he fell for me because I was all cool and collected or some shit, yet here I was beginning to freak the fuck out. If he saw me, would he change his mind, figure out I wasn't the man he thought I—

"Hey, Pearce, take a deep breath for me."

I did so, only wincing slightly that I had to call my mom to get me to sort my shit out. So much for fucking adulting.

"Why do you think she has an infection?"

"Eddie said her wound from surgery is all red. Plus she's sore and was in pain last night. She had a nightmare, and from the state of her bedsheets, I think she'd been wrestling an alligator or something."

"Does she have a temperature?"

"I don't know. We haven't checked."

"Okay, well before doing anything, check that first. You have a thermometer, right?"

She knew I did since when I left home, she and dad had hooked me up with a mammoth-sized first aid kit. Not that I blamed them from the years of mischief and minor scrapes I'd been getting myself into. "Yeah."

"Okay, get that first, then call your doctor's office. But if she has a fever and is in pain, more than her normal soreness, perhaps skip all that and take her to urgent care."

Releasing a breath, I rubbed a hand over my face. "Okay. I can do that."

"I know you can, Pearce. Do you have training today?"

"Yeah. In a couple of hours."

Silence filled the line for a few long moments. "It's important you go to training. You have your next game coming up."

My jaw locked, hating she was right and wanting to argue. If Lottie had to go to the hospital, then how could I just train and behave like everything was okay?

"I can hear your brain thinking overtime there, but Pearce, this is your job. Lottie has her dad, which means she's going to be just fine."

But what about Eddie? The question swirled

around my brain. Who'd be there to make sure he was okay?

I sighed heavily, pissed that I was getting way ahead of myself. Lottie may not even have a temperature, let alone an infection. "I know, Mom. It's just hard."

Mom's voice gentled—she'd pretty much figured out how I felt about Eddie and Lottie, without her ever asking or me ever confirming. "It is, but trust him to do his job, and you focus on yours, okay? Eddie is the last person who'd want you not to be ready. Actually," she said with a quiet chuckle, "make that Lottie. If you don't play your absolute best game, she'll make her feelings known."

The truth of her words tugged a smile from me. Mom was a big Lottie fan, having met her a handful of times over the past few years.

"Thanks, Mom."

"Anytime, honey. Just call if you need me or your dad, okay?"

"Okay."

"And let me know how she gets on."

"Will do."

We said our goodbyes and ended the call. Feeling calmer, I found the contact number for my doctor and went in search of Eddie, thermometer in hand.

I found them in Lottie's room, Eddie listening to an animated Lottie. The sight shot warmth and relief to my chest. To be so talkative meant she'd be fine, right?

"Hey," I greeted, drawing their attention to me. Lottie smiled, as did Eddie. I passed him my cell. "The number to my doctor's office is right there. You want to take her temperature first?"

His gaze dropped to the digital thermometer in my hand before moving back to my face. The tenderness in that one look was enough to have a shaky breath escaping. "Thanks. Can you do that while I make the call?"

I bobbed my head before turning my attention to Lottie. "Hey, kiddo. Let's see what's going on with this temperature of yours."

"Okay, but haven't you got a practice to get to?"

I chuckled. "That I have. I've got time to do this, though, and a little bit extra before I have to leave."

Setting about taking her temperature, I chatted to her about last night's game, or rather she didn't stop describing the game. As she spoke, I grinned, relieved this kid was on my side. She could give one hell of an ego boost while tearing strips off the other team and some of their poor choices.

"You sure you don't want to go into management?" I eyed the thermometer as I spoke, pleased with the 98.5 it registered but wanting a second reading just to be sure.

"Nope." She angled her head again so I could reach her ear. "Managers and coaches have to shout and be grumpy all the time."

I snorted. "You're not wrong. I'll be sure to tell my coach you said that."

She gasped. "You wouldn't."

Easing away to check the reading, I winked. "You're right. I wouldn't." The reading was the same. "Let me just speak to your dad."

I found Eddie in the hallway and showed him the reading. He smiled his thanks, clearly listening to someone at the other end of the call. Before I could turn to go back to Lottie, he held on to my wrist and mouthed, "Go run."

I frowned and shook my head. Sure, I ran most mornings, but today was different. Not only did I get killer orgasms, making the late start so worth it, but I needed to know Lottie was okay. Plus, after yesterday's hard-won game, I deserved a break. I'd still be heading to training in a short while. Mom in all her wisdom was right about that.

The narrowing of his eyes did nothing to change my mind. Instead, I stepped into his space and gave him the briefest of kisses before walking backward with a grin and a follow-up wink. Teasing Eddie was too much fun. With his concern for Lottie, it was only right that I got him to smile, and maybe a little hot under the collar too.

Half an hour later, Lottie had managed to eat something and said she was feeling a little better. Her temperature was the same too, making it easier to step away and go and get changed before heading to training.

As I tied my laces, my bedroom door opened. Eddie entered, gaze on me and an intent on his face that made my heart speed up. Hoping he was here to kiss me stupid, I dropped my foot and leaned back on my palms from my position on my bed. He stopped before me between my open thighs, but rather than lean into me like I hoped, he peered down at me.

There was a beat of quiet, our breaths the only sound filling the space between us. But there was also a crackle of energy too, something that I'd always felt when with Eddie, and something about his features told me he felt it too. The knowledge had my pulse spiking.

"Tomorrow, no distractions. You wake up to your alarm and follow your usual routine, or as much as you can since you're playing in Indiana."

Surprised by the seriousness in his voice, my

brows dipped low.

"You will not break your routine, something I know you rely on, because we're here."

Not sure how to respond to his tone, I quirked my brow at him, maybe forcing a little bit of challenge into that one move.

"I mean it, Pearce."

My smile was instant. "You know, I kinda like it when you're being all growly." I bounced my brows up and down. "Never thought I'd like this domineering side, but it's hot."

Rather than joining in, Eddie tilted his head back and sighed. While a reaction I was used to from others, I wasn't from Eddie. I didn't like it one bit. Eddie always took my shit, my jesting with soft smiles and amusement.

"Pearce," he finally said, gaze back on me again. That one look had me sitting up. He stepped back a little so he could see my face. The distance felt wider than the few inches it was. "I need you to be serious about this. You're playing the best games of your life. Distraction right now is not okay."

He studied me, and for a second, dread landed in my gut, only disappearing when he edged closer and settled on his knees between my thighs. When his palms found purchase on the fabric of my shorts, I exhaled, the unsteadiness unfamiliar.

"I can't be the reason something goes wrong. If Lottie and me being here puts you off your game, I'll nev—"

"No." I shook my head quickly, clamping my hands on his shoulders. "You're not a distraction."

His pursed lips told me enough. He didn't believe me.

"I like you being here," I continued. "And if I screw up or we don't make it any further or don't win the championship, then that's on me and the team." The intensity of his stare didn't waver. Fuck. I forced my muscles to relax and pulled out a smirk. "You know, some studies have shown orgasms help improve a player's game. Something about endorphins and relaxation or something."

He still wasn't buying it, but me followIng up with how he and Lottie being here made my house feel like a home for the first time ever, and me wanting to win for him and to make Lottie proud didn't seem like the best idea. While for me, we had been in the making for years, I knew it was different for him.

"What studies?" The arched brow called bullshit.

"Studies from smart-as-fuck sciency people." I

edged closer, only stopping so I didn't fall off the bed. "I promise I'll go running and stick to my routine," I relented. Not that it was a hardship. Did I want as many moments with Eddie as possible? Of course I did. I also wanted to win the championship.

He studied me, his warm breath brushing across my skin, his mouth deliciously close to mine. "You promise?"

"I promise. And I have fifteen minutes before I have to leave, so I'm happy to seal it with a bj."

He snorted, finally, and my heart raced for a different reason when he leaned in, captured my mouth, and his deft fingers dipped beneath the waistband of my training shorts.

BETWEEN PRACTICE, TRAVELING, KICKING ASS AT GAMES, the buildup to our final round one game, and spending time with Lottie and Eddie whenever I got the chance, I went to bed exhausted each night. Admittedly it was the best type of exhausted, one where I smirked in post-orgasm glow the nights I was home. What didn't happen, though, was sleeping next to the man I was desperate to curl around.

And while I understood his reluctance to share our new, still-yet-to-be-clarified relationship status, it didn't stop me pouting every night when Eddie skulked to his room. It didn't help that he and Lottie were flying back home tomorrow either.

Lottie's temp was right on the normal mark, too, which meant she'd joined her dad for tonight's game. They were courtside. I figured there'd be less chance of her getting caught up in the hustle and bustle of the crowd.

I dragged the towel over my face while listening to Coach. We were in the final time-out of overtime. Perhaps League fans loved the thrill of this extra time in a playoff game, but fuck, I hated it.

The pressure was on, and with sweat rolling down my back and my pulse pounding loudly in my ears, it took every ounce of control I had to focus on Coach's words.

"—let Bradshaw get a touch. Marlow, stick to Hender like glue. You've got a minute to make this happen."

"We've got this, Coach." Ollie's tone left no room for doubt. Like the man, his voice was firm, solid. Damn, our captain held a conviction that was enviable. He scanned our team, making the briefest of eye contact with all of us, then it was game on.

We headed back onto the court. I cracked my neck and focused on Johnstone on the opposing team. The fucker would not be racking up more points if I had any say in it.

The whistle blew, and I moved. The sound of the crowd became white noise as I zoned in on the play, the ball. Seeing my chance, I stole the ball, a rush of adrenaline jolting me into action when my hands connected with leather.

With no time to hesitate, I shifted, dribbled, half of my attention on the pass, the other on Hender, who was coming at me. Cassius opened for me, and I passed, fast and smooth, a leap in my chest turning to fucking joy when he caught, shifted, and shot a three-pointer.

I was already all over Bradshaw like white on rice as their swingman bound ahead. The turn of his shoulder told me his plan, and thank Christ Cassius intercepted. Spinning so fast the room blurred, I met Cassius step for step, covering him as much as possible. Joel broke free, and the sweet fucking genius Cassius was all but flew in Joel's direction, feet barely touching the floor. A split second later, Joel had the ball in hand and scored.

Fifteen seconds, give or take. There was no time to check the clock.

And we were moving, feet hammering, hearts

blazing, desperate for the ball. A rebound, a miss, and we had possession. With each step, each move I made, I counted down, sure any second now, the game would be called.

And we lost the ball, Hender grabbing two points in the next breath. But we were still up. Like hell would I let them score again. Duncan made the pass, and I swiped the ball from the air, long strides taking me toward our basket. Blue jerseys were everywhere, blocking my path. They could blur my vision in color all they wanted. The longer the ball was in my hands, the closer we were to time.

Yellow appeared at my side. Ollie. The ball was in his grip before I could rethink my options, and the buzzer sounded, signaling the end of the game and the Eagles officially in the semis.

I whooped, hollered, Ollie crashing into me, Cassius a second later. "Fuck, man." I ruffled Cassius's hair, grinning wide as we parted. He didn't even swat me away, his own exuberance rivalling my own.

We clapped, and cheered, and did the obligatory rounds. It was at least three long minutes before I sought out Eddie. Still seated, his gaze was already on me, a wide smile on his face. He held Lottie's hand, and I kinda expected that was to make her stay in her seat.

"Where you going?"

Cassius's voice caught me short, not having realized I'd started to move away and in Eddie's direction.

I didn't have time to answer before his attention moved, clocking Eddie, and he snorted and shook his head. "Fuck, man, I really hope you're getting some since you're so damn whipped."

The urge to flip him off rode me, but that was the sort of shit that would end up in the media and get me in trouble with PR. "Screw you," I mouthed, earning me a laugh.

"You wish, Malcolm."

I rolled my eyes. "As much as I wish my ass was on fire from explosive diarrhea."

Disgust colored Cassius's face, as I anticipated. The guy paled at any mention of shit. It was fucking hilarious.

"What?" My tone took on a sugary sweetness. "You're looking a little peaky there, Cass. Need the bathroom? Imodium?"

"Dude, not cool, man. Not cool."

Did I feel even a little guilty knowing what his kryptonite was? Hell no. The fucker gave it back just as hard.

I blew him a kiss, smirking at the thought of the gift I'd left him in his locker. The asshole was going to flip his shit. With that thought, and chuckling to myself, I left Cassius and finally made my way to Eddie.

As much as I want a victory kiss with the man, I settled for a tight hug and a quick inhalation of his familiar scent.

"You were incredible." He squeezed me hard before easing away. "Congratulations, Pearce. The Bulldogs next." Bright-eyed and looking so proud my gut clenched, Eddie grinned widely.

"Thanks," I said, emotion clogging my throat. It wasn't like he'd never greeted me this way before, but now, with everything, his words, the way he stared at me, it felt a whole heap more meaningful. I coughed lightly and focused on Lottie. All but vibrating at her dad's side, she launched at me. I reacted quickly, trying to slow her movement and be careful with how I hugged her back.

"Pearce," she said a little breathlessly, "that three-pointer in the third, and the way you owned Barry, kept blocking his shots...." She pulled away, eyes wide and words trailing off.

"Got your seal of approval, huh?"

She bobbed her head. "Dad got it right. You were incredible."

My heart stumbled at the passion in her tone, and once again, emotion settled in my chest. Jesus, between the two Phelpses, I was going to be ruined. Instead of answering straight away, I hugged her carefully, my gaze traveling to Eddie. His unwavering stare filled with emotion I felt deep inside was something I'd never tire of.

As if seeing my struggle to get my emotions in check, he tapped on Lottie's arm. "Come on. Let Pearce up for air. He needs to go and change so we can head home."

Our eyes connected, and I desperately wished there was more truth to his words. With their flight tomorrow, it was a brutal reminder that they had a life miles away from my own.

Brushing away the ache unsettling my gut, I plastered on a smile and eased away. "Give me fifteen and I'll be right out."

"Okay." Lottie followed up with a loud yawn, not surprising since it was way past her bedtime, and settled her butt back down.

Making my way to the locker room, I tried to focus on the win, and how once Lottie was fast asleep, Eddie and I could have our own celebration. The thought was enough to have my dick taking interest. Since that first night, we hadn't tried to fuck again. Sure, bjs and handies were fucking spectacular, and I was so not complaining, but hell, I wanted to get inside his ass.

The volume in the locker room had me grinning when I stepped inside. Energy vibrated around the room, my teammates talking animatedly and laughing. It was enough to stop me thinking with my dick for a few seconds and instead focus on Cassius.

Standing by his locker, he tugged off his jersey, laughing at something Joel said. Like clockwork, he reached in a tugged out his towel, anal douches springing out and landing at his feet. The one smacking him in his face on the way down, though, had me roaring.

"The fuck?"

About five seconds passed before understanding registered, and the douche he was inspecting flew through the air, smacking Joel on the forehead.

Dead. I was going to die from laughter, but if that didn't kill me, the daggers Cassius shot my way would do it.

"You fucking wankstain." He narrowed his gaze and took a step in my direction.

"Hey," I managed, despite my overspilling laughter. "Hygiene is important. I was being generous. Thoughtful, even, by sharing."

He froze, paling. "For the love of God, tell me they weren't—" He swallowed hard and for a moment there I thought he was going to spew. "—used."

I bit the inside of my cheeks before saying, "They're new." And then he was on me, getting me in a headlock and twisting my nipple. Between my laughter, I gasped for air, tears trickling down my cheeks. "They're new," I grunted, trying to twist away from his bruising fingers, and doing a piss-poor job at reining in my amusement.

"They better fucking be." He loosened his grip and shoved me away, his gaze narrowing. He didn't do a great job at hiding the humor in them, though.

"Yep, and all yours. Have fun with them." I wiped at my eyes, still chuckling.

"You can clear them the fuck up," he ordered, heading back to his locker just as Joel leaned down and picked up one of the douches.

"What you got these for? My sister has one of these, said they're for turkey basting or something." Joel stared at the object in his hand and squeezed the bulb, a whoosh of air seeping from it.

And I lost it for a second time, having no choice but to sit down rather than collapsing, my shaking body struggling to keep me upright.

"What?" he asked incredulously, Joel never seeming more like the sweet, naïve soul he was than in this moment, and glancing around confused as fuck as the whole room overflowed with raucous laughter.

"I swear this is not my job." Ollie peered up at the ceiling, hands on hips. But I knew our captain would step up and stop the kid from squirting himself in the face with the anal douche. He was a good guy like that.

CHAPTER 15

EDDIE

WHILE PEARCE STAYED TRUE TO HIS WORD AND DIDN'T act differently in front of my daughter, every glance, slight uplift of my lips, and the barely there touches when Lottie wasn't looking were enough to make it almost impossible to not race through bedtime. By the time Lottie was fast asleep, I all but vibrated in need.

It was that absolute need combined with the knowledge I was leaving tomorrow that had me dragging him into his bedroom. As soon as the door locked with a heavy snick, I was on him. Between tugging off his suit and tearing my own clothes off, I whispered my need for him.

"You were so incredible tonight." I landed another kiss on his stomach before backing up on the mattress, making my intentions perfectly clear.

"Yeah?" His gaze didn't stray as he watched my every move. When I lay back, I bent my legs, opening myself to him. "Fucking hell," he said with a groan and knelt on the mattress, eyes zeroing in between my legs. With the way his eyes darted around, it was clear he didn't know where to settle—my dripping cock or my aching hole.

"Why don't you get over here so we can celebrate properly?" That I sounded like I'd run a marathon with just how ragged my breaths were was a testament to just how desperate Pearce made me. Watching him play had worked me up to the point of embarrassed discomfort. Then all those small tells over our late supper that let me silently know what he wanted to do to me had been enough to have me craving the man.

I felt wanton as fuck, and it was one hell of a rush I could totally get on board with.

Before he moved, I snatched the lube I'd thrown on the mattress. The opening click and the following dribble of fluid on to his fingers was enough for goose bumps to spring to life.

"You look fucking hot." The reverence in his voice caught my breath, my heart tripping over itself.

And then finally, at last, he moved, angling down, his mouth touching my skin.

Fire chased Pearce's kisses as he worked his way

up from my ankle to my thigh. I groaned, stomach tightening, only to huff out a rumbling sigh when he bypassed my dick and latched on to my nipple instead. He nibbled and lapped, causing me to squirm before combustion was possible, especially with how his fingers stretched as they worked in and out of me. I was nowhere near as ready as I had been that first night, courtesy of the plug, but I wanted the sting, to stretch around his girth so badly, I panted, "I'm ready. Get inside me."

His quiet chuckle reached my ears and drew my gaze to his. With flushed cheeks and blown pupils, Pearce was the epitome of delicious. And I couldn't wait until he was back inside me. This time with no untimely interruptions.

"But that'll mean I can't do all the things I imagined."

"If your imagination went beyond the bounds of your dick in my ass, then it can wait."

A self-satisfied grin beamed on his face as he angled up, this time sensibly reaching for the condom. "Since you look so hot when you're squirming—"

"Not squirming."

"Uh-huh."

I so was squirming.

"Well, since you look so hot when you're

pretending not to squirm, I'm happy to go easy on you."

The way he looked at me, the small smirk, heated eyes, it was enough to get me wriggling. The asshole knew what he was doing. Meanwhile here I was, needier than I'd ever been in my life, and wondering what the fuck I'd been playing at for the past five years.

Rather than share any of that with him, I grinned. "Not too easy on me." Sure, I liked the idea of going soft and slow with Pearce—a couple of mutual hand jobs had already gone down that way—but for this first time of fucking, desperation kept a firm grip on my body.

"That," he said, voice dipping as he edged closer, brushing his covered cock along my taint until it reached my lubed hole, "I can promise you."

Inch by slow, delectable inch, Pearce eased inside me. The stretch, the burn, was everything I needed. It grounded me, and even as I released a shuddery breath, my gaze latched on to his, refusing to let go.

I wanted every reaction, every tender, heated look.

"You're fucking beautiful," he whispered, his tone reverent and enough to make my breath hitch as he bottomed out. I groaned, the sound loud in the otherwise quiet room.

Latching on to his ass with my palms, I stilled him, needing a moment to settle and savor. "And you're perfect," I managed, not hiding the rush of feeling with my words.

His gaze softened, and he angled down, catching my mouth in a blazing kiss, the fierceness a contrast to his gentle words and sweet gaze. Holding on tight, I kissed him back with everything I had, swallowing our combined moans and groans as I squeezed his glutes, urging him to move.

After a couple of shallow thrusts, his mouth left mine. There was no chance to complain, only need when he pushed into me harder, rocking my body and pegging my prostate with the perfect touch. At contact, my gasp turned into a garbled "Nnghh...." Pearce simply smiled and redoubled his efforts.

One thing became crystal clear in this moment: Pearce was giving me everything I craved, everything I desired without me having to make a single demand. And me? Hell, I was along for the ride.

My grip didn't waver as I clung to Pearce, helping him with every thrust and movement. I canted my hips, meeting his, wanting him to go so deep I'd be feeling him for the days to come when we'd be apart. "I need to feel you," I said with a strangled moan, wanting him to know exactly what he was doing to me. "Right there." I grunted as he gave a fast roll of his hips and a deep pump. "I need you to fucking mark me."

I didn't have a moment to second-guess my words, ones that had never in my life fallen from my lips, before he was on me, mouth clasped to the juncture between my shoulder and my neck. Pearce shifted his arm under mine, almost cradling me as he held me close.

Continuing to drive into me, he sucked hard, each pull of skin punctuated by a deep thrust that had me seeing stars. His mouth moved lower to my shoulder, and he shifted his hips, grinding into me, and nipped lightly and sucked. And holy fuck, knowing I'd be seeing the physical evidence of Pearce and what he was doing to me shot a new wave of desire straight to my cock.

My dick pulsed and rubbed against his stomach. The friction spurred me on, and I rubbed against him as much as the position and his weight would allow.

"I'm gonna…"

He let go, turning his face to see me. Sweat dotted his brow, his pupils blown, and then he smiled, and my building orgasm powered through me.

"Holy shit," he said with a throaty groan, renewing his efforts when my body went taut beneath him. "So." He thrust deep and lifted to take his weight on his palms. "Fucking." He dipped his head, looking at the creamy mess on our stomachs. "Hot."

The flash of heat in his eyes when he looked back at me had my hand moving. I trailed my finger along the smooth release, scooped some up, and lifted my hand toward his mouth.

"Fuck." He moaned, eyes closing a second after he drew my cum-covered finger into his mouth, sucked hard, and then he blew. Pearce gasped around my finger, shuddering, ass cheek like granite under my palm as he stilled inside me, dick so far in my ass I knew my wish to feel him for days had been fulfilled.

I withdrew my finger and then he all but collapsed on top of me. I grunted, but when he shifted with a clear intent to move, I held on tight.

"But I'm squashing—"

"You're perfect where you are."

My words did the trick, and he relaxed against me, his weight a welcome comfort as I trailed my fingers over his back, enjoyed his slowing breaths next to my ear as he burrowed his head further into my shoulder. After a few moments of quiet, his tender kisses drew a happy sigh from me.

Pearce angled up a little, focus on my shoulder before our gazes connected. "They look so sexy on you." A wry grin lifted his lips. "When was the last time you had a love bite?" His fingers danced over what I was sure were his marks.

Feeling a little silly for what I pleaded for, I felt color stain my cheeks. His brows bounced high when he took in my reaction, but he waited for my words with satisfaction clear as day on his face. "Never," I admitted.

"Yeah?" Rather than the same self-satisfied tone I expected, tenderness filled his voice. Wordlessly, I nodded. "I like it a lot that you asked for them. Wish like hell I'd asked for the same."

My heart stuttered at the sincerity of the man before me.

"Wish that I had something more than the memory to get me through till the next time I see you."

I angled up and pressed my lips to his before settling my head back on the pillow. This was the first time we'd properly broached the subject that I'd be leaving tomorrow. Other than the logistics about Lottie and me going, we hadn't touched on what's next and when—more from an unspoken agreement not to bring us both down than anything else.

Knowing I needed to suck it up and have a grown-up discussion, but hopefully also have a plan for us both to have something to look forward to, I offered a gentle smile. "How about we shower together and make plans?"

He relaxed a little. I hadn't even noticed how tightly he'd drawn in his shoulders. "I like plans."

I snorted. "Plans for hijinks and being a pain in the ass to your teammates, probably." I indicated for him to lift up, and he did so almost begrudgingly.

"Those types of plans are super important. Do you know how long some of the shit I do takes to get organized?"

I rolled my eyes, keeping up with the low-key jesting despite how sexy he looked pulling off the condom. Maybe I should lick him clean before we showered.

"Ed, you look like you've got a very different plan in mind." Pearce's husky tone had my gaze snapping to his and away from his half-mast cock.

"Just wondering if my mouth on you would get you hard again."

Before I could react, he was in my space, practically attached to my body as he pressed his dick against mine. Holy shit, he was getting hard.

"Just the thought of your mouth gets this reaction."

"Damn. Probably something to do with being in your twenties too."

Pearce's grin turned salacious. "That sounds like

a challenge to me. Give me five minutes, and I bet I can get you so fucking hard again, you'll be desperate to fuck me."

I groaned and pressed my forehead against his shoulder. "That sounds so perfect, but—"

"Yeah, yeah, we have a plan to make."

I angled away from him with an arched brow. "You don't want to know when you're seeing me again?" Amusement came to life in my chest. Pearce was so easy to rile up.

"As if," he shot back, holding my hand and tugging me toward his shower room. "If there was no technical plan, the plan will be for me to be in your bed as soon as humanly possible."

Warmth fluttered to life right alongside my amusement. Pearce wasn't the only one easily distracted, apparently—the thought of sucking him off was proof of that. Maybe I should be worried he was able to tease out this side of me, the one where I'd easily lose focus on the realities of my everyday life.

Rather than overthink and second-guess myself, however, I focused on his tight glutes and stepped into him under the warm spray.

While we didn't manage to get a plan together in the shower, courtesy of Pearce making a spectacular effort at turning my cock to granite, we settled in bed together, both with our cells out and calendars open.

"Let's plan for when you win the conference finals, then make it to the tournament finals," I said, not willing to veer into the possibilities of what-ifs.

When he looked my way, Pearce's smile was surprisingly shy. "Okay."

I offered a firm nod, pleased he was on board. Despite only being six games in, the Eagles had as much of a shot as the remaining teams. "Lottie has school camp during the conference finals."

"She's super pissed she's not getting to miss out on her camp."

I smiled, loving again he was playing along, expecting to keep winning and get through the next games so he'd be playing in the third round.

"Yeah, she's super cut up about that." I shook my head. "I'd like her to head back to school next week if she's up for it. Have a semblance of normality before camp so I know she's going to be okay." While she'd been working on some schoolwork while convalescing, it would be good for her to catch up with her teachers and friends. Plus, she was healing amazingly. After that mild panic when I'd suspected an infection, her health had leveled out, and now she was almost as good as new.

Admittedly, we'd stayed longer than the initial

planned two weeks. But it hadn't taken much for Lottie to convince me we may as well wait for round one to be over. Her argument being she'd be pretty much fully healed by then.

I had to hand it to medicine and the wonders of keyhole surgery. As well as Lottie's ability to get what she wanted.

"Makes sense."

"I won't be able to make it to your next two games for sure, and I'm not sure about three or four either." I watched Pearce's face carefully, but rather than appearing even mildly pissed, he simply leaned over and kissed my shoulder.

"Stop looking at me as though I'm going to kick off and start making demands." His gaze softened, and I kinda figured he was holding back and not mentioning Wayne's name on purpose. We both knew Wayne would have had a hissy fit if I couldn't attend some sort of event with him.

"Thanks."

Pearce dotted another kiss on my shoulder, right over the love bite I needed to remember to hide from Lottie. "You don't need to thank me for under-standing you have a life and commitments. Sure, I know you'd love for me to be the center of your world and strapped to your bed, but all our wishes can't come true, right?" He bounced his brows and grinned.

"That does sound like a wish I would like to get on board with," I teased. Before he could clamber on top of me and pin me down—from the look in his eyes, that was absolutely his intention—I lifted my phone up from where I'd been punching in the game dates.

His not-quite frustrated breath whooshed out of him. "Fine. Remember I'm Mr. Responsible."

I snorted a little too hard at that.

"Hey, you don't believe me?"

There was a touch of uncertainty in his tone that had me angling to see his face better. "Why'd you say it like that?"

Heat colored his cheeks and he shrugged, a gesture that was as alien to Pearce as him passing up the opportunity to pull a prank on one of his friends.

"I'm serious." My brows dipped into a frown, and I danced my fingers down his arm. "Why'd you say it like that?"

He pursed his lips before huffing out a breath. "You said that one of the reasons you didn't give me a chance when I first asked you was because I was immature." He rolled his eyes and smiled, but I could tell he wasn't feeling it.

Guilt sliced through me. The last thing I wanted

was for him to feel like shit. I loved that he was fun and playful. Loved that he teased and enjoyed time with his friends. "You were twenty-four when we first met. Twenty-six when we were in Australia, right?" He bobbed his head. "I thought you were too young for me—" I stopped him from responding with a squeeze to his forearm. "Please let me finish."

"Okay."

"Honestly, the thought that you'd be interested in settling down and want to be serious…." I trailed off, heat racing through me at putting this out there.

As if understanding the reason for my overheated skin, Pearce squeezed my waist. "We are serious."

An embarrassed smile lifted my lips. "Well, back then, I just didn't think you were ready. You're so much younger than me. And then there's Lottie—"

"And you know they're all your concerns and issues, right? Not mine?"

I pinched my lips together as he spoke, not sure what he was getting at.

When I didn't respond, he continued, "I have absolutely fuck-all cares about your age or mine, or the gap between us."

While I knew that deep down, the relief of hearing it calmed a part of the concern that had been balled-up tightly in the pit of my stomach.

"And who knows… maybe you're right. Maybe I

hadn't been ready. Not that I had wild oats to be sowing or anything."

My lips twitched. "Wild oats?"

"Fuck off." He grinned. "You know what I mean. You know I haven't been celibate since you turned down my hot, young body."

I snorted at his waggling brows, giving me a little distraction from the thought of him with other guys. I was the last person with the right to say anything considering I'd been with Wankface. I chuckled internally, refusing to let on that I'd adopted Pearce's name for my ex.

"But I suppose the point is, I am absolutely ready for serious with a capital S."

"Is that right?" This man was so fucking adorable. "The capital S is important…?"

"Because all important stuff has a capital letter."

I couldn't hold back my laughter at his ridiculousness and was grateful as hell he had the uncanny ability to make me feel better about my own grievances and issues.

"And Lottie adores me, almost as much as I adore her."

Of that I was sure. I also expected, and hoped like hell, she'd be happy about Pearce and me together as a couple. Based on her reaction to the news of me and Wayne splitting—a wide grin, followed up with a "He was the wrong kind of weird for us, Dad. Weird is awesome, but Wayne, not so much"—I expected she'd be supportive, especially knowing she'd get more time with Pearce.

"She does." I also wanted to get back to his concern. "I know you can be responsible. You *are* responsible. Just because you have fun doesn't mean you're not those things."

The way he stared at me, looking a mixed bag of relieved and happy, made my heart ache for this man. Hell, ache for me too, as I so desperately wanted this to work. The past two weeks or so had been a cyclone of fast, hot, and heady. But I wouldn't allow the intensity of this time together to stop me from embracing something amazing with Pearce.

"You really think that?" Question filled his brown eyes as he looked for reassurance I'd rarely had to offer.

"I absolutely know so."

I lost sight of his face when he buried it against my neck. He inhaled and kissed my sensitive skin.

"Okay," I said, squeezing him to me. "Let's get these dates sorted so we can sleep."

CHAPTER 16
PEARCE

THE REST OF APRIL AND PRACTICALLY THE MONTH OF May passed by in a blur of games, traveling, and tired phone calls with Eddie. There was admittedly of lot of need and just a little bit of pining in said calls too. But despite my pity party of missing Eddie more than I thought a man could miss another human being, I knew it was all worth it.

Through hard work and a few miracles, the Eagles blasted through the semifinals. By the time it got to the conference finals, the team was flying high while equally dreading the next game—the fifth in the round—would be our last.

Every game in truth tested our strength, our abilities, our absolute doggedness to win the game and push on through.

But fuck, I was tired.

Relief that I had just two more days before the last game in this round kept me going. Then I'd either have the luxury of six whole days before the final round, or I'd be commiserating with my teammates and catching up on a shitload of sleep.

The biggest relief was our final game in round three was with the Jetts, taking place in Eddie's home city, Chicago. It made my bobbing knee even more noticeable, which apparently pissed Cassius off.

"I swear if you don't stop, I'm going to stab you in the thigh with my fork."

Rather than stop bouncing my knee, I angled my head to stare at Cassius, who sat by my side on the hour and a half flight. "I think Coach wouldn't like that so much. Let's ask him, shall we?" My wide grin didn't earn me a smile back. "Hey, Coach," I hollered.

A loud groan preceded Coach's "What is it, Malcolm?"

"Cass is threatening to *fork* me," I whined, earning me a chuckle from some of the guys and a dig in the ribs from Cassius.

"If I have to come over there and separate you, you're not going to like the consequences."

My eyes widened. "Shit." I so did not think this through. Coach was already testy due to Lintman having an injury.

"You're going to be so dead," Cassius whispered, shooting me a shit-eating grin.

I flipped him off, calling out, "Uhm, yeah, Coach. My bad... I totally meant the other kind of *forking*, but since Sutton and Jay-man left, I know you're not actively looking for more on-team hookups."

Cassius spluttered out a laugh. "You fucking wish. Your ass is too pasty for me."

I gasped, acting affronted, and choosing to ignore Coach's threat and plea to God for strength. "Pur-lease. There's not a suntan mark in sight."

"Uh-huh. That's because the whole of you is milk-bottle white. Plus your ass needs more meat on it. Something to grip."

My horror this time was only half feigned. "Take that back. My ass is perfection, just ask—" I slammed my mouth shut, cutting myself off from saying Eddie. We'd agreed to keep our official dating status on the down-low.

"Your hot DILF who you're pining for?"

Of course, all of my keeping quiet was pointless. My friends knew me too well. It didn't help that the last time Eddie had been able to attend a game, I'd played with blatant whisker rash. Yeah, as if any of my teammates didn't call me out on that.

But I'd never confirmed anything. Though in truth, I hadn't denied anything either. I didn't want to outright lie to them. I'd also been trying to figure out who was set to win the wagers on me too. Was it mean of me that I didn't want Cassius to pick up any of the cash? Probably, but the guy threw enough shit my way as it was. I didn't want him drinking the top-shelf booze because he could read me so well.

"Shut up." As far as comebacks went, mine was pitiful. "And you'd better not really think of him as a DILF."

Cassius burst into laughter. "Holy shit." He barely got the words out. "Did you just growl at me?"

"No." My face was aflame, hot enough to toast marshmallows.

"You so did. You were all"—he beat a hand against his chest—"Eddie mine. Grrr."

"Fuck off," I said with a laugh, shoving at him. "I did not sound like... well, whatever that was supposed to be." I looked at him more fully. "Please tell me that was your god of alligators growl." Two could so play at this game. Plus, it offered a fun distraction before we landed and I could finally get my hands on Eddie.

"Sticks, asshole. You know it's all about the sticks."

"Uh-huh. Says the man who has a shit phobia."

He blanched, and for a second there I felt guilty—

though to be fair, he talked about it and ass all the damn time, practically inviting us all to respond. The guilt fizzled away when he settled back in his seat, face turned toward me. "So this daddy kink you have going on, how's that work when you hear Lottie calling him *daddy*?" He arched a brow at me. "Not that I'd dare to kink shame, of course. Just wondered if it gets kinda awkward when you're there all... *Daddy, right there*, and then, what, two minutes later, Lottie's around—"

I slammed a hand over his mouth, turning a little green. "You hush your mouth." I shuddered. "It is so not like that. He's eleven years older than me, not fucking thirty."

Cassius, being the asshole friend he was, licked my palm. It did the trick, and I tore my hand away. He laughed loudly, and despite him being a fucker, I laughed with him.

"You two children want to keep it down?" Ollie turned around and peered at us from the seat in front. "You know everyone can hear you, right?"

I winced. Even though this was my and Cassius's usual back and forth ripping the shit out of each other and mercilessly teasing, not everyone in the team, and definitely not the cabin crew, needed to hear our business.

Clearing my throat, I bobbed my head at Ollie. He

rolled his eyes and turned, but not before offering us a quick smirk. Our captain deserved hazard pay. He also had the patience of a kindergarten teacher.

"But seriously," Cassius said, leaning in, his voice much quieter, "is Eddie meeting you at the airport?"

"Nope. When has he ever met me at the airport when I have a game?" Sure, during the off-season when we'd visited each other in the past, we'd always collected each other, but not when he was taking in a game.

Cassius bobbed his head. "You going official anytime soon?"

I twisted my mouth and studied him, looking to see if he was going to follow up with a joke. When all I read was genuine curiosity, I still hesitated.

Cassius sighed. "Nothing to do with the bet, and you know I can keep my mouth shut." He shrugged, the move a little too casual that I frowned and studied him a little harder. "I just know keeping something completely to yourself can be a lot some-times. It can also feel like shit and get to you."

A level of seriousness that was as unusual as real downtime in the season passed between us. "Sounds like you're talking from experience."

Our gazes connected briefly before he shrugged and glanced away.

"You know I can keep my mouth shut too, right?"

"Not if Eddie's cock is near, I bet," he fired back. And the moment was officially gone.

I snorted, not even bothering to argue with him. When his focus returned to me, he smiled, but his usual cockiness appeared dimmer. My amusement dropped. "I am serious, though."

When he bobbed his head but didn't answer, I felt right to give him something. This trust thing went both ways. "After the playoffs and after we've discussed things with Lottie." Saying the plan aloud made it a little more real. Hell, that could be in two days if we lost our final game. If not, just under three more weeks to go and we could finally be open and move forward. The knowledge shot a flood of warmth into my chest.

I liked the idea a helluva lot.

"Must feel good."

"Yeah, it does."

"I'm happy for you, man. I know I give you hell, but Eddie's a good guy."

Happiness had me beaming. "Thanks, Cass. He really is."

"And if you ever want a third—"

He burst into laughter when I shoved him hard, my own smile not disappearing. "Fuck off, asshole."

Not long after Cassius returned to his usual self, we prepared for landing. As always, we'd be piling onto a bus and transported to a hotel near the Jetts arena. We wouldn't have time to kick back, though, as Coach had organized us court time later this afternoon. Knowing Eddie would be meeting me at the hotel meant I could deal with the hard practice in preparation of Thursday's game with a smile on my face.

THE SOUND OF MY ROOM DOOR OPENING BROUGHT A beaming smile to my face. Immediately I stood, eyes on the man I hadn't seen for six days—not that long in the scale of things, but it was still six days too many for my liking.

"Hey." He closed the hotel room door behind him and dropped the key card I'd left for him at reception on the small unit near the door.

With a handful of steps, I was in his space. "God, it's good to see you," I greeted before I pressed my mouth to his and held him tight. We both moaned on contact, my breath hitching at how amazing it felt being connected to Eddie like this again.

The five long years we'd known each other, many with me actively craving and pining for the man, made moments like these worth the wait.

"Your flight okay?" he asked when he eased away.

"Yeah, all good." I reluctantly released him, and we headed further into the room. "Your day been okay? Get what you needed done?"

He dropped his overnight bag on the floor and kicked off his shoes. "Pretty productive. Got some tasks done. I managed to get Lottie to Sarah's house without too much fuss."

"She doesn't know you're seeing me tonight?"

Eddie shook his head. "Hell no. The fuss she'd make would give me a headache." He picked up the room service menu and smiled. "She's excited for Thursday's game, though."

"I'm glad. Even managed to get your courtside again."

Eddie stepped before me and dotted a soft kiss on my waiting mouth. "Thank you. She'll love them." He lifted the menu. "We ordering, or did you want to go out for food?"

Reaching out, I gripped his waist. "No chance I'm letting you leave this room until morning."

The smirk he sent me had my heart tripping over itself. "That right?"

"Sure is." I shifted my hands to grip his glutes and squeezed, earning me a chuckle.

"I can get on board with that. But food first. I'm starving."

"For dick?" I quirked my brow and brushed my shorts-covered groin against him.

He snorted. "As delicious as that sounds, I need real food."

I sighed and headed to the bed, making myself comfortable leaning against the headboard. "I suppose I can be magnanimous and know that you'll need the energy for what I have planned for you."

Pink colored his cheeks, but the heat in his eyes didn't speak of embarrassment. Eddie liked what he was hearing. He angled to the other side of the bed and joined me, holding the menu out before him. Clearing his throat, he made a good show of perusing the in-room offerings.

"Stop staring and make food choices." His lips twitched when he spoke, but he didn't look my way.

I sighed and leaned into him. "Fine. Let's see what's fast and will give the perfect number of calories."

He snorted and wrapped an arm around my shoulders. I took that as my opportunity to snuggle into him and rested my head on his chest while making an effort to pay attention to the menu.

It didn't take long to make our choice and order on their TV app. Within half an hour, our food was delivered, and we sat on the small couch, food on our laps.

"I spoke to Emily again today at the academy about next month and bringing Lottie," Eddie said after swallowing a mouthful of pasta.

"What did she say?"

"There's definitely space for her at the summer camp."

"That's good, right?" When he winced, I wasn't quite sure.

"She's not sold on the idea, but it was between that or staying with my parents, so..." He shrugged and picked up his bottle of water.

"Yeah, I get it, but at least it's on the same campus, so she gets to see you every day. It's not like you're sending her off into the wild. That's gotta help, right?"

He swallowed and nodded. "It's the only thing that's making her stop behaving like a complete brat." I snorted at that and raised my brows. He chuckled. "She's my kid so I'm allowed to call her out on her shit when the occasion calls."

"But no one else, right?"

Eddie grinned. "You got it."

"I think she'll be fine, though," I continued, returning to Lottie being at the same college as us over the summer. While Montview ran the kick-ass summer program for college basketball players looking to go pro, they ran a whole host of other schemes. The kids' summer school being one of them. Before this year, Lottie had previously spent the time when her dad was training with her mom or her grandparents, so Eddie had never had to worry about being able to dedicate his time to the academy before. "When is it Moira flies in?" I asked, thinking about Eddie's ex-wife.

"Why, going to make sure you're not around and in hiding?" A mischievous smirk followed.

"No," I was quick to say, the word a little more high-pitched than I intended. At the sound, Eddie laughed a little too loudly. "Screw you, jackass."

Eddie's smile didn't calm when he said, "She's flying in the third week in June. She'll bring Lottie to the camp before she heads back overseas. It's good timing really, as Lottie will only miss the first couple of days of the summer school. Not that I think it matters, as it's a fun program, you know?"

"So what you're saying is by making it to the final round, it'll mean there's less chance of seeing Moira. Got it."

He snorted. "She's not that bad."

My brows shot high. "If 'not that bad' means completely fucking terrifying and downright intimidating, yeah, sure." There was only a little exaggeration in my description. I'd only met the woman once. Usually I prided myself on the ability to win people over, if not by my first smile, then certainly by our first conversation. Moira, though, hadn't been won over when I'd spent fifteen minutes talking to her about my CK deal.

In retrospect, it wasn't the greatest topics of conversation, but by that point three years ago, I'd already been having untimely hard-ons for her ex and had been nervous as hell.

And this time, she'd end up knowing about me and Eddie, right? Sweat broke out on the back of my neck. What if she hated me and didn't think I was good enough to help bring up Lottie? Sure, I was getting way ahead of myself with the whole stepdad thing, but that was absolutely the direction I hoped we'd end up. I wanted it all with Eddie, and Lottie was part of that deal.

"Question," I said, while Eddie the ass still laughed about my description of his ex.

He wiped his mouth on a napkin and focused on me, brows lifted in expectation.

While I hated to think of the man, let alone say the dickhead's name… "Wayne," I started, not quite keeping my sneer at bay. "What did she think of Wankface?"

Eddie stilled his movements and examined me

closely. He knew me well enough to not ask me why. "I once let slip your colorful name for him."

"Wankface Wayne?"

His lips twitched. "That's the one. She may have adopted it for herself and mentioned that you were maybe more astute than she originally thought."

I opened and closed my mouth, letting his words sink in. A quick smile broke out shortly after. "Hell yes, I'm astute. She's going to totally love me. She's not going to know what's hit her next time we meet."

Frowning, Eddie shook his head. "Pearce, you don't need to make Moira feel any way for you, and honestly, your tone is freaking me out a little."

"But she has a say in who brings Lottie up."

His gaze softened, and he reached over and held my hand. "I get that you feel like you need to prove yourself or something, but you don't. Honestly. Our friendship, my feelings for you... heck, how Lottie feels about you is enough."

My heart fluttered in my chest at his sweet words and the reassurance in them. I hadn't realized how anxious I was about making sure I was what Lottie needed as well. "Your feelings, huh?" My mouth curved upward.

"Yep." He leaned close and kissed me, soft and slow. While they weren't the words clinging to my heart, ones I was desperate to hear and say, his tender kiss was enough. When he pulled away, he raised a brow at me. "And for the love of all that is rational, please do not plan anything to win Moira over. Just be yourself."

"So I don't need to organize a Wankface hate club so we can spend time bitching about him? 'Cause you know, that could be a bonding experience right there."

Closing his eyes and dropping his head back, Eddie huffed out a defeated breath. "I shouldn't have told you he texted me last week."

I jammed my fingers in his side. "Like fuck you shouldn't have."

An amused smirk was thrown my way when he returned his focus to me. "Huh."

"Huh what?"

"That tone right there…" Heat pulsed between us as he spoke, and he placed his dish on the table before us.

"What about it?" There was no holding back the husk in my voice, not when he looked at me like he wanted to put his mouth on all my favorite places.

"Never thought I'd have a thing for possessive men."

I shook my head. "Not possessive men. Just me. I can be possessive as fuck if you want me to be."

Discarding my plate, I clambered onto his lap, not

an easy feat since the couch wasn't built for two basketball players to fool around on. Not that I cared. I needed my mouth back on Eddie.

"I kinda think I want you to be."

I grinned as I nipped at his ear before pulling back and peering down at him. "All the time?"

Clamping his palms on my ass, he chuckled. "Maybe just in private."

I shifted forward and rolled my hips. His gasp was worth the discomfort of squashing my hard dick. "Cass said I was pretty much a caveman about you."

Eddie's fingers danced up my spine.

"He kinda figured something was going on," I clarified. Not that Eddie questioned me, but I wanted to put it out there.

"I think Neanderthal is pushing the limits of sexy. And if you stop bathing, there's gonna be issues."

Amusement bubbled in my gut. "I missed you so much," I admitted.

Rather than answering, his traveling fingers reached my head. Clasping me tightly, Eddie drew me down, mouth capturing mine in a possessive kiss.

Sweetness went barreling out the window as he devoured me. All boundaries fell away as need pulsed in time with my heartbeat, picking up its pace when I rocked against him.

My "I need you," shattered all resistance. Desperation clung to my words, encouraged me to claw at his T-shirt, seeking his warm flesh.

He pulled away with a gasp and tugged off his tee. "Get on the bed." Each word was punctuated with the vibration of his shaking hands against my body. That his need caused such a reaction had me almost landing on my ass as I attempted to get off him.

It was only Eddie's fast reflexes that had me righting myself. His light chuckle caressed me, warming me up from the inside out as I managed to stand, undress, and walk backward to the bed. His gaze never wavered as he watched every move I made, every inch of skin revealed to him.

Once my ass connected with the mattress, I reached out and palmed myself. It had the desired effect. He was naked and with lube in hand a heart-beat later. A flutter of desire swept through me, knowing finally, we would be going without protection.

"You sure this is okay?" he asked, lubing his bare cock as he spoke.

"Fuck yes."

He grinned and squeezed himself, and both of our breaths hitched.

"You want to pass me that?" I indicated toward the bottle in his hand.

"No fucking chance." And then he was on me, fingers working me over, lips trailing over me, tongue lapping. Stars danced in my vision as I rode his exploring fingers and chased his mouth. "You need more?" he asked, sweeping over my prostate and making me tremble.

"No. Just your dick." I tightened around him, earning me a grunt.

As he eased out of me, his gaze locked on mine while he repositioned himself. I lifted my thighs, opening for him, wanting him so desperately to fuck me into oblivion. With exquisite slowness that was on the cusp of torture, Eddie pushed into me. Each inch left me gasping his name, each fraction deeper had me holding on tight. Bottoming out, he grunted, the sound vibrating into me and settling contently in my chest.

Stroke by stroke, he pushed me to the brink, lips pressing against every piece of skin he could reach. "I missed you so much," he whispered as he angled his chest away and gripped my hips.

I managed a nod, the gesture difficult with my senses going haywire. This was only the second time he'd fucked me, and one thing was clear: I couldn't keep going on without doing this with him all the damn time.

"You feel so good," I grunted. "Can't wait till you come in me."

A hiss escaped him when I spoke, his hips jerking and grip tightening to the point I hoped to God there'd be bruises.

"You want my cum?"

"Uh-huh." I pushed against him and finally gave in and reached for my cock. Any sooner, and this would have been over already. "So fucking much."

"Fuck." Once again, his hips jerked, losing his tempo. I smiled at his faltering, loving how he seemed to enjoy the thought of him coming inside me as much as I did. His gaze snapped to my hand. "Don't come yet."

I grunted and squeezed my dick. Not sure I could hold back.

"I want to suck you off while your ass is leaking with my cum."

"Fuck. You can't..." I shook my head and squeezed a little tighter. "I need to—"

"I know." Then there was no holding back from Eddie. He fucked me fast and hard, pistoned his hips until I grunted and groaned, certain that if I didn't orgasm soon, I would detonate.

With each stroke, I clenched tighter around him, responding to his groans, needing him to let loose.

"You're perfect."

How he even managed the words when I could barely hear beyond the pounding of my heart and the buzzing in my brain was a miracle. Yet I heard them, felt them brush across my skin, leaving a trail of blissful heat in their wake.

His lips once more touched me, taking me by surprise, as I'd since closed my eyes, trying my hardest not to explode just yet. Meeting in a frenzy, our tongues brushed against each other as he fucked me into the mattress. I was coiled tightly—we both were.

Gasping for breath, I broke our kiss, my gaze locking on his.

A smile played on his lips before "Oh fuck... oh fuck..." broke out. His climax burst free. Focusing hard at not following, I stared at his face, watching each movement there. Emotion danced on his features as he filled me up, his hips jerking, body almost rigid with his release.

When he opened his eyes, he kissed me, quick and fast, catching my groan as he pulled out of me. He moved, sealing his mouth around my dick. The gasp tore out of me, the suction tight, the movement so perfect I had no choice but to clamp on to the wrecked sheets.

Stars danced in my vision, and I shouted out my release, my nerve endings spiraling out of control. I was fucking bound, tied so completely to this man that if I believed in soul mates, without a doubt he was mine.

Fuck, maybe I believed after all.

More lucid thought returned as we slowed our breathing. At some point he'd pulled off my dick, and for the first time I felt the remnants of his release, so distinctly different than the mess of lube alone.

"That was amazing." He crawled up the bed, pressing tightly against me, head landing on my chest.

"Need my arms to work to hold you," I managed with a weak chuckle, my limbs refusing to behave.

I felt the whisper of his smile against my skin. "All good. Shower soon."

I grunted something unintelligible. Moving sounded like a lousy idea right now. Not only that, but I was in no rush to wash away the evidence of our lovemaking just yet.

CHAPTER 17

EDDIE

YESTERDAY MORNING WE'D PARTED WAYS SO I COULD attend a meeting with my accountant about some recent purchases while Pearce went about his usual routine when playing away.

We did manage to grab dinner together last night, though. This time with an excited Lottie in tow. Her eagerness to spend time with Pearce, I could completely relate to. It also gave me hope that as soon as we were able to talk about Pearce and me dating, she'd be happy with the news.

While this coming summer—Pearce's off-season —our time together was a given, since for at least six weeks of it we'd be at Montview together, we hadn't discussed beyond that. There was little doubt we knew the reality of our situations and being a flight apart, both with significant commitments and limitations to travel.

As far as I was concerned, I'd keep pleading ignorance. Not trying to work out a plan meant I didn't have to stress or worry about the future. For the time being, I chose to believe we'd figure it out.

Having Lottie with me had meant no sleepover in Pearce's hotel room. It sucked, and I would have asked him to simply stay at my home, but that would have got him in a shitload of trouble with his coach. Instead, I'd had to be content with a sly press of my lips to his neck when I hugged him goodbye, and a lingering look.

The video call last night had helped get me to sleep, though. Much easier when watching Pearce take himself in hand had dragged a spine-tingling orgasm out of me.

We'd texted each other throughout the day. I hadn't been able to head to his hotel between his practice session and tonight's game, but we had the promise of tonight. He'd already got his coach's approval not to travel back with the team tomorrow.

Lottie and I had thirty minutes before we had to leave for the arena. Pearce would already be there, but we had time to kill.

"Lottie. Chair."

The scrape of her fixing her chair and stopping

from balancing the damn thing on two legs followed, right along with her huff.

"Have you completed it?" I peered at her laptop, looking for evidence she'd finished her math homework.

"One more question." She didn't look away as she spoke, a testimony to how focused she could be when being late to the game was at stake.

"Great. I'm just going to sort the washing out."

I left her to it while getting on with the joys of domestic tasks. Admittedly, I had a cleaner who came in twice a week to get on top of my five-bedroom home, but everything else I took on myself. Working for myself as a stockbroking consultant and having invested super wisely during my years of playing pro put me in one hell of a position of privilege. It didn't mean I couldn't handle washing clothes or making dinner, though.

Once the load was in, I made sure Lottie's school bag was ready for tomorrow, as well as her lunch. Tonight would be a late night. Not the first time she'd stay up way past her bedtime to take in a basketball game. No chance I'd let her miss it, though. At least it was almost the weekend, so she could catch up with sleep then.

As I pulled a sandwich bag from the drawer, a loud scream rent the air, followed by a loud thud, then Lottie's cry. Fuck. I dropped the paper wrapper and raced out of the kitchen to the large study area just off the hallway. My heart stumbled in my chest. Lottie lay on the floor, tears streaming from her eyes while she cradled her arm.

The chair that I'd just moments ago told her to stop swinging on lay on the oak floorboards beneath her.

I dropped to her side, eyeing her face while trying to take in her limbs and figuring out where she was hurt and how badly. The thud had been loud. Whether that was simply the chair or her head smacking on the hard wood, I had no idea.

"Baby, where are you hurt?"

With her legs still draped over the chair, she looked fragile and so small. Add in her snotty tears, and it took everything in me not to simply scoop her up.

"Baby," I repeated. She sobbed, her breath stuttering as she stared up at me. "Your arm, is it hurt?"

"Yeah." She barely got the word out between her tears.

"Anywhere else?"

"My h-h-head."

I carefully moved aside the strands of hair latched onto her wet cheeks. "Shh… it's okay, baby." I glanced at her legs. "What about your legs?"

"Th-They're okay." A shuddered breath tore from her, and her tears settled.

I bobbed my head and refocused on her arm. "You think you can stand up if we go super slowly and I help you?"

Her face looked stricken. "Okay."

I moved to the other side of what I thought was her injured arm and helped her up. She cried out, and fuck if my heart didn't break. This kid of mine was having a shit run of it. "You're being so brave, Lottie. We need to get you in the car and to the hospital, though."

That she didn't frown or cry that the hospital was the last place she wanted to go clued me in to just how much pain she was in.

We made our way slowly to the car, figuring her slow steps caused less jostling than if I swooped her up and carried her. I couldn't see any blood or cut on the back of her head, nor did I want to start prodding around.

My focus was getting her safely to the hospital. I'd seen enough injuries in my years of pro sports to recognize a break when I saw one. I just hoped it was clean and didn't require surgery. Two of the damn things in six weeks was a shitshow I didn't want for my girl.

Once I'd settled her in the car, wincing at her

small sob when I had to strap her in, I hurried back into the house to swipe up my car keys, my wallet, and my phone. A press of a button once I was strapped in opened my garage door, then my mission was getting to the emergency room.

As I drove, I murmured words of encouragement. She'd since settled down, only the occasional shuddering breath drawing out of her.

"You doing okay?"

"Yeah. It really hurts, but I'm okay."

I stole a glance in the rearview mirror and my shoulders relaxed a fraction when she attempted a watery smile. "You're a regular badass, kid. You know that?"

"I try."

A laugh huffed out of me as I returned my attention back to my route. I sighed at the ridiculous amount of traffic. "Come on." I tapped at the wheel, wishing the cars in front would magically drift apart so I could race on through. Gritting my teeth when I had to brake for the fiftieth time, I wondered if it made sense to get off this route and work my way around.

A flash of color, a ribbon on a car, caught my eye, and my heart plummeted.

The game.

Pearce.

Holy shit, we were going to miss the game.

The car in front edged forward. I put my foot on the gas, hoping this time we'd get some movement. With my gut churning, my worry for Lottie slammed hard and fast with the ache in my gut for letting Pearce down.

It didn't matter that he'd understand. Tonight's game was make or break time. And what would I do if I couldn't get hold of him? How the fuck would he react when he took to the court and spotted our two empty seats? Our courtside tickets would leave an aching gap.

Fuck. I squeezed the steering wheel. Pearce would be distracted, confused... fucking *distracted.* Everything I never wanted him to feel because of me.

Making a decision to turn off the main route, a few minutes later, I exhaled in relief. Thank Christ it was the right call. The traffic was easing, and it should mean it wouldn't take much longer to get to the hospital.

A few moments later, Lottie interrupted the quiet. "We're going to miss the game." Distress pitched her voice high.

I winced. "I know, baby. Pearce will understand." Nausea swirled in my gut as I tacked on a silent *I hope.*

"I really wanted to see him. Maybe we could go to the hospital after."

A laugh punched out of me. "I don't think that's the best idea."

"But I can be brave, and I can ignore how much it hurts for a while. I haven't cried in ages."

Love for my girl caught in my throat. "That's because you're brave, but all it'll take is one jostle and it'll hurt lots again, and ignoring it could possibly make the damage worse." I didn't add that she also needed to get her head checked out. She could be concussed for all I knew. "Is your head okay?" I wanted to punch myself for not thinking to ask before.

"I don't think there's any blood, but I don't want to check."

The emotion clogging my throat threatened to spill over. "I don't think there's blood. But does your head hurt? Do you have a headache? Are your eyes fuzzy?"

She was quiet a beat. A glance in the mirror showed me she was thinking, no doubt cataloguing her injuries, knowing my girl. "My eyes are sore," she eventually said. "But they always are when I've been crying." She scrunched her nose, as if the very fact that she'd cried in the first place offended her.

"Okay. And headache?"

"My head's sore where I hit it, and my head hurts a little."

"Okay." I nodded. At least she wasn't saying her head was killing her or anything. "We're just pulling into the parking lot now, okay?"

"'K."

We found a spot almost immediately, a rarity for this busy hospital. After pocketing my phone, I helped Lottie out of the car, locked up, and we headed to the reception. With every step, my phone called to me, desperate for me to at least attempt to reach out to Pearce. It would be my next move as soon as possible. I just hoped he'd get the message beforehand.

WITH JUST TEN MINUTES LEFT ON THE CLOCK, THE JETTS were dominating.

Lottie kept up a running commentary as she livestreamed the game on my phone while waiting for the results of her X-ray. The whole time, I could barely look at the footage.

Unsurprisingly, Pearce hadn't picked up his phone before being on court or responded to my messages. Knowing he'd gone out expecting to see us sent a wave of guilt up my throat.

Routines were important. I'd lived and breathed basketball for so long that I was more than aware that when something shifted, it could impact your focus. While I definitely wasn't part of Pearce's regular game routine, when I did attend, without fail, Pearce always sought me out as soon as his feet hit the court.

There'd always be a chin uplift, a tweak of a smile. That was it. Nothing especially significant or earth-shattering, but on games I attended, I became part of Pearce's routine. Me not being there would impact him.

"Urgh. I can't believe Wallumby missed that shot." She started to shake her head but halted and winced.

"Your head hurting more?" It was easier to focus on Lottie rather than the guilt refusing to dislodge from my chest.

"A bit."

"We'll be able to get you painkillers as soon as the doctor sees what's going on with your arm," I reassured. The emergency doctor expected it was a straightforward break just in need of casting. Hopefully the X-ray would confirm that. The good thing was it didn't appear Lottie had a concussion, but I'd still been advised she needed to take it easy and to keep a close eye on her over the next seventy-two hours.

"They're taking forever. We could have been at the game," she grumbled.

"Uh-huh. Just think how quiet and relaxing it is at a game. Nope, that wouldn't have made your head hurt worse or anything." I quirked my brow, trying to make my levity believable.

"Pearce just missed a shot."

I huffed out a breath and rubbed the back of my head. Tempted to look, I instead stood under the pretense of stretching my legs. If I saw his face, saw his distress, how could I possibly break free from feeling so damn responsible for what was likely going to be a loss.

Pressing my lips together, I breathed heavily through my nose. The Eagles were more than one man. Rationally I knew that. It didn't stop the reality of the team's dynamics going wonky from one player being off their game.

"I don't think I can watch any more."

Concern had me whipping around back in the direction of Lottie. "Does your head hurt so much?" I stepped back to her side, examining her face closely.

"The only thing that's painful is this game."

In any other circumstance, I'd likely laugh my ass

off at her quick answer, but not this time. I pursed my lips together. "Maybe just turn it off."

She stared at me then, her eyes wide, full of reproach. "I can't do that to Pearce."

This time I snorted, despite the fresh blow of shame for me suggesting she should turn off the game. "I know." I slipped into the chair beside her, feeling anything but the adult.

"It will take a miracle for them to pull this back. There's less than four minutes on the clock and eighteen points between them." She sighed. "But we should still watch. Even though we're not there, we can support Pearce."

Jesus. I was being schooled by a ten-year-old. Clearing my throat, I bobbed my head. "You're right. We're there in spirit, right?" My smile was tight, but I focused on the screen.

Between now and when I saw Pearce again, I needed to get over myself and make sure my focus was on him and how he was coping with the result. I just wasn't sure how to stop the dread in my gut from gnawing away at me.

Just as the buzzer went, the game officially won by the Jetts, the doctor returned, X-rays in her hand. "Good news," she said.

I took the phone off Lottie and closed down the app. "Yeah?"

"Sure is." She held up the X-ray against the light box attached to the wall. "A nice clean break here, so no surgery. Just six weeks in a cast and you should fix right up."

Relief released some of the tension weighing me down. "That's great news."

The doctor smiled kindly at Lottie. "How about we get you set up for a cast, then you can get out of here?"

Lottie smiled for the first time since hurting herself. "Okay."

As we set about getting Lottie in a cast, I held on to my cell, checking it every thirty seconds, hoping like hell at any second now, I'd receive word from Pearce.

CHAPTER 18
PEARCE

THE GAME WAS A SHIT SHOW. I WAS OFF MY GAME FROM the moment my Nikes hit the court and didn't see the smiling faces of Eddie and Lottie. Worry had churned my gut, making it hard to concentrate, but basketball was my job, and I'd been determined to give it my all.

We all missed the mark a hundred and ten percent. Add in Cassius taking a hard foul in the first five minutes and Ollie fumbling the ball, something he never did, it wasn't a surprise it was a clusterfuck.

I glanced at Ollie as he stood in front of the sports news crew and I winced, feeling sorry for the guy. I was so fucking relieved I wasn't the captain. With a nod at a couple of the guys, we headed silently to the locker room. Misery was thick in the air. It clung to us as we waited for Coach to enter and give us a reaming I knew we all deserved.

Cassius threw his Nikes on the floor, punctuating it with a loud "Fuck."

A few grunts of agreement joined in, and I sighed, rubbing a hand over my face.

"I don't give a shit if we've got an early start for our flight tomorrow," Joel grumbled, taking a seat on the stool beside me. "I'm getting wasted tonight."

"Fucking A," Cassius responded.

"You in?"

It took me a beat for me to realize Joel spoke to me. Before I could respond with my excuse, which combined with a legit pang in my chest wondering what had happened with Eddie, Coach stepped into the room. All thoughts of checking my phone and making some calls fled.

Coach Jenkins appeared eerily calm, his face a mask of not quite indifference, but it seemed carefully neutral. And fuck if that didn't get a fresh knot forming in my gut.

Standing in silence, Coach peered around the room. I did the same, noting that Ollie had joined us. He looked hollowed out. Drained.

"Round three," he started, arms folded, and taking his time to look at his team, "it's one hell of an achievement." I swallowed hard while Joel shuffled uncomfortably in his seat. "One game away from the finals." He nodded and took a few steps, standing more central to where our lockers were. "It's been fourteen years since the Eagles got so far in the play-offs." Coach pursed his lips, and fuck, if he said he was prou— "I'm proud of each and every one of you for getting us this far."

And there it was. Tears sprang to life in my eyes. I lowered my head and stared hard at the tiled floor before squeezing my eyes shut.

"Was tonight's game your best?" Rather than any acknowledging chuckles, dead silence greeted his words. "I can't say it was. Ollie, one thing. Go."

I lifted my head and focused on my captain. My friend deserved my attention.

"We need to make the plays."

Several of us bobbed our heads, and we went around the team, all of us contributing. Highlighting our errors, taking responsibility, reflecting on a loss was never fun. It was painful as fuck. Disappointment sat like a heavy weight, threatening to crush each of us. It was only Coach's plain-spoken reactions, countering every single thing we'd screwed up with something each of us had aced that kept me, hell, all of us from spiraling. He was an amazing coach.

When our debrief was over, Coach reminded us

to be ready for seven in the morning for the bus to the airport, which immediately made my heart race once again.

Eddie.

Where the fuck was Eddie?

I scrambled for my phone as soon as Coach left, nearly dropping it in my haste.

Something had to be wrong, right? Eddie wouldn't just not show. But the thought of something not being okay I didn't like any more.

"Damn, Malcolm, slow your roll. What's the rush?"

My teammates were blissfully unaware of the anxiety that accompanied every beat of my heart since I'd realized Eddie's seat was empty. Telling them would be a pretty clear signal about one of the reasons I'd been off my game tonight. I felt like shit, knowing I was going to disappoint them.

"Eddie and Lottie didn't turn up to tonight's game," I admitted, risking a side-eye to Cassius, who'd spoken to me.

A frown dragged his brows low. "Why not? Something wrong?"

I gripped my phone. "That's what I'm trying to work out."

Rather than bitch me out, Cassius waited, clearly expecting me to check and tell him what was going on. I woke my phone. A missed call, a voicemail, and three text notifications. Seeing them, I exhaled.

He'd contacted me.

"All good?"

I shrugged at Cassius. "Not sure." I opened the texts first, reading through them all. The first was sent forty minutes before gametime—when my phone had been on silent.

"Shit."

Cassius's chest brushed against me as he peered around me. "Something wrong?"

"Lottie broke her arm. They're at the hospital."

"Damn," he said. "Sucks. Poor kid. Bet she's pissed she missed the game."

I bobbed my head. "I expect so." I read Eddie's last message again, telling me he was waiting for the X-ray, and he'd be in touch when he knew more. But it was his *"I'm so sorry I wasn't there. This is exactly what I didn't want to happen"* that had me frowning.

With no idea what the hell he was talking about, I hit his name in my phonebook, not bothering to step away for some semblance of privacy.

He picked up on the first ring. "Hey."

The sound of his voice took the wind out of me. I'd been more freaked out than I'd realized. "Hey, she okay?"

The sound of him swallowing reached me before

his "Yeah. The doctor just left, saying it was a clean break."

I rubbed a hand over my face. "That's good. A relief."

"It is. We just have to wait for someone to organize the cast. Not sure how long that's going to take." Exhaustion caressed each word, making my heart pang.

"Where are you? I'll come as soon as I've showered."

When he didn't respond, I glanced at my phone, making sure we were still connected.

"Eddie, you there?"

"Yeah," he croaked. "You don't need to come here. I have no idea how long we'll be. We could be just thirty minutes or five hours. You must be beat." His voice dipped low. "I'm so sorry about the game."

"Yeah, me too. Sucks. But it is what it is, right?" I said, aiming for upbeat but not sure I pulled it off. "But I don't mind coming and waiting with you guys." I tensed, waiting for his answer, suddenly nervous at his quiet responses. Sure, he must have been shitting it, worried about Lottie, but there was something off in his voice that sounded like more than general exhaustion and parental fear.

"I know you don't." A huff of air traveled down

the phone. "But it's late. We're both exhausted. Plus, you need some food in you before you crash."

This man was always looking out for me, but who took care of him?

Clenching my jaw, I steeled my resolve. It didn't make sense that he'd be trying to push me away, and if he was for whatever jacked-up reason he had in his head, he could fuck right off with that. "Let me worry about what I can handle. What hospital are you at?"

"Grace Memorial."

"That wasn't too hard, was it?" I pushed levity I didn't quite feel into my tone.

"Pearce—"

I cut him off, saying, "Just know when to shut up. See you soon." I ended the call and turned back to my locker, catching Cassius's gaze.

"Well, that's one way to end a call." Wide-eyed, he snorted. "Sweet-talking like that is not going to help me win the cash, you know, Pearce. You need pointers? I'm always here for you."

A real chuckle tore out of me, surprising us both if the startled laugh from Cassius was anything to go by. After tonight's epic loss and my very real concern over Eddie and Lottie, I hadn't thought I had a laugh in me.

"I can just imagine what your advice would be," I

fired back, trying to shake off the post-game funk pressing down on the locker room. I stripped down and grabbed my towel.

"If it includes dicks and mouths, you're on the money."

I rolled my eyes and laughed while Joel threw a sweaty sock at Cassius. Our very straight young friend was more than used to Cassius's oversharing and often warped advice.

"Says the man who has more knock backs than a drunk." Joel angled to look at me. "You going to the hospital?"

I expected the whole locker room had heard my discussion, and if they hadn't, they'd soon hear what my deal was. Shit rarely remained a secret on our team.

"Yeah."

Joel frowned. "You think that's a good idea?"

"What do you mean?"

He waved his hand in my general direction. "You're hardly going to blend in and go incognito. Sure... *that* won't piss off the hospital staff when they're dealing with crowd control."

I groaned as I wrapped my towel around myself, ready to get showered. "Fuck." I shook my head, sounding a little petulant when I said, "Well, Eddie's there and isn't swamped by the press." At least I didn't think so.

At my side, Cassius snorted. "No offence to your hot DILF, Malcolm, but he's been out of the League for a fair few years now."

"And he didn't just get knocked out of the championship," Joel added. He followed with a sad shrug that I felt all the way to my disappointed bones.

"So you're saying it'd be selfish of me to race on in there?"

Joel shrugged again. "I don't know, man. I suppose it's about why you're going in the first place. Do you need to be there? You going for yourself or for Lottie and Eddie?"

My answer was quick. "I need to make sure Lottie's really okay." The truth of that statement made my chest squeeze. The fog and the mess of the last two hours was finally lifting, leaving behind concern for a kid I loved and her dad who I needed more than fucking oxygen. "Eddie must have freaked and been worried sick. He needs me." Whether he realized or even admitted it or not was left unsaid.

Joel shot me a shit-eating grin. "Holy shit, you're so fucking loved up it's disgustingly sickening." He glanced around the room. "Miles, it's time to call it, right?"

Miles whooped. "Fucking finally." And the assholes around me clapped.

I couldn't hold back my grin. "You fuckers. Coming off a loss and you're celebrating like you're all fucking winners." I didn't conceal the warmth in my tone.

"With Cass picking up the bill tonight, you bet your ass we're all celebrating." Miles high-fived Wilkes.

"For fuck's sake." Cassius shook his head. "Malcolm, you couldn't have waited one more week?" He launched his sweaty shorts at me.

"I don't get it," I admitted, making my way to the shower. These guys were too distracting with their motivational love talk.

Miles answered for him, "Cass decided to make a new wager. He was the one who made the stakes a night out for the team."

"I don't even want to know." I flipped Cassius off, shouting, "Serves you damn right, alligator dick. But…," I stretched out the word, "I'm not actually confirming anything either."

Cassius seemed happy. The others not so much.

I washed quickly, spoke to Coach, then hightailed it out of the arena. Bronwyn, one of the Eagles's all-round miracle workers, was able to organize me a car and a way out, away from the crowd, so I could head out without fanfare.

While I still had no idea how I'd get into the hospital without causing a fuss, the important thing was I was going, and not for me. Well, not just for me. Eddie and Lottie were my priority.

My cell rang. I answered immediately. "Hey, Bron."

"Ask the driver to take you to the east-side emergency exit. There's someone from security there waiting to greet you. They'll get you to Eddie," she explained in her no-nonsense voice.

"You're amazing, Bron. Thank you."

"Uh-huh. Just remember this next time you even think of a prank anywhere near my vicinity."

I chuckled. "You've got it."

"And don't forget your sit-down with the team on Saturday night, okay?"

I cracked my neck, having completely forgotten our official end-of-season meal with the team. We'd all been hoping it wouldn't happen for another two and a half weeks. "Yeah," I responded, sobered by the reality of tonight's loss and being out of this year's playoffs. The reminder was a sucker punch.

Bronwyn's sigh preceded her. "Just try to relax the next couple of nights, okay? You guys did amazing to get this far."

"Yeah, thanks, Bron. I best speak to the driver, as we're getting close." I said goodbye, disappointment and failure threatening to overwhelm me. Truth was, I was devastated by tonight's loss. Add in how poorly we'd played, it made the loss even more cutting.

We should have done better. The fact that every single player was able to pinpoint so easily something that went wrong, or what we should have done better at, made that crystal clear. Losing sucked majorly.

I tried to shake off my funk as I spoke to Mark, the driver, and worked hard at reining in my pity party so I could be there for Eddie. This grown-up shit, behaving all responsible and less of a selfish asshole, took a lot of energy. The thought made me want to slap myself.

I hadn't eaten, and I could feel my energy flagging as quickly as a spent dick. Jesus. And there I'd been on the phone to Eddie earlier, acting like I could handle it all and be responsible, implying I could look after myself perfectly fine as well as him.

"I don't suppose there's a drive-through we pass before we get there?" I asked Mark, trying to salvage some of my self-respect. Food was food, right?

Mark met my gaze through the rearview mirror. "I can make that happen. Anything in particular?"

"What's good around here?" I asked.

"There's a Susie's just ahead. Their chicken cheese fry bowl is pretty good. Add in some extra chicken and it hits the spot."

I smiled, relieved. "Sounds great, thank you. Will you order three and shakes, and whatever you want for yourself?"

Mark bobbed his head and grinned back. "I sure can."

"Thanks. You're a lifesaver."

It didn't take long for our food to arrive, and we continued on to the hospital. The fried tortilla shell filled with fries, cheese, chicken, and veggies made my tastebuds sing. I devoured the food and made far too much of a mess. Mark simply laughed and handed me a supply of napkins and some wet wipes.

"Good, right?" he asked as he pulled over to the side of the hospital while I frantically tried to clean up my mess.

"Hell yes. Good choice. Thanks, man."

He indicated toward the hospital door that opened, a security guard appearing. "You need extra help getting in there safely or you good?"

I reached out and shook his hand. "I'll be fine. Thanks, though." I opened the door. "You got Venmo?"

"Yeah, man. Thanks."

After I sent him a healthy tip, I stepped out of the car and went directly to the waiting security guard.

"Right this way, Mr. Malcolm. Mr. Phelps is in a private room with his daughter. I'll take you right there."

"Thanks." With food and drinks tray in hand, I followed him along corridors, cap in place. Though with my height, Joel had been right about me not really blending in.

"Here we are, room 408. I've been requested to wait out here until you're ready to leave."

I smiled at the security guard, taking note of his name tag. "Thanks, Terry." I shook his hand before knocking lightly on the door.

Hearing Eddie's familiar voice, I entered. My gaze snagged his immediately, and seeing the flicker of emotions on his face confirmed I'd made the right decision by coming here. He stood immediately, then hesitated, looking toward an internal door I assumed was a bathroom.

"Where's Lottie?" I asked.

Eddie indicated toward the door. "She'll be out in a minute."

With that knowledge, I didn't let his initial hesitation stop me. After placing my goodies on the table, I was in his space, holding him tight, lips pressing against his warm neck. When he sagged in my arms,

I squeezed, allowing relief to trickle into me, loosening the grip on my heart.

"She's really okay?" I asked, easing back just enough to read his face.

"Yeah." A sweet smile followed. "Hopefully we won't be much longer, then we'll be out of here."

"That's great. How'd it happen?"

He sighed and rolled his eyes. "Swinging on a chair of all things. I swear I've lost count of the number of times I've asked her not to do it."

I winced and rubbed circles on his back with my thumb. I wasn't ready to let him go just yet. "Shit happens. The important thing is she's going to be fine. A break sucks, especially as it's almost her summer vacation, but it could have been a whole lot worse, right?"

"Yeah." A frown appeared, drawing his brows low. "It just made my heart stop there for a moment." He swallowed. "Her being hurt like that, in more pain..." He shook his head. "This year's been one for it."

Rather than respond with words, I pulled him close, dotted a brief kiss on his mouth, and hugged him again. He embraced me back, tighter than before, and then we heard the bathroom door snick open.

With one last squeeze that made my heart sigh in welcome relief, Eddie stepped out of my hold. He looked over my shoulder, saying, "Look who I found roaming the hospital."

I turned to Lottie. Her arm was currently in a sling. She also shot me a wide grin.

"You came." She stepped toward us, her smile never dipping.

"Of course I did, kiddo." When she reached me, I dropped a kiss to the top of her head, too anxious to hug her like I wanted in case I hurt her. "I needed to make sure I was the first person to sign your cast. I get dibs since I'm your favorite."

"Cool. Perhaps you can write a limerick."

"Uhm…"

"We've been working on them in class, and there's some really fun ones. Lester at school told me a rude one."

"He did, did he?"

We both looked at Eddie, who didn't appear especially happy with that new piece of information.

With an exasperated sigh, Lottie said, "It only had the word 'ass,' Dad."

I snorted. "I'll see what I can come up with, okay?"

Her expression sobered. "I'm sorry about the game."

The sadness in her tone made my gut clench. "It's

just the way it goes, right? Getting all the way through to the third round was pretty cool."

While Lottie nodded solemnly, I side-eyed Eddie. His expression was shuttered, lips a little pinched, and he seemed to be looking anywhere but at me. Before I could think about it further, a knock on the door preceded it opening.

A doctor headed inside the room, alongside a nurse pushing a metal cart filled with supplies. When the doctor's gaze landed on me, it widened slightly before she refocused on Lottie. "Right, Lottie, let's get your arm supported so you can get going home. It's pretty late so I'm sure you're ready for bed."

Lottie bobbed her head. "Okay." She then looked at me. "Is that milkshake for me?"

"It sure is. There's food too. I thought the two of you might be hungry."

Returning her attention to the doctor, she asked, "Can I eat and have my shake while you're doing my arm? My stomach is going to eat itself."

The young doctor chuckled. "You definitely can."

"Thank you."

While the nurse and doctor got Lottie set up where they wanted, I dished out the food, offering the doc and nurse some fries. They refused politely and started work on Lottie's arm.

Once they were focused, I dragged a chair over to

the corner of the room next to a second chair, and the furthest point away from the doc and nurse, attempting some semblance of privacy.

"Come and eat," I ordered Eddie.

He raked his gaze over my face before offering me a small smile. Once he sat, I placed the taco-like shell in his hands. "Have you already eaten?" he asked.

"Yep. It's amazing but messy. Like all good things in life." My wink earned me a blush.

"Thanks for the food," he said, and took a bite. His moan was sinful. "What?" he asked around a mouthful when our gazes met.

Lifting my brow, I said, "You know exactly what. Noises like that in public should not be allowed."

Wide-eyed, his lips twitched, color once more appearing in his cheeks. He took another mouthful, looked me dead in the eye, and moaned. The sound was too quiet to reach the other people in the room, but fuck if it didn't have my cock jerking awake.

"Dude... you really want to play that game?"

He tilted his head, and a familiar warmth flooded his gaze when he answered, "Always."

Air rushed out of my lungs. Fuck, I so needed to hear that. Today had been an unequivocal nightmare. Eddie's strange, almost wary reactions adding fuel to my nerves. That one word helped unravel the pit of dread sitting heavily in my body.

He finished eating in silence, while I kept half an eye on Lottie, watching the progress of the cast.

The rustling of wrappers drew my attention back to Eddie. "I didn't realize I was so hungry. Thanks for bringing us food."

"You're welcome. Feeling better?"

After flicking his gaze in Lottie's general direction, he answered, "Yeah. Less panicked. More human."

"Good. My work here is almost done."

"Almost?"

"When Lottie's fast asleep, I can show you."

Eddie shifted in his seat, sent me a look of warning, and glanced quickly away. I chuckled quietly, loving I could distract him so easily.

"Okay, we're all done." The doctor stood, drawing our attention her way.

Both Eddie and I eased out of our uncomfortable chairs and made our way over. Lottie was supporting a bright red cast. Despite her drooping eyes, she smiled. "Thank you."

"I would say anytime, but hopefully this will be the last time you have to pay a visit to the hospital," the doctor responded kindly, then peered up at Eddie. "Nurse Madison will just collect the necessary paperwork you'll need to sign, then you'll be able to head on home."

Eddie responded with a tired smile and shook the doctor's hand. "We really appreciate you taking such good care of her."

My heart stuttered and I extended my hand for a shake, realizing the "we" included me. "Absolutely. Thanks, Doctor."

"My pleasure. You all take care." She turned back to Lottie. "And how many legs do chairs have so they're stable?"

Pink trickled into Lottie's cheeks, and a shifty smile appeared. "Four."

"That's right." She followed up with a wink and headed out of the room.

I set about tidying away our takeout containers while Eddie got Lottie ready. By the time the room was straightened up, the nurse returned with the insurance paperwork and discharge papers. And then finally, at close to midnight, we were being escorted to Eddie's car before we were making our way back to his home.

A comfortable silence filled the car on the drive, the three of us flagging after our stressful evening. I was relieved Eddie's place was so close, else I was sure I'd have been snoring with the lull of the moving vehicle.

By the time we pulled into the garage space, Lottie was barely awake. Eddie guided her out of the car and helped her get ready for bed, while I grabbed us two bottles of water and said goodnight to Lottie with a kiss on her brow before making my way directly to Eddie's room.

I just hoped like hell he wouldn't kick me out to sleep in the spare room. Not tonight. We both need the comfort of each other's arms.

"Hey." He entered his bedroom and closed the door behind him. I took that as a good start and made my way over to him.

Pressing my mouth against his, I sighed into the kiss, bubbles of relief coming to life when he kissed me back, wrapping his arms around me. Our kiss was slow, tender, gentle brushes of our lips and swipes of our tongues.

When he eased out of the touch, rather than breaking free, Eddie buried his face against my neck. Warm breath tickled my skin, and I squeezed him closer, knowing he needed this as much as I did.

"I'm so sorry we missed the game." There was a tentative husk to his voice that I didn't like, but I wasn't quite ready to let him go yet.

"You don't need to apologize for Lottie hurting herself."

At my words, he pulled out of my hold, an

unhappy expression on his face. He sighed and offered me a fake-as-fuck smile as he stepped around me and made his way to the bed. When he sat down on the mattress, he clasped his hands and stared down at them.

"What is it?" I asked.

Without meeting my eyes, he said, "You were off your game."

The statement, while true, was a fuck of a thing to hear from him, especially with such a despondent voice. Something twisted in my chest, but I remained silent.

"Did it…" He huffed out a breath, giving me the quickest of glances. "Were you distracted?" Once again, his gaze connected with mine. Whatever he saw in my expression had him continuing. "I mean, it's so unlike you, and you didn't play like you usually do." A shadow of remorse flickered in his eyes, and understanding slammed into me.

Guilt encompassed him.

"While I like the fact that you only have eyes for me," I jested, hating the heaviness between us, "you know I wasn't the only player on the team, right?"

He didn't laugh. "Pearce, I'm serious."

"That's pretty obvious," I said, feeling suddenly awkward standing in the middle of his room.

Nothing about his body language screamed he wanted my comfort.

A frustrated line appeared on his mouth.

"Eddie, just say what's on your mind and stop dancing around it, okay?" Him taking on this kicked-puppy look freaked me out. In five years I'd never seen him behave this was before.

"I think," he started, sitting up straight and making a valiant effort to meet my eyes, "you were expecting me there and when I didn't show, it put you off your game. I *know* you're not the only player, and I watched enough of the game to see there were a variety of decisions that were poor ones, but I'm focused on you. My concern is for you and how this thing between us messed up your chances at getting to the finals."

"Thing?" I jolted back, my eyes widening as hurt flared to life. "What the fuck's that meant to mean? Thing?"

Eddie blanched. "I didn't mean…" He shook his head. "This has just been all so fast and now it's impacting your game. Your dreams."

Emotion, thick and fast, threatened to bowl me other. At the pinnacle was a punch of incredulous anger. "Five fucking years I've been in love with you." The words shot out. "If that's fucking fast, we need to work on the definition." I clenched my jaw and pulled in a deep breath.

"I'm sorry. I'm not trying to ignore our time together, our friendship—"

"Really?" I gave a humorless laugh. "'Cause I have to say, Eddie, right now it feels like the past five years were completely irrelevant and my feelings are invalid."

"No." He stood up quickly and I was so, so tempted to take a step back. This was not how tonight was meant to go down. "Of course your feelings are valid, and real. I'm sorry. I'm doing a shit job at apologizing and a worse job at telling you how I feel."

I loosened my tight jaw and took a big breath. "And how do you feel?" My voice was tight and low while my pulse picked up speed, freakin' terrified at what would fall from his mouth.

Automatically, my muscles contracted, and I held my breath, preparing to protect myself.

"I love you so much that just the thought of you hurting because of me breaks my fucking heart."

A fast, unsteady breath whooshed out of me. "You're a fucking idiot," I whispered shakily and took the necessary steps to engulf him in a hug. "Jesus, I thought you were trying to end this *thing* between us."

He squeezed my waist. "That's the last thing I want." He shook his head and blew out a breath. "I just wish you'd been able to see my message before the game so at least you knew what was happening. I wasn't trying to say you're incapable. My head's just a mess and I freaked the fuck out. I'm sorry. I definitely don't want to be ending things between us."

I swore my heart tripped over itself at his words. "It's a good job, as there's not a chance I'm letting you go." I searched for his mouth, capturing it a second later, pouring everything I felt for this man into every touch.

Passion burned in my veins, fueling me to show Eddie just how much his words meant. Dragging my mouth away and panting, I stared at him, realizing I hadn't said the words back. Sure, I'd shouted them at him, but that wasn't quite the same.

"What?" Confusion furrowed his brow, but he didn't lose the desire in his gaze.

"I swear it feels like I've loved you forever."

His mouth curved at my words. "Forever, huh?"

I grinned, affection clogging my throat. "Five years… forever… same difference."

Rather than answer, he drew me back in for a kiss, our lips exploring, never letting up. Each movement, each taste seeped beneath my skin, burrowing its way even deeper into my soul.

The clusterfuck of a day didn't matter. Not when Eddie in my arms was so right, so perfect. More than that, it was everything. And I could barely get my head around the fact that we were finally here.

When I pulled away for the second time, he growled, the sound scorching my skin in the best of ways.

"Tomorrow," I said, once more capturing his gaze. "I want us to tell Lottie that we're together tomorrow." I held my breath, waiting for his response. While his telling Lottie was ultimately his decision, it didn't mean I wasn't prepared to push or plead if necessary.

I wanted to be able to hold this man's hand whenever and wherever. I wanted to share his bed and wake up beside him. Sure, the reality of my career was a huge fucking elephant between us, let alone in the room, but I had to believe we'd figure it out.

"Okay." He nodded. "We can tell her first thing."

"Yeah?" The grin on my face was wide and so full of relief, his smile softened.

"Yeah, definitely."

"Thank Christ." And then I was on him, tearing free of our clothes, our kisses fast and messy as we stumbled while undressing, trying to get to the bed. "I want inside you."

His breath caught and body shuddered at my

words. "Yes." Eddie clambered onto the bed, turned so his ass was before me, and dug around in his bedside drawer.

"Holy fuck, yeah, just like this."

A sultry smirk that told me he'd known exactly what he was up to when he'd searched for the lube lifted his lips as he glanced at me. He threw the lube on the bed, and I swiped it up, opening the cap as I kneeled behind him and showered him with kisses.

A soft sigh slipped from his lips when I finally inserted a slick finger. He leaned further, head resting on his hands on the mattress, his perfect ass in the air, waiting for me to take good care of preparing him.

"Be fast. Little prep. I just need you inside me," he said with a wispy sigh as I inserted a second finger.

"I don't want to hurt you," I said reverently, loosening him up.

"You could never hurt me."

The conviction in his words embraced me, shrouded me so damn tight that I swallowed hard and trembled. Slicking myself up, I pressed more kisses to his back before whispering, "I love you so much." A moment later, I eased into him, pausing at the tightness, carefully easing in further until his muscles loosened, welcoming me in.

And finally, fucking finally, I entered him fully, as deep as my dick could go. Not giving him time for an extra breath, I pulled back before penetrating him in long, sure strokes. With each drag of my cock in his ass, he gasped and groaned, getting to the point he all but vibrated beneath me.

"So fucking hot," I praised, driving into him.

"I need…"

I leaned over him and pulled him back up with me, his back to my chest as I thrust deep and hard. "I've got you." Gripping his cock, I smoothed my fingers over him, rubbing in the slick still on my fingers.

Eddie's trembling increased, and he gasped as I jerked him off in time with fucking him.

"That's it, baby," I whispered against his neck, kissing up his jaw, chasing his mouth.

The groan when he angled and captured my mouth was so fucking hot and dirty that I sucked on his tongue, wishing I could do the same to his dick. My kiss was possessive, full of need, and filled with so much love that my heart clenched and threatened to explode.

I'd gladly let it happen, too, if this was the beginning of the rest of our life. "I want this with you forever," I whispered after breaking our kiss. I didn't give a shit that I was spilling my guts as easily as I spilled my cum. Eddie deserved all of my truths.

"Okay." He followed up with a kiss, but I pulled back, my heart hammering in my chest.

"No, I mean it." I stilled, the reality of what I wanted so bright and clear in my vision that I had no choice but to continue.

Eddie frowned, staring at me wide-eyed from his awkward angle.

Shit, I really needed to do this. Now.

I pulled out of him.

"What the—"

I cut him off by manhandling him so we faced each other. Concern bled into his eyes, but all I focused on were his flushed cheeks and just how amazing and gorgeous he was.

"Marry me." The words tumbled free. When he startled, his brows lifting, I held on tight. "I mean it. I love you so fucking much. Marry me."

His mouth fell open before closing again, his gaze darting around my face. "But…" He trailed off, still staring, still trying to read me.

"*But* marry me."

And then it happened. The slightest curve of his lips. The flare of his eyes. The added tremble in his hands as they clutched me back. "You mean it? You want this with me…?" He paused before saying, "With Lottie?"

With my heart in my throat, I managed a nod,

smiling so wide it hurt. "I've never been more certain about anything. Ever. I think we're an amazing family."

His gaze softened, hearing the present tense of my words. It didn't matter that we hadn't been romantically together for long. We'd been a family for over five years.

"I think we're an amazing family too," he whispered, tears springing to his eyes.

My tear ducts took note and reacted in kind when I asked, "So… marry me."

"Yeah… yes… okay." The last word came out on a broken laugh, and I fell against him, pushing him deep into the mattress.

Wordlessly, my chest so full of wonder and love, I positioned once more at his entrance and pushed into him. I caught his gasp with my mouth and kissed him slowly, tenderly, so fucking reverently that I knew it would leave no room for Eddie to not feel soul-deep the depth of my love.

CHAPTER 19
EDDIE

WITH THE EARLY MORNING SUN FILTERING THROUGH THE blinds and Pearce's warm body draped over me, I smiled. Legit full-on grinned.

Maybe the story of how Pearce proposed to me would have to change slightly for public hearing, but with every beat in my heart, I knew it wasn't a question asked in the heat of the moment. One asked in lust or the panic of the stress and disappointment of yesterday.

No. When Pearce had asked me to marry him, I'd looked into his hazel eyes and beyond the heat in them. I'd felt his love encompass me, reflecting my own.

There was no confusing that with misplaced passion.

The gulf of what would happen next remained

between us, but having the next step, the knowledge he'd be my husband, settled the worry that had refused to be at peace since I'd admitted that Pearce was so much more than my best friend.

Foolish or not, I wasn't even concerned about telling Lottie. I trusted that I knew my daughter well enough that while she may initially be surprised by this development, she'd be happy for me. For us.

"You're grinning."

Pearce's sleep-heavy voice licked against my skin. I angled to see him as he moved his head off my chest and reached for me, seeking out my mouth.

I kissed him, slow and sweet, barely able to keep the same grin he'd pointed out off my face.

"I'm happy," I said easily, so matter-of-factly that there wasn't a hint of embarrassment in me for saying something so honest aloud.

"Thank fuck. I was worried about opening my eyes in case I dreamed it."

When he sighed, I realized he spoke the truth. There wasn't a hint of teasing in his breath. I shuffled down so we lay on our sides, face-to-face, and stroked his messy hair from his forehead. He practically preened at my touch, edging in even closer.

"No dream."

Opening his eyes, he studied my face, his

emotions front and center for me to absorb. "How do you want to tell Lottie?"

"Over breakfast."

"And about you being my fiancé?" Pink flushed his cheeks as he followed up with a chuckle. "Fuck, that sounds weird, but so fucking amazing."

I nodded, knowing exactly what he meant. "We tell her everything." His brows shot high, amusement glinting in his eyes. "The PG stuff that she needs to know."

"And then we need to figure everything out."

My heart beat a fast tattoo in my chest at his word. "Damn…"

"What?"

"Being engaged makes you all assertive and a certifiable grown-up." I bounced my brows. "It's hot."

In response, he licked my face. "Yep, totally grown up."

"Ew." I shoved at him, laughing loudly. "I take it back."

The wind was knocked out of me before I could bat an eye. He had me pinned, hips and arms trapping me.

"Take *that* back." He narrowed his eyes at me, though he couldn't disguise the humor filling them.

"No chance I'm taking back my yes, but the official grown-up status is on hold."

"Fair enough." A sweet kiss followed, one that thickened my cock. "Mmmm." He rocked against me. "Morning frottage sounds like an awesome way to wake up."

I squeezed his ass cheeks, only to pause when I heard movement down the hallway. "We're going to have to put a pin in that amazing idea."

His gaze softened, a nervous smile tugging at his lips as he peered down at me. "She won't freak out, right?"

I wrapped my arms around him, finding his nervousness ridiculously adorable. "You know she loves you. It'll be fine."

"You really think that?"

"Let's go find out. She'll be finished in the bathroom in a tick." Leaning up, I traced his lips with mine for the briefest of kisses. It was time to get dressed and speak to Lottie. I wanted to get this out there. That way we could work out what came next.

Once we both pulled on tees and shorts, we left my room. Nervous excitement fizzed in my stomach. But before I plowed right in with our announcement, I needed to check she was feeling okay and wasn't in pain.

During the night I'd paid a couple of visits to her

room, relieved to find her sleeping solidly. With a fresh new day, I hoped she'd be feeling brighter after her awful night.

"Hey, kiddo," I greeted, dotting a kiss on her head. The TV blared out sports reports, and her gaze remained fixed to it as she sat on the couch with her feet tucked under her. "How are you feeling this morning?"

When she pulled her attention away from yesterday's League game overview, which I winced at, she bobbed her head. "Okay. My arm hurts a bit, but not as much as yesterday."

I examined her face, happy to see no dark rings under her eyes, amazing since she didn't get to bed till midnight. It reminded me that I needed to call her school. Lottie had missed so much school already this semester, which she wasn't that cut up about, but I didn't like the thought of her falling even further behind.

"Let me get you some anti-inflammatory pills, then I'll make a quick call to your school. Back at school on Monday for your final week, though, if you're up for it."

"It's the last week so we only play games, so it wouldn't matter so much if I didn't go."

I chuckled. "Uh-huh, but I think it's best if you go in anyway."

"Fine." She dragged the word out, and Pearce's chuckle caught my attention. Standing in the doorway, he looked so fucking delectable and at home.

On seeing him, Lottie grinned. A split second later, her smile slipped, and she glanced at the TV. "I can turn it off."

God, I loved this kid so damn much.

Moving away from the doorway, Pearce shook his head. "It's okay. Watching this stuff helps me improve my game." He took a seat next to her, and whether she realized it or not, she shuffled closer to him, leaning in enough that she made her intentions clear.

Pearce sent a quick look my way, his eyes soft as he wrapped his arm around her. Immediately, she leaned against him, injured arm away from his body.

"That's good. It wasn't all bad. Jetts were the stronger team in this game." She angled to peer at his face. "But you made it all the way to the conference finals, Pearce." Her brows lifted high. "That's incredible. I'm proud of you." Lottie followed up with a pat on his chest, near where her head leaned.

The sweet gesture, the compassionate words were more than I thought any ten-year-old capable of. Emotion flooded me, and from the expression on Pearce's face, he battled with emotion of his own.

"Thanks, kiddo. That means a lot." He placed a kiss on the top of her head, flicking his gaze at me.

I shot him an emotional smile before huffing out a breath and clearing my throat. "Okay. Breakfast?"

"Yes, please," Lottie answered. "Pancakes. They'll make my arm feel better." There was no missing her crafty grin.

"Uh-huh. In that case, pancakes it is."

"I'll come help." Pearce made to move but I waved him off.

"You stay here with Lottie. I'll call you when food's ready."

Snuggling back next to Lottie, he shot me a grateful smile. "Thanks. I've already put a pot of coffee on."

"You're the best."

I left them to it and set about making breakfast while trying to think about what to say to Lottie. When Pearce and I spoke about it earlier, I'd pushed confidence into my response. Wanting to reassure him and ease his anxiety had been easy. But it didn't stop my stomach from twisting or my heart from galloping.

There could be no sugarcoating what was happening. Not that our news needed sweetening. How could it, when it made me so happy? The shock factor would be there, though. It was the surprise of it all that had me dropping an egg on the floor and burning one pancake.

Once I finally managed to make a decent stack and crisped up the bacon without incinerating it, I called Pearce and Lottie, figuring we'd sit around the smaller kitchen table just off to the side rather than at the breakfast bar. This way I could read Lottie's reaction.

They filed in.

I placed a couple of pancakes and bacon on Lottie's plate, cutting everything up for her.

"This is so annoying," she grumbled.

"It hasn't even been a day." I quirked my brow at her. "Your pills are there too."

Anyone would think I was offering her something toxic by the way she scrunched up her nose, but she dutifully swallowed them with her juice, knocking her head so far back to swallow that I had to work to not laugh.

"You'll be able to cope with cutting your own food. I promise. You're just sore and a little awkward at the moment. The weeks will fly on by," I said sympathetically.

"And at least you won't be stuck in Alabama," Pearce supplied, cutting off a large piece of pancake. "You have time with your mom, then get to come and spend some time with us." He finished with a flourish of his fork and crammed the syrup-dripping pancake in his mouth.

I had to look away, too tempted to lean in and swipe a drip of syrup from his mouth.

"That's true. And at least it's my—" She looked at her hands and made an L-shape with her pointer finger and thumb. "—left hand."

"True." Pearce winked at her before glancing at me. The expression told me enough. He was nervous and wanting to get this done. Giving a barely perceptible nod, I cleared my throat and placed down my utensils.

"Lottie, I've… that is, Pearce and I have something we want to talk to you about."

As she chewed, she bobbed her head, eyes bright and so unaware.

With my pulse picking up speed, the sound drummed loudly in my ears. Jesus, my nerves were ridiculous. "Actually, there's also something we want to tell you." I swallowed hard and opened my palm toward Pearce.

His cheeks flushed immediately, but he quickly placed his hand in mine and squeezed. A small, nervous smile lifted his lips, and he turned his attention to Lottie. My gaze followed in the same direction, landing on Lottie. Wide-eyed, her head moved as she drifted her focus from our faces to our hands and back up again.

"Pearce and I—"

"For real?" she interrupted. While her face was hard to read, I didn't hear anything bad in her tone.

"We've been together for a little while."

"And you didn't tell me?" I wasn't sure if it was hurt, surprise, or a simple statement. Hell, this kid of mine would make a killer poker player.

"Well," I responded, appreciating Pearce's encouraging squeeze, "I know our relationship affects you, but we wanted to be sure we were making the right decision by getting together. And that's something only we could navigate through."

"So you're what, boyfriends?"

My heart crashed against my rib cage so hard, I could barely hear myself think, let alone the words coming out of my mouth.

"We were," Pearce cut in. My gaze whipped to his, and his focus was already on me, a brilliant smile directed my way. "Last night I asked your dad to marry me."

Our eyes stayed connected. Only the sound of Lottie's fork hitting the tabletop broke the eye contact. I focused on Lottie. Her cheeks were pink, and tears swam in her eyes.

"Baby," I whispered, standing and moving over to

her. Kneeling before her, I stroked strands of hair out of her face. "You know how much I love you, right?"

She bobbed her head while I quietly started to freak out. My girl was rarely this quiet. She had an opinion about everything.

"Me too," Pearce added, shifting to my side. "I love you so damn much, kiddo."

And holy shit, she smiled. This headstrong, whirlwind child of mine smiled so damn big that my heart exploded for the second time in twelve hours.

"And you did say yes, right?" she asked with a sniff.

"As if your dad could say no to me." Pearce chuckled and squeezed Lottie's leg. "Do you not see how irresistible my face is?"

Rubbing at her nose, Lottie sniffed again. "So you're really getting married and we're all going to be together?"

Fuck. Emotion beat at me as I tugged her into my arms, only remembering at the last moment to go easy on her. But there was no holding back my tears. I held her tightly, Pearce's comforting hand pressing against my back. "Yes, we are." I didn't get into explaining how that would look, but she didn't need to worry about any of that for now.

I eased away, looking at my girl's sparkling eyes.

"You're happy about this? Pearce and me getting married?"

"It's amazing. I'll be able to go to all of Pearce's games now." She grinned.

"Uhm…" I winced. "Remember your job at the moment is school. That means no missing it."

"Urgh." She sighed dramatically, exactly the way I expected her to.

"You need all that schooling to make a kick-ass agent, right?" Pearce supplied diplomatically. My heart warmed. He totally had this parenting gig sorted. "Nobody will pay a dumbass the big bucks."

I opened and closed my mouth like a fish before snorting and shaking my head. Not what I would have said, but maybe Pearce spoke Lottie's language better than I did, since she nodded solemnly and finally responded, "True."

THE FORCE OF NATURE IN PEARCE WAS STRONG. LIKE crazily so. I liked a little too much how caught up he got in getting us matching engagement rings. There was little doubt he used his name to get us an appointment with a designer in the city who had a range of men's rings in stock.

I'd suggested we just wait for our bands, but I

wasn't joking about Pearce being a force of nature. Who knew him insisting on getting a ring on my finger could be so hot? It was also ridiculously sweet. Lottie didn't help calm him down either. Nope. Between the two of them, I was railroaded into jumping in the car and being their chauffeur.

Admittedly, as I looked down at the ring, nothing but happiness floated inside me. A quick glance at Lottie, and my heart filled further. She hadn't stopped playing with her necklace since Pearce had gifted it to her. It was a simple gold chain, but a diamond, the same cut as the ones in our matching ring, hung from it.

It had been the sweetest of gestures, and if it were possible, I would have loved Pearce even more for the tender moment between him and my girl. We'd flown into Minneapolis late this morning to attend Pearce's end-of-season meal.

Each club tended to run these events differently. In the past I'd attended anything from black tie to red carpet, to family-focused fun, and more low-key events. Pearce reassured me the Eagles were hosting the dinner for immediate families, and that all the players with partners and kids would be attending too.

That didn't stop me from being nervous.

We were stepping out officially to his friends, and inevitably, the public too.

Thankfully, we'd already spoken to our parents before we left my place this morning. To say they were surprised was grossly underplaying it. I swore Pearce's mom nearly burst our eardrums. But at least she was excited.

My parents were a little more reserved in their enthusiasm, but once Lottie took over the call, effectively bigging up the news with the excitement only a ten-year-old could manage, by the end of the call, my parents warmed up, asking for us to all make sure we got together at some point over the summer.

But I needed to call Moira before the news broke all over social media. Pearce was ranked in the top ten in the country. The game from two nights ago was still a popular talking point too. There wasn't a chance this would stay under the radar.

"I can't believe you're leaving it till now to make the call." Amusement filled Pearce's voice.

We had ten minutes before we had to leave for this evening's event. It was officially a wussy move, but this way, I wouldn't have to get into anything with my ex-wife. I could drop the news and run. That I spoke to her yesterday to tell her about Lottie and maybe, unashamedly, made Lottie promise not to tell her mom about my news didn't strengthen my case for bravery.

"I told you she's terrifying." Pearce straightened his tie. "You need me to step in and do it for you?"

My hesitation as I legit considered it made him laugh too loudly.

"Just make the damn call. What's she gonna say or do?"

The truth was, there wasn't much she could say about anything. While Pearce would be Lottie's stepdad, Moira wouldn't truly be concerned about that. I prided myself on being the best dad possible. While I wanted to ignore the blip of Wayne and what a mistake he was, I deliberately didn't spend much time at all with my daughter and Wayne together. Even if I hadn't admitted it aloud, I'd known he wasn't stepdad material, and I hadn't wanted to expose Lottie to him unnecessarily.

That didn't stop me from feeling like an idiot for not breaking it off with him sooner, but shit happened. And it was one decision I had to live with and was happy to bury deep in the back of my mind alongside all of my stupid decisions.

"I know. I just don't like talking to her at the best of times."

Pearce chuckled and stepped behind me, wrapping his arms around my waist. "I know Moira can be super self-centered and… difficult." I huffed out a humorless breath. That was one word for it. "But you two both try hard to remain civil for Lottie, and honestly, it's impressive as hell." He dotted a kiss on the back of my neck above my collar. "Just get it over and done with."

I sighed. "I will."

When he stepped away, I eyed him appreciatively. "You look hot."

"Yeah? You'd do me?" He bounced his brows up and down.

"Every chance I can get. We could do that now if you want."

"Ha." He stepped out of reach. "No using me to put off the inevitable."

"I could just text her." At his raised brow, my shoulders sagged. "I know she does shit like that to me all the time and I hate it."

"You're better than that."

"Maybe I don't have to be."

He stalked toward me, intensity in his gaze that had my breath catching. "You are the best man I know. You're honest and loyal and have so much integrity it gets me rock-hard."

My laugh burst free at his sweet words being followed up with his usual horny self. "Thank you."

With a swat of my ass, he backed away. "I'll go and make sure Lottie is ready to head out."

Once alone, I stared at my cell before finally pressing on Moira's contact details.

"What's wrong?" she greeted.

"Why would there be anything wrong?"

"It's not even seven in the morning."

"Shit, sorry, I didn't think."

Silence filled the line.

"Moira, you there?"

"Yes, of course I am, but you always call knowing what time it is here." I could imagine her pursing her lips, a frown between her eyes. "So," she drew out, her tone on the cusp of exasperation, "I'll ask again. What's wrong?"

There was little point beating around the bush.

"I'm getting married."

One, two, three beats she remained quiet. I waited her out.

"I can't say I saw it coming. I didn't think you and Wayne were heading down that path."

"Ah, actually," I interrupted, realizing I hadn't told her about splitting with Wayne. In my defense, why would I have? Our communication was always centered around our daughter. The only time we shared or discussed anything else was when it was significant. It was another clarifying moment—the knowledge that me ending things with Wayne hadn't been significant enough to mention. I winced. Not sure I liked at all what that said about me.

Fuck, Moira was going to think I was fickle as fuck and that this was rushed.

"Actually what?" she prompted when I got lost in my thoughts.

"Wayne and I called things off months ago." "Months" sounded better than seven weeks or whatever it was, right?

"Right," she said slowly. "Oh please God, don't tell me you knocked someone up."

I barked out a laugh, not even feeling indignant or telling her it was none of her business if that had happened. "No chance of that happening."

"So, a man. Don't keep me in suspense, Eddie. You know I was never one for guessing games."

I sighed, thinking about the impatient woman Moira was today. She absolutely was no longer the woman I'd once fallen in love with and married. "It's Pearce. He asked me to marry him, and I said yes."

"*Pearce* Malcolm?"

"One and the same."

"Your friend? The basketball player?"

"Yes." I swore my sighs were coming thick and fast.

"Isn't he barely out of college?" There was no actual venom in her tone, just general curiosity.

"Not at all. He'll be thirty at his next birthday. Not that his age matters," I was quick to add.

"Right, well, congratulations. I know Charlotte speaks of him fondly."

A fast breath raced out of me, tension I hated to admit had held my shoulders rigid dissipating. "Thank you," I responded.

"It's hardly like you were seeking my approval."

"You're right, I wasn't, but since there's Lottie to think about, I thought it right you should know before the news breaks."

"Ah," she said, and I could hear the smile in her voice, "now that is something I don't miss about being a League wife." Laughter followed, taking me by surprise. It had been years since I'd last heard it. "Just think, Eddie, you'll be a League husband. Get to hang out with all the other players' partners. Have fun with that."

I snorted at her glee. "I think you're having a little too much fun with the idea."

Her laughter died down. "You know I didn't enjoy the whole fame or wife thing." A quiet sigh slipped down the line. "But you've been on the other side. I'm sure you'll handle it all just fine."

Surprised by her words, my eyes widened. "Uhm,

thank you?" Moira was both congratulating and reassuring me? What freaky dimension had I fallen into?

"And on that note, before you curl over in shock that I'm able to impart wisdom, please let Charlotte know I'll call her tomorrow."

"Yeah, will do, Moira. Have a great weekend."

"You too, Eddie."

She ended the call, and I stared at my cell screen.

That hadn't gone at all like I expected.

Pearce found me still staring at my cell. "You all good in here?" He wrapped his arms around me and kissed my cheek.

"Weirdly, yes."

"Huh. That's good, right?"

"She congratulated me."

Pearce snorted. "Ah, so you're wondering if she's been abducted by aliens and brainwashed or something."

I snickered. "Maybe a little."

After a quick squeeze of my waist, he stepped away. "Well, I'm pleased she didn't give you any shit. I love you, Eddie, but I seriously wouldn't want to go toe to toe with your ex."

Amusement trickled through me, and I faced my hot fiancé. "And I love you too much to ever ask you to do that."

A mouth-splitting grin pulled at his lips. "You see,

a perfect match." As his gaze raked over me, he gnawed on his bottom lip. "You seriously do look hot in that suit."

Pleasure warmed my chest. "You can show me how hot you think I am when we get home. Is Lottie ready?"

The mention of my girl's name had him nodding and taking a deep breath. A glance at his pants showed a twitching bulge, one he was clearly trying to settle.

"Let's get going before you make us late."

I stepped past him, not daring to tease him further or even smack his ass like I was tempted to.

"Fine," he whined. "If we must."

With a roll of my eyes, I slipped my hands in my pockets and pulled the material forward a little, knowing full well my ass would be where his gaze drifted to.

When his "Fuck, Ed, you don't play fair," greeted me as I headed down the staircase, I chuckled, loving teasing my man a little too much.

A couple of minutes later we were all strapped into Pearce's SUV. He was driving us there, and I'd offered to drive us at the end of the night. It wouldn't be a late one as Lottie was exhausted after another crazy forty-eight hours. Not that she'd admit such a thing.

It didn't take too long to reach the venue, the thirty-minute drive filled with banter and Pearce still figuring out his limerick. They were ridiculously abysmal. A poet, he wasn't.

When we pulled up outside the hotel, Pearce eyed me speculatively. And considering the way my pulse rocketed as soon as he hit the brakes, I figured he knew the reason why.

"I love you." The words, smooth and easy, helped to ease my nerves. Since I retired, I'd enjoyed being out of the limelight, only chasing it when raising awareness for the charity foundation I was heavily involved with.

As soon as I stepped out of this car, I'd be putting myself out there, and more significantly, Lottie too. I had to have faith she could handle it, as could we all.

"I love you," I responded, then peered over at Lottie. "You ready, kiddo?"

She bobbed her head, her eyes a little wide from the bunch of cameras outside.

"You hold my hand or Pearce's, okay?"

She turned to me, a patient smile appearing on her face. "I know the drill, Dad. Promise."

"All part of your agent prep, huh, Lottie girl?" Pearce winked at her through the rearview, and a moment later, we exited the vehicle.

As soon as Pearce reached my side, our gazes

connected. My small smile was all the reassurance I seemed to need as he reached out and held my hand, Lottie moving around to Pearce's other side and clasping his hand too.

The camera flashes seemed to double, and Pearce's name being hollered out reached a peak. These events weren't about stopping and chatting to reporters, so with smiles and a few nods, we held on tightly to each other and reached the door, held swiftly open for us.

Exhaling slow and steady, I shook off the first layer of tension. Next up were Pearce's friends.

CHAPTER 20
PEARCE

Pride. That's exactly what encompassed me and made my heart swell and my chest puff. Getting to redefine my relationship with Eddie and Lottie and introduce them as my family was a heady emotion.

The way his palm settled in mine, the way our shoulders brushed, each touch sending delicious shockwaves of belonging through me, all of it guided me step-by-step into the large function room.

While tonight was a semiformal affair, there was nothing somber about the laughter and conversation we walked into. The loss had been a hit to all of us, but how far we'd reached, all the way to the conference finals, made me as proud as punch.

I expected come the finals and watching the Jetts play the Starlings there'd be a hit of melancholy, but I didn't plan for that to be the last time we entered the playoffs. There was always next year.

And God willing, a few more seasons after that.

As we entered, I smiled and nodded at a few of the support staff, making a beeline to Coach. I owed the man a big thanks in person. Thank Christ he was a family man, and once I'd told him about Lottie's injury, and also mentioned my new relationship status, he'd taken it in stride, with a promise from me to meet with the team on Tuesday morning.

"Coach," I greeted, releasing Eddie's hand, and shaking the Coach's.

Eddie did a follow-up shake, while I kissed Coach's wife, Edna, on the cheek. "You're looking pretty damn gorgeous tonight, Edna. It's about time you traded up from this old man," I teased, earning me a sigh from Coach.

"You know how we have a follow-up debrief before off-season on Tuesday?" Coach quirked his brow at me. "Carry on, Malcolm, and you'll be responsible for a training session."

I grinned. "Nah, that's just mean. You wouldn't do that to us."

Both his brows shot high. "Wouldn't I?"

"Uhm… hey, Lottie, come say hi to Coach." The small group laughed as I shielded myself with Lottie.

With a shake of his head and roll of his eyes,

Coach turned his attention to my almost stepdaughter. And damn if I didn't get a bubble of delight at that label. "Hi, Lottie. If you need any help keeping this guy in line, you just reach out to me, okay?"

Lottie grinned in good humor. "You got it, Coach. I think I've got him handled, though."

He snorted in amusement. "I have no doubt about it." He indicated toward the side of the room and double doors. "We've set up a games room if you want to check it out. I'm sure that arm of yours won't hold you back too much."

Lottie looked at her dad. "Can I go?"

"Let me go with you to check it out, okay?" he responded. "I'll be back in a second," he said to me, hesitating for the briefest of moments before leaning in and placing a sweet kiss on my mouth.

Hot-cheeked and grinning, I watched them leave, a flood of happiness swelling in my chest knowing I was lucky enough to call Eddie mine.

"Jesus H. Christ, Malcolm." Coach's voice tugged my attention to him. "So it's really true."

"It really is."

He huffed out a small laugh and retook my hand in a shake. "Congratulations. Eddie is a good man."

"The best."

When he released my hand, he studied me, a small frown appearing on his brow. "You're not looking at leaving the Eagles, right? Shopping around? Looking for a place with the Jetts?"

I clamped my mouth shut, not sure how to respond.

"Keith, leave the poor man alone. It's a night to celebrate and wind down, not talk shop."

I could have kissed Edna but I sensibly didn't. Not with the way Coach narrowed his gaze at me. The truth was, it was something I'd been thinking about… or admittedly more than thinking. I'd flicked off a brief email to my agent, letting him know about my engagement to Eddie, and asking what the likelihood of jumping ship to move to a team closer to Eddie and Lottie was.

In typical, efficient fashion, my agent had responded: *Congratulations. Leave it with me.*

That was yesterday, and something I hadn't shared with Eddie yet. I didn't want to get his hopes up.

"Maybe we can sit down on Tuesday?"

Whatever he read in my tone didn't make Coach any happier, but rather than question me more, he sighed. "Fine. Before the team meeting, though."

"You've got it, Coach."

"Now go and put your teammates out of their misery."

My brow scrunched in confusion. Looking over

my shoulder, I searched the busy room, gaze settling on the group of my closest friends. Literally every pair of eyes was on me. I grinned and gave them a finger wave, earning me a finger from Cassius.

I chuckled. "Thanks, Coach, I'll make sure they behave."

"God give me strength if you're the one reining them in."

My butter-wouldn't-melt grin stretched wide. "I'm also responsible now. Didn't you get the memo?" Before he could answer, I said goodbye to Edna and sauntered on over to my teammates. "What are you jerkoffs gossiping about?" I got pounding back slaps from the five guys I'd approached.

"Just figuring out where I'm going to be spending all my winnings." Cassius folded his arms, looking thoroughly impressed with himself. "These dicks said game night wasn't official, as you hadn't confirmed you and Eddie being a thing, despite rushing off like your dick was on fire." He quirked his brow. "But you walking in holding hands, that's me hands-down winning."

I rubbed my mouth with my middle finger, making sure my ring was front and center to his smug face.

"And what in the ever-loving fuck is that?" On cue, Cassius's wide-eyed gaze snapped to my ring.

"Holy shit!" Ollie exclaimed. "You're engaged?"

"Yep." Every inch of happiness I felt lifted my smile.

"When?" Ollie asked, humor in his eyes I didn't quite understand.

My brows drew together. "Why?"

As if frustrated, Ollie flapped his hand at me, indicating for me to hurry the hell up and answer. "Just… when?"

"Thursday," I answered carefully, feeling almost like this was a weird sort of trap or something.

"Fuck" came from Cassius. At the same time, the rest of my teammates burst into loud laughter and hollers.

Joel clapped me on the shoulder. "Congrats, man. You've made me so damn happy."

"I'm confused." I glanced around, looking for some sort of explanation.

Jax tugged me into a hug. "Seriously, Pearce. Best news ever."

"Uhm…" Okay, something funky was going on. "As much as I obviously agree that it's fucking amazing news, what gives?"

Ollie, the good captain he was, clasped my hand and pumped it a couple of times, saying, "It's a double celebration, as an engagement vetoes boyfriends, which means Cassius doesn't win."

I grinned at that news. "Sucks to be you, Cass." I bounced my brows, earning me another middle finger. "But weren't there multiple bets or something?"

"There were. We voted a few weeks back to pile up the pot. Just one winner now."

"And who's that?"

"Coach."

My jaw dropped at Ollie's answer. "You're kidding?"

With a snort, Ollie shook his head. "Nope."

"But Coach never gets involved in this bullshit."

"Right," Cassius responded, sounding seriously put out, complete with a pouty lip. "That's what I said."

"If you wanna tell Coach he can't get in on a bet, have at it," Ollie said pointedly.

Cassius's eyes widened. "Uhm... that'll be a hard pass."

"Damn." I turned and tracked down Coach. When our gazes caught, he held up his beer and winked at me. I laughed in response and saluted him. When I focused back on my friends, I asked, "How big was the pot?"

Cassius sighed. "Thirteen grand."

"Holy shit." Impressed, I nodded for good measure. "Never mind, Cass," I said with sugary sweetness, "let me buy you a beer."

"Fucker. It's an open bar."

I grinned, knowing that. "Well, I am going to get a beer. You want me to fetch you one?"

When they all piped up about "favoritism" and calling out their drink orders, I sighed. "Cass, come with me to get the drinks."

With a lot of loud fuss, he followed me to the bar where we ordered everyone's drinks. As we waited, I looked back at the small group of my single teammates. Over the years, we'd had a helluva lot of fun together. Knowing that life had unequivocally changed, I waited for the pang to hit, but it never came.

"I really am happy for you and Ed," Cassius said at my side.

"Thanks. I'm happy too."

His focus followed my own, looking at our tight group. We did hang out as a whole team fairly often, but over the years, we'd sort of navigated to singles versus those with families.

"We're going to have to take back your single card," Cassius said.

"You reading my mind?" I asked, and Cassius laughed.

"You're hardly the best at keeping your thoughts off your face. It's a wonder that Ed didn't know how you panted over him all these years."

My lips twitched. "He knew," I admitted, no longer feeling as crappy about that time when Eddie shot me down. How could I when he'd since said yes to being my husband? "Fuck, I'm getting married. Can you believe it?"

Cassius released an amused snort. "I wouldn't have, but considering I saw you together all in love and shit, I suppose I can."

"I can give up my card, but don't think you're dissing me now." As soon as I said the words, a different pang in my chest had me pausing. If I did leave the Eagles, then it would change everything.

Movement to my left caught my attention.

Eddie.

The man knew how to make an entrance, looking all suave and sexy as hell. My heart leapt to my throat as he headed toward me, thoughts of leaving the Eagles no longer seeming so dire. How could it if it meant fewer days apart from this man?

"Urgh… your being outrageously loved up is going to get old fast."

"Fuck off." I shoved at Cassius and welcomed Eddie to my side, wrapping a possessive arm around him. "Lottie happy?"

"She is. There's a heap of stuff she can do, and about ten other kids in there." He turned his attention to Cassius. "Hey, Cass." He reached out and shook my friend's hand. "Good to see you."

"You too, Ed. Congrats on the big news."

Color dotted high on Eddie's cheeks. "Thanks."

"Whenever you need to talk shit about Pearce, I'm your man."

"Uhm… thanks?"

Cassius nodded as though he was happy to be of service. "And you'll totally need a best man, Pearce, since you know, I'm your *second* best friend."

I snorted. "You are?" Though he did have a point. Since I was marrying my best friend, I'd need someone to have my back.

"Dude." He grabbed at his chest. "You wound me. You need me there. I will have a killer best man speech."

"Uhm, yeah, that's what I'm kinda worried about and why I think I need to keep you as far away from the wedding party as possible."

Before he could respond, our drinks order appeared, and the three of us carried them over to the rest of the guys. We handed them out as Joel finished talking about his vacation plans.

As he spoke to our group, I leaned into Eddie. "You okay?" I whispered close to his ear. While he seemed more relaxed than when we first entered, I needed to be sure.

"Yeah." He squeezed my waist. "Are you?"

"I really am. After Thursday's game, I wasn't expecting a downer, since the fact we got so far is cause to celebrate."

Eddie's gaze softened. "It really is. You did amazing to get so far."

Not only did it feel good hearing the praise from Eddie, but I felt good about the whole season too. I smiled, pushing warmth into my voice when I said, "That the guys are rolling with it, happy for all we've achieved, is awesome, but I have to admit, I'm fucking ecstatic with just how okay I am. And you have everything to do with that."

"I do, huh?"

"I didn't ever expect to attend one of these events with you… like this. More than just friends," I admitted, getting caught up in the emotion of sharing.

His smile lost some of its shine. "I'm sorry I made you wait so long."

I tugged him a little away from the group, not expecting to be having this conversation. Not the ideal place sure, but I'd do anything for his happiness to return. "Hey." I leaned in a little closer, inhaling his scent and relaxing into the warmth of his body. "I don't need you to say sorry. We're exactly where we're meant to be. Every move we made was the right one, because it led to us wearing matching rings."

He searched my gaze, the seconds intense as we stood so close, his warm breath caressed my skin. "So no wrong moves, huh?"

My heart stumbled at the lightness in his tone and the way he quirked his lips. "That's right."

He glanced around us, taking note that we had a little privacy. "We still need to discuss what happens after the summer." The hand he held my forearm with trembled a little.

"I know. And there'll be no wrong moves there either," I said, stealing his words.

"Okay." As he exhaled, a bright smile lit up his handsome face. "Let's get back to your teammates. I have a feeling they're a little too invested about who's going to be your best man."

I side-eyed my friends and snorted. Eddie was right. And knowing these guys, especially if Cassius was at the center of it, I expected a shitshow of chaos.

"—a point system." Cassius tugged out his cell.

"What are you doing?" Ollie eyed Cassius.

"Making notes."

Lips twitching, Ollie looked our way. "I hope you're ready for this."

"Do I want to know?"

"Probably not," Joel answered, "but we'll tell you anyway." A mischievous smile spread quickly, and he rubbed his hands together.

"Oh God, is this about being my best man?"

"Obviously." Cassius didn't bother looking in my direction when he answered, his stare fixed on his cell, his fingers flying over the keyboard. "Right," he said, finally looking up, "when's the date so we know how much time we have?"

"Uhm..." I turned to Eddie, who wasn't looking as shell-shocked as I expected. He'd heard enough stories of my teammates that maybe he had immunity to their special kind of enthusiasm. "Eddie?" I shrugged.

Since we hadn't sorted out our joined lives in general, the reality of a wedding hadn't even made our list of life-changing decisions to discuss. As far as I was concerned, I just wanted him to be mine forever. Wanted us to exchange vows and live our lives together, as a family. I didn't really care how that came about.

"Well," Eddie said, his voice noticeably careful as he peered back at me, "I've already had the big wedding thing." He eyed me carefully, watching for a reaction.

I offered a reassuring smile. While I didn't like thinking about him married or with any ex, at least his marriage had resulted in Lottie. That wasn't anything I could be jealous or even pissed off about.

"I don't need a big wedding." My palm slipped from his wrist, and I held his hand. "Or even a long engagement."

Eyes widening, Eddie stared at me, his grip on my hand tightening. "Really? You're okay with skipping out on the big stuff?"

"You sound surprised."

Eddie glanced around, a reminder that every pair of eyes in our group was on us. Rather than tugging me away, he released a soft huff of a laugh, as if simply accepting my teammates' involvement was a given. "I thought maybe you'd want to. You were in a rush to get our rings."

"That's because you wearing my engagement ring is fucking hot."

My friends chuckled, and Eddie's cheeks turned pink as he joined in.

"So," Cassius intervened, "are we thinking shotgun wedding? Trip to Vegas? Marquee in the backyard? And how soon? This summer?"

Tickled by Cassius's complete investment, I focused on him. "Jesus, you'll be trying to organize the damn thing next. Why are you weirdly all over this?"

As soon as the words were out there, his face lit

up, and I realized my mistake.

"Shit," I mumbled at the same time Ollie snickered and Cassius said, "Yes, I'll do it. I fucking love organizing shit. All I need are a few details and leave it with me." Legit joy lit his face. "Man, right here, right now, I've got a heart-on for you something fierce, Malcolm."

"What—?"

"I don't think—"

But Cassius had stopped listening to Eddie and my attempted protests. He hushed us both. "Let me make a call. This is going to be fucking epic." In the next breath, his cell was at his ear, and he greeted someone with a "Stop whatever the fuck you're doing. We've got a project…" as he walked away, leaving us with gaping mouths.

"What the hell just happened?" Eddie sounded as confused as I did.

I shook my head, not sure how Cassius had railroaded us in spectacular fashion. It was pretty impressive, to be honest. Not that I'd admit that aloud.

Staring around at my friends, they were all in varying stages of amused and highly entertained.

"Right, new wager," Joel started, while I was pretty certain Eddie was having second thoughts about saying yes.

CHAPTER 21
EDDIE

AFTER TUCKING LOTTIE INTO BED, I MADE MY WAY TO Pearce's bedroom with tonight's craziness buzzing through my brain. To say it had been an interesting evening was an understatement. But it had also been seriously fun.

Pearce had been in his element with his friends and teammates, and they'd all seemed to have moved on from their loss with a grace that kinda surprised me. That made me sound more jaded than I intended, but I'd experienced a heap of losses over the years playing pro. And honestly, there were many a team and a player whose reaction had been down-right embarrassing and less than gracious in their loss.

It made me even prouder of Pearce and his team-mates who he called family.

When I entered the bedroom, I heard the shower running. Steam rolled out of the ajar door, an invite if ever I saw one. Cock thickening, I freed it from my tight suit pants and stripped in record time. The thought of a wet, naked Pearce waiting for me was a good motivator to move quickly.

After locking the bedroom door, I pumped my cock and didn't delay in getting to Pearce. Whatever he wanted, he could have it.

And what I saw momentarily took my breath away.

Pearce stood under the spray, back to me, angled forward, pumping two fingers in and out of his ass.

"Fuck." The word burst out of me, catching his attention despite the noise of the shower.

He glanced over his shoulder, not moving his ass, allowing me a view that caused precum to form on my rock-hard dick.

"I'm almost ready."

I groaned but refused to close my eyes at the spectacular fantasy before me. No way was I missing a second.

"You want me to take over?"

Biting his bottom lip as he pushed back on his fingers, he shook his head. "I want you to watch." There was a hitch to his voice before his stare shot to the hand on my cock. I gripped myself tightly, willing myself not to explode. Like this, Pearce looked undeniably sexy, almost wanton.

Forcing air into my lungs, I got myself under control and stroked myself in time with Pearce riding his fingers.

"So I was thinking…"

I released a surprised laugh, my words wispy when I responded, "You can think while doing that?"

Latching on to his lip again, he smiled and gave a single nod. "Mm-huh." A shuddery breath chased the word.

"What were you thinking?" I remained rooted to the spot, knowing if I dared move, I'd be buried in him so fast, he wouldn't have time to blink.

"We should get married." When I quirked my brow, he continued, "Soon. As in as soon as we can. Like tomorrow."

"Tomorrow?"

"Well…" He closed his eyes and shuddered before saying, "Well, not really *tomorrow* tomorrow, but yeah, soon. I don't want a long engagement. I want to make you mine forever. Be yours forever."

Somehow I kept my focus off his fingers and solely on his expression. "We can do that."

"Yeah?"

"I want to be your husband."

A brilliant smile broke out, hitting me so hard in

the chest that my hand froze. God, he was magnificent.

"What else do you want?" Levity caressed his words, completely in contrast with the heat in his eyes.

I swallowed hard, gaze trailing down his perfect body. "My mouth on your ass. You riding my tongue."

"Nngh." His body trembled, and I took that as my cue.

With long strides, I was behind him, on my knees, removing his hand and spreading his cheeks open.

"Holy fuck. Yes, that. You can do whatever the fuck you want," he garbled.

Heart stuttering, I licked a line from his balls, across his taint, until I reached his hole. As soon as I made contact with his pucker, he shivered. When I latched on, giving open-mouthed kisses, he gasped. And then I went to fucking town.

I devoured him. Feasted on his soap-scented hole that tasted of watermelon lube. Beneath that was everything that was uniquely Pearce—my favorite taste of all.

Tongue probing, his hole loosening, I focused on working him up to the point he'd be begging. From the grunts and groans and the way he clawed at the shower wall with one hand and clamped his other on my head, it wouldn't take long.

But I was in no rush.

Tonight really had been a whirlwind, and his team's enthusiasm had sent my head spiraling a little, but at the center of it all was their devotion to Pearce. To my man. The thought was grounding.

"Eddie," he gasped. "Need your dick."

I chuckled against his ass, earning me a grunt and a shiver.

"Did you just laugh in my ass?" The words were gasped and filled with incredulous amusement.

The only way to respond was to chuckle again, pressing my lips against him. Another groan pulsed out of Pearce.

"Seriously. Dick in my ass."

With one last kiss, I eased away, taking my time to kiss his cheeks, then up his back, settling with my mouth on his neck. "When's your CK shoot?" I asked around my kisses.

Giving me better access, he angled his neck. "Thursday."

I grunted, weighing up the likelihood of a hickey disappearing by then. With the way I was worked up, it was unlikely I'd go easy on him, so I pulled back. "Next time," I murmured against his skin.

Without seeing his face, I knew he was grinning

when he said, "Pretty desperate to mark me up, huh?"

"Yeah." And I didn't even care that it made me feel ridiculously like a teenager either.

Turning his face toward me, he smiled, eyes sparkling. "After the shoot, you can mark me wherever you want."

My cock twitched against his ass. At the movement, he pushed against me, back tight against my chest.

"Anywhere?" I teased.

He narrowed his amused gaze. "Not on my head."

I quirked my brow.

"Well, that head, go for it." He rubbed his ass against my cock. "But my forehead or face."

"Deal." I angled for a kiss, capturing his mouth with mine while trailing my hand over his skin and reaching for my cock. "Lean forward," I instructed, pulling away from the kiss.

Complying immediately, I swiped more of the watermelon lube he kept in the shower, slathered up, and positioned at his entrance. I slid right home. The combination of his fingers and my tongue working their magic had opened him perfectly.

I grunted but didn't pause, didn't wait for him to adjust. I knew what Pearce needed. Had known from the moment I found him finger-fucking himself. My hips moved, smooth glides in and out of his tight channel. With each entry, he clamped around me, almost begging me to let loose, trying to draw my orgasm out of me.

But not yet. I wanted all the moments with this man. Wanted to cherish every cry and plea. Above all, I wanted to wring him dry and watch his cum paint the shower walls.

"Harder," he grunted.

Gripping his hips, I pounded into him, hard and fast, listening to his sharp breaths and the accompanying hitches. And then I caught the stuttered moan, the contraction of his ass cheeks, the tell I was looking for.

Fighting the tightening of my balls, I homed in, slamming into him at the same angle, determined to keep pegging his prostate until he called my name.

"Holy. Fucking. God." The words were broken, each caught on a grunt.

"Hands on the wall," I ordered.

Immediately, he released his dick, a sweet sigh following, and he dropped his head, completely letting go as I fucked him hard.

There was no relenting. No slowing down. Just focused pushes as I slid in and out.

"As soon as you come," I said breathlessly, aiming

for the words needed to push him over without touching his cock, "we'll set a date. Get fucking married. Make you mine forever."

He gasped. Moaned. Groaned so loud that the sound echoed around the room, my name on his lips.

His taut body clamped down. I called out, cum shooting out of me, implanting itself deep inside him. I couldn't do anything but hold on to Pearce, prepared to catch him when he sagged in my arms.

"God." A whole-body shudder followed, and a gasp slid out of me as another burst of cum pulsed out of my cock. "I just…" He shook his head and leaned back against me. Low and breathy, the words "Holy fuck" fell from him as he pressed his head against my shoulder.

Breathing heavily, I wrapped my arms around his chest, my own words struggling to surface.

"You still alive?"

In response, I kissed his temple, the closest surface I could find.

"That's good." A flimsy pat on my arm followed, his limbs no doubt as limp as my own. "You need to move before your legs give way?" His amusement was back.

I managed an exhausted, satisfied smile. "Your recovery time is impressive." I would have laughed if I had the energy.

"I'm not hard yet, but give me five."

I snorted, wincing at the way it jerked my spent dick still in his ass. "I meant your legs." Because, holy shit, the trembling in mine made it highly likely I legit would fall down any moment.

Angling to catch my gaze, Pearce smiled, soft and sweet with an extra hint of teasing. "Kiss me, and we'll move before we crash."

That I could totally get on board with.

I teased his lips with mine. While I intended on a brief kiss—knowing my legs weren't up to the task of keeping me upright—as soon as his tongue swiped mine, I sighed into him. Kissing Pearce was like experiencing sunshine for the first time after storm season. He radiated warmth and happiness, and I would never get tired of this.

Of him.

When my knees almost knocked together from exertion, I had no choice but to pull away.

"I love you."

I searched his gaze as he spoke, loving the curve of his mouth and the softening of his expression.

"I love you."

He dotted a kiss on my nose. With a smile, he pulled off me. We both winced, and I pressed a hand against the shower wall for support. "You need a hand?" Teasing entered his tone.

"Hell no. You go anywhere near my dick," I said as he picked up the body wash, "and there's no chance I'll be walking out of this shower."

Pearce chuckled, eyes alight. "Would that be so bad?"

"If you don't want to be dragging me out by my legs, then yes."

With a snort, Pearce passed me the shower gel and we cleaned ourselves down. We made quick work of it, keeping our hands to ourselves, and me giving him pointed looks in warning to keep himself in check. Much to his amusement.

By the time we fell into bed, it was past midnight. In the morning we had a lot to talk about. We'd been putting off the conversation for too long, both of us using "we'll figure it out" all too readily.

After tonight and our agreement on a short engagement, we could no longer avoid the serious talk. Holding back my sigh and worry about what the reality of our future would look like, I held on to Pearce's arms when he got in position and spooned me. For the next few hours, I'd embrace the ease of avoidance with a smile on my face and Pearce's soft cock snug against my ass.

OUR FLIGHT WAS BOOKED FOR LATER IN THE AFTERNOON. Despite Lottie's sulking and trying to convince me she should just skip school, I put my foot down. We'd be making the flight, and Lottie would go to school come hell or high water.

It seemed like a long time since we'd had any semblance of normality, and with me heading out to Montview in a few weeks, I was beginning to forget what calm looked like.

We'd finished breakfast. While Lottie sprawled out on the couch, Pearce and I drank coffee outside on his back patio. It was a beautiful morning. The sun touched my skin, tugging a relaxed sigh out of me.

I couldn't wait for a whole week of nothing but stillness and no injuries. No traveling.

"You need me to leave you alone with your coffee?"

I blinked one eye open, taking in Pearce's teasing smile. "Fuck off."

He chuckled. "Not sure if I should be jealous of the blissed-out look on your face or not."

Fully opening my eyes, I stared at him, running my gaze over his shirtless body, appreciating every curve, divot, and sharp line.

A shit-eating grin broke out before he said, "It's all good. You can carry on."

"Huh?"

"You looking at me like that makes me know you think I'm more irresistible than coffee."

"Only just."

"I'll take it." He bounced his brows, continuing to eye me, his gaze losing some of its shine.

"What is it?"

"Just trying to figure things out in my head."

I nodded. "I know." A light sigh escaped. Just thinking about working out our future was exhausting. It didn't stop excitement from buzzing around my body, though. Pearce was worth every sleepless night and possible dilemma. "We need to talk this shit out. Work out how to make this work together."

When he pulled his bottom lip between his teeth, I frowned. He was nervous and I didn't know why. As he continued to study me, still gnawing away on the flesh of his lip, my heart stuttered. He'd already had a thought or gone ahead and done something.

After so long with this man as my best friend, I knew when he was battling something. And I figured he felt guilty.

"What is it?"

"Huh?"

I waved a hand in his general direction. "You can't keep shit from me. What have you done or are thinking about doing?"

"You have ninja mind reading skills."

That wasn't awe in his voice. It was a piss-poor attempt at distracting me.

My arched brow called him on it.

"Okay, so don't be mad... Hey, no frown, you don't even know what I'm going to say."

"Anytime anyone starts off a sentence with 'don't be mad,' I think it's safe to say a frown is right on cue." With a smile, I shook my head. "The number of times I've heard that from Lottie..."

"You saying I have the maturity of a ten-year-old?"

"She hasn't said it for at least two years," I deadpanned.

Pearce flipped me off, and I grinned wider.

"So what shouldn't I be pissed off with?" I pushed.

The tip of his tongue darted out, and he licked his slightly swollen lip where he'd been gnawing. "I emailed Rick about the possibility of a trade."

"What?" I sat bolt upright in my chair, heart hammering in my chest. "Where? Why?"

"Something close to home."

My brows pulled tight as I shook my head. "I don't understand. What am I missing?" The Eagles were situated within a perfect distance to his home, hence the reason he'd bought the house not long after we became friends.

"I've asked for the Jetts, or the next closest team."

I snapped my mouth shut, pulling back, completely startled.

For the first time in a super long time, I was completely speechless. But fuck, my heart expanded, filled so much with love and affection and so much respect for Pearce that I struggled to contain the way it pounded against my ribcage.

"You…" I shook my head and blinked back tears. "I don't know…." Fuck, my words wouldn't form. How could they, when I was a certifiable mess of love and gratitude? I swallowed hard, my breath catching on a weird sort of choke that I should have been embarrassed about.

"Hey." Pearce knelt before me, palms on my knees and concern in his gaze. "If I can make this happen, it's a great thing."

I nodded, my heart feeling the truth of his words. "And you're okay with a possible move. Leaving the Eagles?"

"For you, absolutely."

A fresh wave of emotion threatened to take me under. Clearing my throat, I stared at the man before me through a watery gaze. "Won't you miss them?"

"Of course, but hell, I've only played with these

guys. It's not like a change won't do me good, maybe help improve my game." He cradled my cheek, and I leaned into his touch. "But I'll miss you a hell of a lot more than my team if we don't get to live with each other and call your place home."

"You're amazing."

A smile lit up his face.

"Don't stop." He bounced his brows, finally tugging a chuckle from me.

"You are." I frowned, admitting, "I feel like I should be stopping you and offering to move to you."

"It's a possibility," he said carefully, stare never wavering from my face, "but we have to make sure Lottie's at the center of every decision we make."

"FUCK." I CLUNG TO PEARCE AND DRAGGED HIM INTO my arms. He straddled me, the chair creaking under our combined weight. "Thank you for being incredible." My kiss followed, sweet and soft.

He sighed into the connection, opening his mouth and kissing me back, tangling his tongue with mine in a gentle, slow exploration. When he eased back, my head remained spinning, and I blinked open my eyes, absorbing the perfection of my fiancé.

"Am I right in thinking Lottie would struggle with the move?"

Wincing, I hesitated, earning me raised brows. "Maybe," I admitted. It didn't matter how confident my girl was, or that she was a whirlwind, she was still ten, and I'd do all I could to protect her. "On one hand, as long as she has us, I know she'll be fine, but when Moira left... she struggled there for a time."

Pearce nodded. "I remember."

"I want her to have stability."

"And already, me not being home all the time will be disruptive enough."

"Well, maybe. But in fairness, she's not used to you being around anyway. I haven't really thought about it."

"I have," he said softly. Hell, how this man ever thought he wasn't responsible enough to step up boggled my mind. He was fucking incredible.

"And what if a trade isn't possible?"

There were just two teams between the Eagles and my home. The Jetts and the Blackhawks.

The chair creaked again, making us both still. When it didn't collapse, we chuckled, but Pearce took that as his cue to get off my lap and return to his chair. "It's only a six-hour drive," he stated, "and a flight with drive and wait times takes, what... three hours?"

"Yeah, about that."

"So it's not undoable. Any chance I get, I'll fly home to you, and I'll keep pushing for a trade. I'm speaking to Coach on Tuesday and will see if he'll support me and make something happen. I'm still contracted with the Eagles for another year, which will make things easier after that." He searched my gaze. "If we have to wait it out, will that be a problem?"

I shook my head immediately. "Not at all. If it's one season, we'll be fine. It doesn't mean I won't miss you like crazy, though."

And then he was back out of his seat again, clambering on me and kissing me senseless. There wasn't even a warning before the legs decided they couldn't cope with our combined weight. We slammed to the deck with a yell and loss of breath, Pearce on top of me.

I groaned, chuckling despite my sore ass.

"Holy shit," Pearce wheezed. "You okay?" His laughter spilled out as he shifted off me, peering down to take in my sprawled form. "Did I break you?" He reached out and snagged my hand, tugging me up.

I grunted, rubbing my back. "Jesus." I chuckled. "You know if you kill me off before we're married, you won't get any inheritance, right?"

He crushed me into a hug, grinning wildly. "About that."

"Yeah?" I quirked my brow, my pulse picking up speed.

"How about making this official in three weeks?"

"Three weeks?" My brows shot high. While we'd said we didn't want to delay, three weeks was... well, three weeks away. That was soon.

"It means Moira will be here." I frowned at that, wondering why on earth he'd want my ex around. "So," he continued, "she'll be here so we can enjoy a real honeymoon, and I can have my wicked way with you the whole time."

My dick twitched, on board with that plan.

"It'll also save those college guys' lives during academy training, since you'll be wearing a wedding band."

"What?"

"You seriously don't know there's always at least one guy at the camp who's constantly eye-fucking you?"

"What?" I sputtered. "No, of course not."

Pearce shook his head. "Oh, dear, sweet, naïve Eddie. You're hot as fuck, and when in coach mode, you're practically irresistible."

I rolled my eyes. "You're so full of shit."

"Uh-huh. Just ask any number of guys on my team, even the straight ones."

Heat filled my cheeks. "I don't think I want to know."

"Right answer." He pressed his mouth to mine. "And if you hear any of the guys mentioning you're a DILF, just let me know, and I'll defend your honor."

I snorted out a laugh, a little bit mortified and maybe just a little bit intrigued. "Maybe you should give me the names of your teammates who call me that." When he narrowed his gaze, I grinned. "You know, just so I can be on guard."

"Uh-huh." He squeezed my ass cheeks and tugged so my groin rubbed against his. "That'd be a no. I'm the only man you need to be thinking about fucking."

I relaxed in his hold and smiled. "Deal."

Seeming happy with my response, he buried his face in my neck, inhaling deeply and dotting kisses over my skin. When he pulled away, he shot a grin my way. "Right. I'm going to go give Cass the date."

"Noooo," I gasped, shaking my head. "You can't be serious?" My tone seesawed somewhere between concern and edging-on-hysterical amusement.

"Damn straight I am. The guy wasn't lying about being an organized freak of nature."

"Really?" I struggled to marry that information to what I knew about Cassius.

"Yeah, really. Surprised the shit out of me a time or two."

"Okay." I winced as the word left me, not sure I'd be prepared for what I was getting myself into.

"Excellent." He stepped away, grabbing his cell from the table, his gaze landing on the collapsed chair. "Do you mind...?"

I waved him off. "It's fine. I'll do this. You go deal with whatever Cass is doing." I glanced at the time on my watch. "We don't have to leave for another three hours."

"Thanks." He backed away, moving his cell to his ear.

"Pearce," I called. When he stopped and peered back at me, I said, "Do we need to, I don't know, rein him in or anything? Give him a 'hell fucking no' list?"

"Nah." He scrunched his nose and shook his head. "Leave this with me."

And then he left me standing over the broken chair, hoping like hell Cassius's idea of a quiet wedding wasn't one that would give me nightmares.

CHAPTER 22
PEARCE

WHILE COACH HAD LISTENED TO WHAT I HAD TO SAY, I wasn't surprised that he wasn't interested in me breaking my contract. I tried to see his no as an ego boost and clasp tightly to his praise for the strong season we'd had and how essential I was to the team and next season.

Fuck, it sucked, but unless Rick managed to come up with a spectacular offer from the Jetts that Coach would be interested in, I'd need to swallow down my disappointment and make this year a killer one.

Free agency next year after an even more spectacular season would have to put me in an even better position, right?

What I hadn't done was tell any of my teammates about my request or hope to be traded. I didn't want to piss them off or cause any waves next season. It made joining in with the guys' conversation a little more work, and I was beginning to think they'd started to notice.

"Who the fuck pissed in your cereal?"

Called out on my grouchy mood, I snorted. Joel frowned over at me. We'd headed to a local bar that was our main haunt for chilled drinks after our final meeting with Coach. Most of the team was here, a few taking over the pool table while the rest gathered around a few tables.

Cassius, though, was fixed to his phone, tapping away, every now and then making calls. He was in total planning mode. It was enough to have me smiling and my stomach flipping. In less than three weeks, I'd be getting married.

"Earth to Pearce."

"Shit, sorry, man." I glanced at Joel. "Nothing's wrong. I'm okay."

He studied me a beat before nodding. "If you say so. You just missing your thirst trap?"

I snorted while taking a pull of my beer, quickly covering my mouth to stop the spray. "Shit." I coughed. "Really, thirst trap?"

Joel grinned and bounced his brows. "You know it."

I shook my head, still smiling at my straight friend having the confidence to acknowledge how fine Eddie was. The moment of nearly choking eased some of my tension and did a decent job at pulling me out of my funk. "Yeah," I answered, "of course I'm missing him."

"It's a good job we're around to keep you entertained. When are you heading to Montview?"

"The first week in July. I'm driving down to Chicago on Sunday. Means I can get that photoshoot wrapped up and organize some other shit. What about you? You sticking around or jetting off somewhere?"

"Plan to spend some time with my family. Promised I'd take my kid sister on a vacation to celebrate her graduation."

"You get on well with her?"

He bobbed his head. "Yeah. She's the only sane one in my family. She's pretty cool. Plus I said she could bring a couple of her friends." He grinned.

"Like that, huh?"

"Hell yes. Her best friend, Tilly, is fucking hot. She's also smart as shit and loves giving me hell. Pretty good foreplay, I reckon."

I chuckled. "Well, have fun with tha—"

"Yes!"

Cassius's loud holler grabbed my attention. When I looked in his direction, his gaze was on me, and he wore the smuggest grin I'd seen to date.

"You are going to want to suck me off so bad," he said, standing and heading over to our table. "But of course I'll say no, as I don't mess around with attached men."

"Geez, thank goodness for that. I was so tempted," I deadpanned.

He flipped me off before taking the seat in front of me. "Whatever." He shoved his cell in my direction.

"What am I looking at?"

"Only the perfect wedding venue that's idyllic as well as private. Room for three hundred guests."

My brows shot up. "Quiet and low-key, Cass."

He waved me off. "Yes, yes. Just saying that's the capacity, but I have your half-assed guest list."

"Which you'll stick to," I said pointedly.

"Uh-huh."

"I'm serious, Cass."

"Yes, I know." He rolled his eyes.

Ollie snorted from beside him. "Bet you're wishing you flew out to Vegas and eloped right about now, huh?"

"There's still time," I said, with a little too much hope.

"No chance in hell. This, my friend, will be perfect for your day. Low-key, measly guest list. I know the parameters."

I held his gaze and hoped like hell he wasn't going to screw me over. When I didn't see anything beyond impatience in his gaze, I returned my focus to his phone. I raised my brows. "Damn. The place is nice."

"You don't want to know how many strings I pulled to get you in."

When I flicked my attention to him, he attempted an innocent grin, which I absolutely was not buying. I focused back on the incredible barn and flicked through the pictures. "Shit, how did you get this place?"

He shrugged, offering an indifferent, "I'll send you the bill by email."

Ollie broke into laughter, and I sighed, but seriously, the venue was gorgeous. "We can have the ceremony outside?" I stared at the tree-lined aisle, thinking it would be pretty cool to get married in a forest.

"Yeah. It also has views of the lake just behind that. The reception will be in the barn."

Searching through the photos, I found the barn with exposed beams. It looked rustic and romantic as hell. "Cass," I said, something close to awe in my voice, "this is seriously incredible. Thank you."

For the briefest of moments, a soft smile traced his lips, and a slight flush reached his cheeks. Then it was gone in a blink, a wide grin appearing. "Told you. I'm a fucking rock star at this."

There was no debating that. "You pull this off, I'll never doubt you again." I grinned as I passed him his phone back, a rush of gratitude forming in the pit of my stomach that Cassius was so eager to do this for me. "Actually," I said, wondering whether or not Eddie would have me certified for making this call, "I think you were right."

"I usually am," Cassius sassed, "but about anything in particular?"

"About you making an awesome best man."

Surprise flitted across his features before he shut his reaction down and smirked. "You know it."

I chuckled, saying, "Cass, you wanna stand up with me and be my best man?"

"Hell fucking yes." He whooped, stood, and tugged me up, patting my back in a hug.

A chorus of "no" surrounded us, followed by potato chips and peanuts being thrown at our heads.

Cassius pulled back, flipping off our team, shouting, "Best man, fuckers. We'll save the competition for his bachelor party. No way I'm letting that go to waste."

I tilted my head back and looked at the ceiling. I'd kinda hoped he'd forget about the competition he'd been organizing. I should have known better.

My cell vibrated in my pocket. I pulled it out, my whole body lighting up when I saw Eddie's name.

"Hey, you," I answered with a smile.

"Hey, how'd today go?"

"It… went," I settled on, stepping away from the tables and toward the small yard out the back where I expected it would be quieter.

"That sounds a little ominous."

I chuckled and looked around the outside space. Finding it empty, I stepped out and settled on one of the chairs. "Not deliberately." I wiped my hand over my face. "I just miss you." My gut tightened, knowing I had to tell him the bad news about Coach's response.

"I miss you. Only a few more days and you'll be here. We can handle that."

"Yeah, I know. It's just going to take some time to accept that it's all not happening now, you know?"

The sound of his light breaths traveled down the line as he listened to me, pausing a beat before saying, "So I'm guessing Coach Jenkins wasn't keen on a trade for next season?" Despite the gentleness of his voice, I didn't need to see his face to know he was upset.

"No. The team's strong."

"It is."

"I'm still hoping Rick pulls something out of the bag at the end of June."

Eddie released a slow breath. "I know, and I want that too, but I think we best prepare to expect lots of commuting next season. It'll all work out, though."

"Yeah," I answered, my voice quiet. Shit, I needed to pull myself out of this funk. If I couldn't get to grips with staying put, it would make next season unbearably depressing. I didn't want that. I loved my job, was so blessed to have it and be living the dream. "We have a venue," I said abruptly, changing tack, wanting to focus on something amazing.

"Yeah?" This time I heard the smile in his voice.

"It's amazing. A farmhouse on a lake." I continued to tell him all about it, describing the photos I saw, and promising to send him the link as soon as I got it from Cassius. I also admitted to making him my best man. Thankfully he only groaned a little, but he did laugh a lot.

By the time we finished discussing our wedding and how Lottie was coping with one arm out of action, Eddie cleared his throat, quickly followed by an "Uhm…"

"Are you going to bring my good mood down?"

"Not deliberately."

"And now you're the one who's sounding all ominous. What's on your mind?"

"I ran into Wayne today."

I didn't have to look in the mirror to know an impressive sneer had formed on my face. "Bet that was thirty seconds you wish you could get back."

A strangled laugh escaped him. It didn't have the teasing humor I expected. "I actually… uhm… he was there when I had lunch."

I opened and closed my mouth, having no idea how to respond. While my gut clenched and I wanted to spit venom, I exhaled instead, holding on to his tone and the resignation I heard there.

"It wasn't planned, and it wasn't welcome," he rushed to say. "It was actually awkward as fuck." This time an exasperated sigh fluttered down the line, and whether he knew it or not, his frustration eased some of the building emotion sitting on my chest.

"What happened? Was he his usual asshole self?"

"You could say that." Eddie sighed. "I met up with Graham and Tim. Apparently Tim told Wayne we were meeting and ended up inviting him. He did apologize a shit ton afterward. Told me he'd felt cornered."

I grunted at that. "There's a lot to be said about the power of saying 'fuck off.' More people should try it."

"I expect after lunch that's something Tim will

agree with. The guy's too well-mannered for his own damn good."

"So what did Wankface have to say for himself?"

"Spent most of the time bragging about bullshit. It was at the end that was, uhm… awkward."

I gritted my teeth. "Do I need to get on a plane and kick his ass?"

Eddie snorted. "You think I need defending?"

"Well," I smiled, visualizing the huge wall of limbs and muscle he was, "not exactly." But he also was nowhere near as quick-tempered as I was and could be too forgiving. "Just wondering if I needed to defend your honor or something." My tone turned lighter.

"Ha. And people say chivalry is dead."

"They clearly don't know how chivalrous as fuck I can be, especially when Wankface is involved." My shoulders untensed, listening to his warm laugh. I wasn't really worried about any conversation Eddie may have with any of his exes. What pissed me off was that I didn't want him to deal with dickheads. "So what was so awkward?"

"He suggested we get back together and that he'd even consider being exclusive."

My sneer was back. "Big of him."

"Uh-huh. I reminded him I was engaged, since I'm sure as shit am sure he's read the gossip columns about that announcement, and that in no universe would I ever consider getting back with him."

A smile stretched big and wide on my face. "Did you also make clear I'm the best you ever had and that you're so ridiculously in love, you'd die without me?"

"Yes," he deadpanned. "That's exactly what I did. I even used props and a piece of theater. You know, add in some drama to the moment."

"Sweet. I hope you recorded it. Right along with his reaction."

"You're such a dickhead."

"I'm your dickhead." I grinned, wishing like hell the week would hurry up and be over so I could kiss his face off.

"You are. For better or worse before you know it."

"Less than three weeks." As I said the words, my heart tripped over itself. In three weeks we'd be married. "I can't fucking wait."

A soft sigh reached me. "Me either. And Cass has really found something great and not too OTT?"

"I think it could easily be over the top, but it won't be. The place is stunning. There are cottages too for everyone, which will make everything easier."

"Sounds perfect. Are you still out?" he asked.

"Yeah. I'll head back soon. Get my beauty sleep

before Thursday's shoot."

"About that…" He cleared his throat. My interest piqued at the rumbly tone that followed, but rather than push, I waited him out. "Uhm… you think I can get some of the proofs?"

I quirked my brow, tempted to switch to video so I could see the blush I knew would be spreading across his cheeks. "You want pics of me in underwear?" I teased. "I could have sent you plenty before now."

"I wouldn't be, you know, averse to seeing a few of those." I heard the smile in his voice, and my dick twitched.

"Maybe I should head home now, get a video call going, and make sure we record it."

His needy moan drifted to me, threatening to turn my cock rock-hard.

"Well, uhm…"

"You like that idea, huh?"

"Maybe."

I grinned wide and stood, absolutely on board with this plan. "In that case, give me thirty minutes."

"Yeah, okay." His voice dropped, all growly and sounding delectable. Hell, video sex would absolutely help the growing ache I had to endure between now and the weekend. I just hoped he realized I was deadly serious about recording.

CHAPTER 23
EDDIE

"THIS IS INCREDIBLE."

Hand in hand, we stood at the edge of the lake. Admittedly, I'd been dubious about Cassius organizing our wedding, but props to the guy. Not only was the location perfect, but everything I'd been involved with had blown me away.

The man took organization and wedding planning to a whole new level. And pulling all this off in under a month was mind-blowing.

"Right? I can't think of anywhere more perfect for tomorrow." Pearce squeezed my hand, the whimsy in his voice impossible not to react to. I leaned over, pressing my mouth to his neck, smiling when he angled to give me better access.

"You sure we should have separate rooms tonight?" I asked, rubbing my nose along his neck, enjoying his slight shudder and the fresh goose bumps breaking out.

He chuckled. "That was your idea. Not mine."

"I'm an idiot." I pulled away, and he turned toward me. "I've changed my mind."

A smirking, cocky grin lifted his lips. "Nuh-uh. I had to listen to your whole speech about why you thought it was a good idea. I didn't put up with that for nothing." He reached out and squeezed my waist. "Plus you've got a special night with Lottie."

He was right. It had been ridiculously sweet when he'd suggested I spend the evening with Lottie before our big day. My room for the night was already set up. We had a feast of sugary goodness waiting for us, and a batch of fun sports movies to watch. We were having an indoor daddy-daughter night, complete with mattresses on the floor. Lottie had tried to hold back her excitement when Pearce had suggested it, but while she thought she was a teenager at times, she was still very much my ten-year-old little girl.

"I know. You're right." Since we were actually having ten child-free nights starting with our wedding night, missing the chance to spend the time with my daughter, the last as a single dad, was not really up for negotiation.

"We should be getting back. Our parents will be expecting us."

Both of our parents had arrived this morning. Tonight we were having a family meal, just the seven of us. There were already a few other of our guests here, but legit only around thirty. Neither of us had been lying when we said we wanted a quiet wedding. There'd still be twenty or so more arriving tomorrow. Combined, it seemed like a chilled, low-key number.

"Come on, then." I tugged him in the general direction of the main property, heading toward the conservatory where the owners had organized for us to have a meal.

"You think your 'rents have survived spending time together this afternoon?"

I chuckled, only feeling slightly guilty we'd thrown our parents into the deep end. I'd met Pearce's parents a handful of times, and he'd met mine a little less than that. Today was the first time they'd met each other. But between Pearce's mom being as outgoing as her son, and the clear fact that like my parents, they doted on Lottie, it had been enough for them to spend time making calls to each other since we announced our wedding date.

"I think they've been fine."

Pearce grinned. "Mom told me today she had a wine-fueled video call with yours last week."

I snorted, relieved they were both making an effort and seemed to be genuinely getting along. Like me and Pearce, there was a small age gap between our parents. I'd worried it would mean a possible divide, but I'd been happy to be proven wrong.

"One of many, I expect."

In the distance, the farmhouse came into view. Immediately my gaze zeroed in on Lottie. Bouncing a basketball, she was laughing and calling out something. From the clear amusement on Brice's face, she was smack talking. "I hope your dad knows what he's in for." I gave a chin lift toward their general direction.

"Dad... well, let's just say I didn't get my sporting gene from him." He chuckled as his dad dodged, tried for the ball, and missed spectacularly. "If it wasn't for his grandad being a certifiable giant, he said he would have doubted my parentage a time or too."

I grinned. "Uh-huh. That and your smile."

Pearce glanced at me. "You think?"

"Your dad's a handsome guy. I'm pretty sure I chose well if that's how you're going to look when you're gray."

"He is rather dashing, huh."

"Dashing... sure, let's go with that," I teased, earning myself a shove and a "Fuck off."

Tugging Pearce close, I wrapped an arm around him, dotting a kiss on his cheek. I didn't need to see his face to know he was smiling. The pair of us were giddily in love and excited for tomorrow. We didn't need any of our friends to tell us that. I saw and felt it whenever we spoke, touched, in each smile and soft gaze.

The sound of a car engine drew our attention. I recognized the rental from yesterday and wondered if we could cut off the path and find an alternate route. To be fair, Moira hadn't been pissed that our wedding fell in the first few days of her being back, even though it meant we were stealing Lottie away for a couple of days.

She'd taken it in such good grace, it had taken me a while to pick up my jaw off the floor.

"Eddie," she called once she'd exited.

"And I might just go and check on the 'rents," Pearce said, making a move to abandon me.

Before I could mumble, "Chickenshit," Moira's "No, I need to speak to the both of you," stopped him in his tracks.

As always, Moira looked elegant in a pantsuit. Not quite the outfit for relaxing by a lake on a beautiful acreage property, but then I couldn't remember the last time I'd seen or even heard of Moira letting her hair down.

I smiled, still making sure there was no mistaking my gratitude that she was being so cool with everything. She wasn't attending the wedding—even though I'd felt compelled to invite her, since she was here for Lottie.

"Can I have a word before you get to your plans?"

"Sure," I responded, dropping my arm from around Pearce's shoulder and clasping his hand.

"I haven't discussed this with Charlotte yet, but I'm intending to stay in Hong Kong permanently."

My brows shot high. When she'd moved there full-time last year, it was with the expectation it was for a three-year contract. "Okay...," I dragged out, already trying to figure out any damage control needed, unsure how Lottie would respond to the news.

"I've met someone."

I froze, muscles turning rigid. My brain buzzed to life, heart thumping in my chest. If she thought she'd be taking Lottie.... I swallowed hard, not even able to finish that thought.

When I didn't speak, Pearce rubbed his thumb over my hand and said, "That's great news. We're really happy for you." Caution traced every word.

"I've already been in touch with my Stateside lawyer," she continued, and I struggled to focus, my rapid pulse almost deafening. "I've asked her to draw up paperwork so you have full custody—"

"Fuck me," I interrupted, clasping my chest, gripping Pearce's hand so hard I wasn't sure he had any blood circulation. "Thank Christ."

Moira arched a brow and continued as if I'd never spoken. "I think it's best. I've asked my lawyer to ensure I have a minimum of two weeks with her a year, and hope that when she perhaps turns sixteen, she'll be able to fly out for visits."

"Yes, sure," I said, certain I would have agreed to almost anything if it meant I could get full custody of Lottie. "If you can make sure my lawyer gets the paperwork, I'll reach out to him and let him know to expect it."

While her smile wasn't warm, it didn't appear painful. She turned her attention to Pearce, and I felt him pull his shoulders back. "I expect you'll want to ensure you have legal guardianship."

As my eyes widened in surprise, I angled to look at Pearce. Heat flushed his cheeks, and he was bobbing his head. "Yes," he croaked. "I'd love nothing more." He turned his attention to me, our eyes connecting, nothing but love in their depths. "If you want that? If that's okay?"

"Absolutely." Happiness slammed into my chest, so grateful I'd found this man and opened my heart to him.

"Good. That's settled then." Was it strange that I wanted to hug the shit out of Moira? Not that I'd ever try. And whether her decisions were selfish or not, I chose to think of her as being selfless for once and doing the right thing by our daughter and for me. Having joint custody hanging over my head, knowing at any time Moira could have demanded equal time with her, had been a challenge.

Admitting that to myself was shit and selfish as fuck, as Lottie loved her mom, but hand on heart, I knew I was best for Lottie. Scrap that. Pearce and I were the family she needed.

"I'll discuss it with Charlotte when we're alone, after the wedding." I cringed, wanting to be there. Her gaze narrowed. "If there's an issue, I'll call you."

"Fine," I reluctantly agreed, not quite convinced, but if Lottie needed me, I'd be there as fast as humanly possible.

She nodded. "Right, well, good luck tomorrow. Charlotte and I will leave the day after. I'll make sure she says goodbye."

"Thanks, Moira," I said, still a little shell-shocked with the bombardment of emotions in the last few minutes.

And then she was gone. High-heeled shoes clipping on the concrete. Chanel mixing with the fresh lakeside breeze.

Once she was out of sight, Pearce stepped in front of me and wrapped me into a tight hug. "Fuck," I whispered, "I thought…"

"I know. Me too." His soft voice caressed my skin, helping to slow down the erratic beating of my heart. "But it's okay. Amazing even."

I nodded against his shoulder.

"How do you think Lottie will handle it?" He didn't disguise the concern in his tone.

"Hopefully not badly. She's been amazing this year, well, certainly the last six months. I just don't want her to feel abandoned."

Pearce's hold on me tightened. "If she does, we'll support her. It's no hardship reminding her every day how much she's loved and wanted."

Easing out of his hold, I slowly shook my head, nothing but wonder making my heart beat anew. "How'd I get so lucky, having you be mine?"

With a softening gaze, a small smile appeared before it kicked up on the right, forming into an expression very much Pearce. "Because we're fucking magic together, and try as you might, I'm a stubborn asshole who never gave up hope."

"Who thought stubborn could be a good quality?" I teased, resting my lips against his.

He nodded against the kiss. "I hide it well."

I chuckled, pulling away. Pearce was one of the most easygoing people I knew. He seriously wasn't stubborn at all. "You hide it remarkably well."

"It's because you're dazzled by my wit and sparkling personality."

I kissed him again, absolutely agreeing with him.

"And how my ass looks in a pair of CKs."

Abrupt laughter spilled out of me. "That right?"

"The bookmarks on your computer tell me as much."

"Fucker," I said with a laugh, shoving at him with my right shoulder but refusing to let him go.

"Seriously, best bookmarks ever. I think it's adorable. It also explains the wet wipes you keep in your office."

I groaned and rested my head on his shoulder. "I take it all back."

"Too late for that, Ed. Tomorrow you'll be mine forever."

I embraced the rightness of the words, the perfect happiness they created, and settled into stealing him away in the fifteen minutes we had before dinner, to show him exactly how wonderful we were together.

Pearce and I were just at the start of an amazing

life together. And whether we had a year or more of commutes ahead of us, we'd make it work. The truth of that settled in my chest, encompassing me in warmth and certainty. And tomorrow, when we exchanged our vows, it would be the perfect reminder that there were no wrong moves between us.

How could there be when everything had led us right here?

EPILOGUE
PEARCE

EIGHT YEARS LATER

"Don't you dare do it."

Whether Lottie was talking to me or her dad, I had no idea. Probably both of us.

The boxes had been unloaded, the minifridge filled, bed made, yet we were still hanging around. We'd reached the point that there were no more ridiculous excuses for us to be here, and I expected she'd have thrown us out of her dorm room at least an hour ago if she'd been physically able to move us on.

"I don't know what you're talking about." Eddie glanced away, staring pointedly out the window. Without a doubt, I knew tears would be threatening.

The urge to tease fell flat, my own emotion sitting high in my throat.

"Geez. I mean it. I'm going to be known as *that* girl with two blubbering dads. It's hardly like you're doing a great job of blending in." The exasperation in her voice was strong, but since I hadn't looked away, her struggle wasn't as invisible as she hoped.

That was my cue to step up, wrangle her dad, and let her start living her college life.

Without tears.

At least until we were three blocks away.

"Right." I clapped my hands. "It looks like you're all settled. You know how to organize your app for campus meals, right?"

Rather than rolling her eyes at me, Lottie's gaze softened. "I'm all set, Pop-Tart." Before I could ask the next question on my mental list, she stepped into my space and wrapped her arms around me. "I've got this. I know what to do in an emergency. I have a campus map. I have my schedule. I've got the credit card in my Apple Wallet."

"*Emergency* credit card," I said with a smile, hugging her hard.

"I promise I'll be fine. I'm more worried about you."

I dotted a kiss on her head and pulled away

chuckling, aware since I'd indicated it was time to leave, Eddie had faced us. "Me? Why?"

"You're going to have to put up with the old man. You know he's going to pine, right?"

"Pining. Pfft…"

I smiled at Eddie's attempt to deny her words. "Yeah, there'll be pining, but I have ways to distract your father."

"Ew." She stepped out of my hold, wrinkling her nose. "And that's something I am so not going to miss."

I gasped, keeping up with the levity. Anything was better than tears at this point. "We're adorable."

"Uh-huh. You guys keep telling yourselves that. You know how much I'm looking forward to not having to wear my headphones at night?" Lottie arched her brow high, looking scarily like her mom when she did so.

"Uhm…," I said with a laugh, trying to cover up the mortification of even thinking about our daughter hearing me and her dad going at it. "Now that's our definite cue to leave." I shot a glance at Eddie. The poor guy looked miserable as hell.

Lottie wasn't wrong about the pining. Eddie was going to be a nightmare. But I really did have all the best plans to distract him.

"Go say goodbye to your dad, and then I'll get him out of here."

She sent me a grateful smile and hugged me hard. And fuck if a new wave of emotion didn't sweep over me. Who knew letting go could be so damn hard?

When I'd left the Eagles seven years ago, it had been an emotional, bittersweet goodbye, but being able to spend more nights at home than not with my family, once I'd joined the Jetts, had been worth it.

And the Championship I'd won with the Jetts five years ago had been even better.

Even then, with my emotions high, they'd been nothing like this. Add in my retirement three years ago, which had taken Eddie some work to convince me didn't mean I was past my due date, and each of those moments had been a breeze.

A black hole of fear sat in my chest that Lottie would be at college eight long hours away. Fuck, I was going to miss her so damn much.

"Dad."

Lottie's strangled voice caught my attention. I pursed my lips, understanding Eddie's inability to release her, while trying to hold on to my amusement at Lottie's panicked plea for help as she stared my way.

"Come on, Ed. Time to let her go." I reached out

and rubbed his back, my palm landing on the nape of his neck where I gave a reassuring squeeze. "We need to leave. Lottie will be fine. She's got this. You know that."

His panicked gaze met mine, and I smiled softly. "Come on, baby. It's really time."

With a shuddery sigh and a bob of his head, he released Lottie and cleared his throat.

"Jesus. I think you broke a rib." Lottie rubbed at her side and rolled her eyes. "Butts out of here." Her bottom lip trembled, and I swallowed hard.

"We love you," I said quickly, snagging Eddie's hand and tugging. Lottie's struggle to keep herself together was crystal clear. I didn't want her tears. I wanted to leave her happy and smiling, excited to be here.

"Love you, Lottie girl." Eddie's words were soft, but he followed my lead and allowed me to tug him toward the door.

A glance at Lottie showed me her brave smile. "Love you both. Text when you get... home," she said after a moment of hesitation, her gaze flashing to mine. The smile eased into something more genuine.

I'd already told her we were taking a short break. Just five days in a luxury resort to try to distract Eddie. I hadn't told him, sure he would have balked at travelling even farther away from Lottie's college.

Fully expecting this, I deliberately kept our trip in the States.

"Will do." I winked and squeezed Eddie's hand, finally hauling him out of her room and down the corridor.

He remained silent the whole way as I smiled at the wide eyes and gaping mouths of students and some of the other families still setting up their kids. Poor Lottie was right about our giant forms not being the best at blending in.

Once we made it to the car, I pulled Eddie's keys out of his pocket and ushered him into the passenger seat. A couple of minutes later, I pulled out of the campus grounds, shooting worried glances at my husband.

It was at least ten minutes before he spoke, the sound of his voice making me jump. "Shit, we left?"

I snorted. "Yep."

He sighed, glancing around the small town we were heading through. "This isn't the way to the 90."

Smiling, I side-eyed him before returning my attention to the road. "Nope."

"Where are we going?"

"It's a surprise."

"But Lottie mig—"

"Lottie will be fine, but if she needs us, she'll call, and we'll make sure she's okay," I reassured.

A huff of breath escaped him. "I can't believe she's in college. The house is going to be so quiet."

A pang hit my chest, and I reached out for him. He took my hand immediately, and I rested our joined hands on my thigh. "I know, but I don't think she was joking about the headphones." I chuckled and glimpsed his face turning red. "That means we don't even have to attempt to keep it down. A win, right?"

His lips twitched, and my shoulders relaxed.

"Tonight I'm going to fuck you so hard into the mattress, you won't be worrying about a thing other than when you can come again," I promised.

When he shifted in his seat, I grinned, happy to distract him.

"Yeah? Is that after you eat me out?"

"Fuck," I groaned, hand contracting on the wheel as blood rushed to my cock. "Yeah. I can definitely do that." Tightening my hand on his, I cleared my throat. "It's actually a bit of a drive, so maybe you should look on your phone and see if there's a motel close by."

He snorted out a laugh. "Can't wait, huh?"

"Fuck no. Not when you say you want to ride my tongue."

A quick glance his way and our gazes connected. "We're going to be okay, huh?"

My heart clenched, smile tender when I nodded, lifting his hand to my mouth to kiss the back of his hand. "We really are. Just a first for us." And hell if I wasn't excited about the idea.

Lottie was starting a whole new adventure, becoming independent and beginning her college life. For me and Eddie, we'd be living by ourselves for the first time ever, working out new routines. From the heat in his eyes, all wrapped in the love he was quick to tell me he felt every day, this next journey together would only get better.

And that would start in the next fifteen minutes if he hurried up and found us a motel.

Go Bears! Want to read the cheeky bonus scene of Pearce's bachelor party? You can get the link in my Facebook group, RoMMance with Becca & Louisa or by subscribing to my newsletter. GET READY for book four, Cassius's fun story. Yet to meet the previous Bears players? Now is the perfect time to check out No Take Backs.

ABOUT THE AUTHOR

I live and breathe all things book related. Usually with at least three books being read and two WiPs being written at the same time, life is merrily hectic. I tend to do nothing by halves, so I happily seek the craziness and busyness life offers.

Living on my small property in Queensland with my human family as well as my animal family of cows, chooks, and dogs, I really do appreciate the beauty of the world around me and am a believer that love truly is love.

To check for updates head to my website:
HTTPS://BECCASEYMOUR.COM
Join my mailing list:
HTTPS://LANDING.MAILERLITE.COM/WEBFORMS/
LANDING/R9F0I4
Plus, join my Facebook group:
WWW.FACEBOOK.COM/GROUPS/
ROMMANCEWITHBECCALOUISA/

facebook.com/beccaseymourauthor

tiktok.com/@beccaseymourwrites

twitter.com/beccaseymour_

instagram.com/authorbeccaseymour

bookbub.com/authors/becca-seymour

CPSIA information can be obtained
at www.ICGtesting.com
Printed in the USA
LVHW011608151022
730779LV00005B/595